CHINATOWN ANGEL

CHINATOWN ANGEL

A. E. ROMAN

Minotaur Books ⚏ New York

This is a work of fiction. All of the characters, organizations, and events portrayed in this novel are either products of the author's imagination or are used fictitiously.

A THOMAS DUNNE BOOK FOR MINOTAUR BOOKS.
An imprint of St. Martin's Publishing Group.

www.thomasdunnebooks.com
www.minotaurbooks.com

Library of Congress Cataloging-in-Publication Data

Roman, A. E. (Alex Echevarria)
  Chinatown angel / A.E. Roman.—1st ed.
    p. cm.
  ISBN-13: 978-0-312-37500-3
  ISBN-10: 0-312-37500-X
 1. Private investigators—New York (State)—New York—Fiction.
2. Hispanic Americans—Fiction.   3. New York (N.Y.)—Fiction.
4. Murder—Investigation—Fiction.   I. Title.
  PS3618.O566C48 2009
  813'.6—dc22

2008034164

First Edition: March 2009

10 9 8 7 6 5 4 3 2 1

This book is for Alicia Roman.

Down to the closest friend every man is a potential murderer.

—Henry Miller

Thou shalt not kill.

—Exodus

CHINATOWN ANGEL

ONE

I try not to judge, but from the get-go, I didn't like Albert's friend. Kirk Atlas, not his real name, was twenty-seven years old. He was already rich but that wasn't enough. He wanted to be famous. It was 9 P.M., January, a cold winter. I was sitting under red lights in the overheated cabin of a luxury yacht called *La Pinta,* docked at City Island, not far from what used to be Tito Puente's Restaurant. The music of 50 Cent banged out from overhead speakers, filling every corner of the room. Atlas sat, bopped his head and waved his arms in time to the music.

"I aim straight for your head!" sang Atlas. Then he whispered in Albert's ear.

Kirk Atlas was of indeterminate ethnicity, with a shaved head that glistened like a dull gold. His torso was the size of a mini fridge, packed tight into a five-foot-six-inch frame. He was bare-chested under a white gym suit with maroon stripes.

He wore Puma sneakers on his feet and dark Versace sunglasses, a tattoo of a black panther etched above the word "Gangsta" on his forearm. On the long glass coffee table was an empty bottle of Havana Club, dirty ashtrays, a can of Coca-Cola, and a .45.

Like I said, I didn't like the guy.

Atlas was a phony. Not a gangsta, a wangsta: wannabe gangster. Phony shouldn't bother me. I've chased all kinds of folks, from Queens to Brighton Beach, from Brooklyn to Southern Boulevard, from the South Bronx to St. Marks, from Manhattan to West Brighton.

A lot of people are phony and wicked and cruel. It shouldn't bother me. But it does.

Atlas finished whispering in Albert's ear and sat back smugly on the plump leather sofa, smoking a Cuban and drinking rum from a crystal glass. He beamed at me like I was a camera ready to snap his picture.

I put my Coca-Cola down on the long glass table. Albert, still in a red waiter's jacket and black bow tie, puffed nervously on his fat cigar and slapped my knee. "Chico here can be trusted. He was one of my best friends at St. Mary's."

"When was the last time you and Albert saw each other?" Atlas asked, turning down the hi-fi system by remote.

"New Year's Eve with you on Fordham Road," I said. "At your restaurant."

"I mean, before that?" said Atlas.

I looked at Albert. "Over twenty years ago."

"Still live in the Bronx, right?" said Atlas.

"I was raised on Brook Avenue," I said. "But I live in Pelham Bay now."

"What were you doing on Fordham?"

"I go on a walkabout around the Bronx every New Year," I said. "Been doing it since I was a kid. Clears my head."

Atlas took another puff of his hand-rolled cigar. He studied my face. "What're you, Dominican?"

"Puerto Rican."

Atlas laughed and looked at Albert. "A Puerto Rican from the Bronx. That's rare, huh?"

"Yeah," I said, glancing at Albert. "Like unicorns or Bigfoots."

"I like you, Chico," said Atlas. "I think we can do business."

"What kind of business?"

"I need you to find a girl for me."

"Who doesn't?" I said.

"Sense of humor," said Atlas, leaning forward. "I like that, too."

Atlas examined my face again. "So you're *pure* Puerto Rican?"

"No such animal," I said.

"Well," said Atlas and put his feet up on the long glass coffee table, "when you walked into my restaurant, you looked kinda like a black guy to me."

"Sometimes a spade is a spade," I said. "What's your story?"

He smiled. "I'm a lot of things."

Kirk Atlas removed his dark sunglasses and stared at me with cold green eyes. He looked like a *blanco*, a white man, maybe northern Italian or Russian, or maybe some kinda Spanish. There was an almost imperceptible accent in his voice.

"What's the accent?" I asked.

"What accent?" He looked as if he was going to jump out of his skin.

"I hear an accent. It's slight, but it's there."

"I don't have an accent!"

Atlas looked at me like he wanted to kick my teeth in and gave Albert an annoyed glance. Albert tapped my knee and said, "Chico, relax."

"I thought we was all friends here," I said.

Atlas got up violently and stomped across the cabin to the rectangular window.

Albert laughed and said, "Chico, relax. Marco—"

Albert stopped himself. Atlas turned and glared at him, because Albert had slipped up and started to say Atlas's real name—Marco something. Real cloak and dagger stuff.

"I need your name, Atlas," I said. "Your real name or I hit the yellow bricks."

Albert looked at me, sweating like a man who had stolen something. "Kirk here is one of my oldest friends, after you, Chico. Kirk's got his reasons fer bein' so stingy with information. He's got a career to think about."

I had bumped into Atlas and Albert on Fordham Road at the Chinatown Angel, a restaurant owned by Atlas. Albert, a waiter there and a wannabe filmmaker, announced that his old buddy and current boss Kirk Atlas was on his way to fame. Atlas had just appeared in a commercial for salad dressing, and was now producing and starring as the action-hero in a low-budget science fiction flick. Albert was directing. It was called *Doomsday*.

I'm not sure what being an action star has to do with salad dressing, but I'm not in show business. I'm a private investigator. Or, I was. Before my wife, Ramona, kicked me out. I quit my job at the private investigator's agency St. James and Company and buried myself in a basement apartment for six months. The good news? I quit smoking and drinking. I had only just come up for air on New Year's Eve. That's when I bumped into Kirk Atlas and Albert Garcia.

It seemed to me that Albert was acting strange. He looked anxious and irritated. If you were a lightning bug on the wall of that yacht, you'd see that Albert Garcia didn't match the ritzy surroundings at all. Albert was short, like Atlas, but older. He had crooked teeth and a scraggly beard. His oily hair stood up on his head like porcupine quills.

I knew Albert from back in the day at St. Mary's—he was a moody street kid, a fearless little South Bronx Napoleon with a bad temper who wasn't ashamed to scratch, bite, and deliver a nut-shot in a fight with a bigger kid if he had to. Also, he was one of the few boys at St. Mary's who knew comic books and movies as well as I did.

"I'd like to keep my real name private," Atlas said. "It's not personal, dude. I gotta watch the ol' publicity machine. My agent wants me to be an enigma."

I thought maybe being an enigma had something to do with being a liar. I didn't say that, though. "Name."

"Marcos Rivera," said Atlas, grinning tough. "I'm Cuban. Well, my folks are Cuban. I'm American. Kirk Atlas is my Hollywood thing."

Atlas turned to check his shaved head in a giant mirror hung between two framed movie posters: Harrison Ford's *Blade Runner* and Vin Diesel's *Pitch Black*. A collection of Kirk Atlas's Hollywood dreams and fantasies, which included himself at the center.

Albert went into his jacket and came up holding something. He handed it to me. It was a photograph.

I studied it. It was a publicity shot of a stunning young girl playing a violin. She was Asian with dyed blond hair and green eyes. She looked a bit like that movie star of another era, Veronica Lake.

"She's Asian?" I said, holding up the photo.

"Yeah," said Atlas and turned from the mirror, eyes narrowed. "Chinese. What? Are you prejudiced?"

"Only between the hours of nine and five on Monday mornings. I'm workin' on it."

"She's only half Chinese," said Albert.

5

"Half Cuban," said Atlas. "Her name is Tiffany."

"A half-Chinese half-Cuban girl with dyed blond hair and green eyes called Tiffany," I said. "I thought I had issues."

I looked at the photograph again and then at Kirk Atlas.

"What do you want with her?"

Atlas's mood changed. He got a depressed look on his face and took a slug of his rum. He paused.

"Tiffany is my cousin," said Atlas.

"She's my girlfriend's little sister," said Albert.

"I'm looking for your girlfriend's little sister?" I asked Albert.

Albert got a tense look on his face, and then he relaxed. He winked at me.

"Tiffany's sister Olga is at Columbia University. Pre-law. Brainy and high strung. I don't want her involved in this."

"Never mind about Olga," said Atlas. "Tiffany and I are very close. More than blood, more than just family. At least, I thought so. Before she quit school and ran off. I just want to know that she's okay."

"If she's missing," I said, "why don't you call the police?"

"Not that kind of missing," said Albert.

"She's eighteen," said Atlas. She took an official leave of absence from Julliard. She packed one bag and a violin. She left a note. Doesn't wanna see or talk to anybody. No family. Not even her closest friends. She writes postcards to say she's fine. But there's no return address."

"Smart girl."

"Smart?" Atlas bragged. "This girl can ski, snowboard, ride a horse, shoot a gun, and play a violin like an angel."

"An angel that shoots guns?" I said. "Bro, obviously, we grew up in different churches."

Atlas pulled out a wad of cash. He placed it on the glass table. I picked it up. Five grand to start. Not too shabby. Once upon a time I had the luxury of turning down investigative work, but now I was behind on the rent, the light, the cable, the cell phone, the car repair bills, and gas was going up to twenty dollars a gallon. I had quit my job, and I counted only eight hundred dollars in the sock I kept under my bed. I still had a choice, you always have a choice, but the wiggle room was tight.

Albert handed me a small passport photo of a man in a dark business suit along with a card.

HMD Financial
Samuel Rivera, President
43rd Street, 5th Avenue

"Samuel Rivera," said Albert. "Tiffany's father. Kirk's uncle. Ever hear of him?"

"No," I said. "But I travel in small circles and low places."

"Tiffany is Samuel's favorite," said Atlas. "I don't believe he doesn't know where she is."

"You follow Tiffany's father," Albert said. "I think you'll find her."

"All I want from you is an address," Atlas said and pushed a red button on the wall. "I'll do the rest."

A pretty black girl wearing a snug tuxedo that accentuated her ample curves entered. She was holding a second bottle of Havana Club. She smiled flirtatiously at me, and Atlas gave her an irritated look. She appeared so quickly that I knew she must have been standing outside the door, listening.

"Allo, Albert," she said, with a sweet giggle. *"Tudo bem?"*

Albert didn't say anything. He just nodded his head politely.

Tudo bem. I recognized it. Brazilian. My wife, Ramona, and I used to go to Little Brazil or Rua 46 in Midtown for black bean stew and caipirinha.

"Everything's fine," said Atlas, glaring at Brazil, as he held out his empty glass: "Pour!"

She looked at me with a lingering and confident eye. I checked out her hips as she passed and poured Atlas some more rum.

As I grabbed and sipped my Coca-Cola, Atlas threw Albert a second wad of money. Everybody was getting a taste. But I noticed that Albert was scowling as he pocketed the cash.

He looked agitated as he talked excitedly about some of the films that had been shot on City Island. *Butterfield 8* with Elizabeth Taylor, *Awakenings* with Robin Williams, *A Bronx Tale* with Robert De Niro. Brazil pretended to just be clearing the glass table. But I could tell she was eavesdropping. She came over and tried to fill my glass.

I shook my head. "I don't drink anymore."

"Cigar?"

"Don't smoke anymore, either. Thank you."

"What your name is?" she whispered.

"Chico. You?"

"Pilar," she whispered and winked at me with very dark brown eyes. "I go off soon."

"In that case," I said, "I'll wait for you outside."

She smiled and nodded.

I looked over at Atlas, who was flexing his muscles for Albert. Oh, yeah, Kirk Atlas was a real prize.

Atlas, grinning, suddenly hopped over and slapped Pilar's bottom with a hard *thwack*!

Pilar didn't even flinch. She just kept smiling. Albert opened his mouth as if he was going to say something in protest. But he didn't. Albert wasn't saying a lot of things.

As Pilar left with the first empty bottle of rum and a dirty ashtray, she bowed to Atlas. She actually bowed—bent at the waist, head down, eyes to the floor, walking backward, behind up in the air, primed for kicking. But hell, the things I've done for money. Who knew what her story was? *Uno nunca sabe*, one never knows, as my mom used to say.

Albert and Atlas raised their glasses to me. I raised mine back. I try not to judge.

But sometimes it gets real hard.

TWO

Servants know everything and I had a hunch that Atlas and Albert weren't telling me everything. So I thought I'd buddy up with Pilar Menendez , drive her home from City Island, and fill in the blanks.

At midnight we were seated in my 1972 Dodge Charger heading to Queens. Otis Redding on the radio. The car had belonged to my old man. The white racing stripes were pretty much faded away but the sea blue paint job was in good condition. Except for a questionable transmission, fuel system, and suspension, it ran like a dream.

Pilar, leaning into me, offered to take me around to the Noguchi Museum and the Museum of the Moving Image, Astoria Pool, and Bohemian Hall, the last original remaining beer garden in New York City, built by Czech immigrants. She said that we would sit under trees behind high walls and drink beer and eat goulash outside in the summer and it was feeling dangerously close to a date except she kept calling me "police."

"You are good police or bad police?"

"Actually," I said, "I'm no police at all. I'm a private dick."

Pilar gave me a funny look as we crossed the Triborough Bridge. We drove into Astoria, past Greek diners, Indian restaurants, Middle Eastern cafés, and Korean fruit markets under the elevated N train platform, and rode up the lamplit streets of Ditmars Boulevard. Manhattan shot up in the distance over the East River, beyond the gray winter trees clawing the sky. A dog barked as we got out of the parked car and walked toward her building.

There I was with Pilar plastered to my arm, when I spotted two suspicious-looking men. They wore long leather coats, black winter hats and gloves. They stood on the corner, across the street and down the block, outside Astoria Park. They were watching us.

The smaller guy was pacing and pretending to be talking on a cell phone. The bigger guy leaned against a parked car, a red Mustang, and smoked a cigarette. I couldn't make out the license plate. Pilar didn't seem to notice them.

"Just so you understand," I said. "This is a professional visit. We're gonna sit down at your place, you're gonna tell me everything you know about this Tiffany. It's just a friendly interview. Okay?"

"I will tell you all about."

She nuzzled close to my face, which reminded me that I needed a shave, and said, "I like you."

We stopped in front of her building. It was a five-story limestone box with windows, clean but uniform, the kind you'd find in any part of Queens. She searched her little white handbag and said, "I lose my key!"

"How we gonna get in?"

That's when a potbellied man, short, bald, smelling of garlic, wearing a short-sleeved shirt and black slacks, more hair on his chest than on his head, came out of the building, carrying a glass jug full of thick liquor, held the door and yelled, cheerfully: "Ouzo!"

"Ouzo!" Pilar yelled back and laughed. "The Greek love ouzo!"

"How are you doing, *Samba?*" asked the Greek.

"I am no good," Pilar said. "I forget my key."

"Again!" the Greek said, holding the door open for us. "Have you seen Irving?"

Pilar grabbed the door. "I no see anymore."

"Well," said the Greek. "His loss. Not ours. He'll be back."

The Greek slapped me on the shoulder, saluted, and whispered, "Forward, captain, forward," and quickly walked off into the dark.

"Who's that?" I said.

"My good friend," said Pilar.

"What's he doing here?"

"You too many question," she said.

"Who's Irving?" I said, ignoring her.

"Irving. Nice boy. Smart men. He was good friend. Now no more. Happy, meester?"

"You have many friends."

"No," she said with a shake of her hips. "I no have many friend. The world is my friend. I am Samba. I am Brazil."

We went inside. I heard voices in the hall, coming from behind closed doors, talking loudly, and smelled the sharp remains of all the foods boiled and baked and fried that night for dinner.

All the way up to the fifth floor I kept watching Pilar's skirt below her white winter coat. I could feel every step of her five-inch heels, red on the marble stairs, and I could taste her perfume in my mouth. I knew that I was fooling myself that this was *just* another part of the investigation, and I thought about Ramona, and I cursed my lying rotten self.

When we got to the fifth floor, Pilar stripped off her coat and headed up one more flight to the roof.

"I be back," she said as she threw me her coat. I felt the fur. It was a fake.

I waited maybe five minutes outside Pilar's apartment until I heard a small dog barking and then a window opening. Someone was walking around inside. I knocked three times and the door opened and there was Pilar, holding a trembling Chihuahua.

"Tah-dah!" she said. "Magic!"

"I'm impressed," I said. "You'd make a great cat burglar."

When I said the word "cat" the Chihuahua went crazy barking at me like I was some secret spy come to take him back to the hell he sprung from.

"Baby," Pilar said. "Is all right. Is only Chico."

I never liked Chihuahuas. People might imagine that if the devil has a dog, it's a Doberman pinscher or a pit bull or a rottweiller. But I know better. Chihuahua.

"Come," Pilar said.

I followed Pilar into her apartment. It was all white: the walls, the couch, the lamps, the coffee table, the carpet— everything white.

A makeshift altar (a familiar sight of religion at work or mumbo-jumbo up-close-and-personal, depending on who you asked) stood in a corner of the room. It was a white table stocked with white candles, water, dried fruit, cigars, coffee grounds, blue beads, feathers, black dolls in white dresses, and a statue of Saint Lazarus. Above the altar was a large laminated headshot of Kirk Atlas, looking impressed with himself in his tight T-shirt and jeans, grinning like a god. There was a DVD (*Dead Poets Society*) and a piece of paper with a poem on the altar, "Mad Girl's Love Song" by Sylvia Plath. The poem was inscribed: *To Pilar, Wishing you success & happiness over the next year. Love, Irving and Olga.*

A freezing wind came in through the open window. Pilar shut it.

"I have good house, no?"

"Yeah," I said and she kissed me. I pulled back.

"How old are you?" I asked.

"Twenty-two," she said. "Everybody say I look older. But I have hard life in Brazil. My family is poor. No money. No shoes. No books. I beg on street in São Paulo."

She looked away. "I do many bad thing."

I couldn't even imagine, so I didn't try. I touched her dark face. Poor kid.

"You're doing okay now," I said and pointed around the living room.

Her eyes got wide. "Kirk."

She kissed my cheek and turned on some music. A husky woman's voice sang "The Girl from Ipanema. . ."

"Come," she said, sitting, and slapped the plastic cover on the white couch.

The dog started barking at me again.

"Baby!"

Baby, that rat in dog's clothing with its big head and bigger ears, popping satanic eyes, and buzz saw teeth, ran around me, all nervous energy and trembling, barking like Lassie on crack. I stood there looking at Pilar as she bent over, grabbed the dog, and locked him away in the bathroom with a kiss. I knew what was happening. It was wrong, unprofessional, illogical, I know. But I hadn't been with a woman in almost a year. Six months is *almost* a year. Pilar stood before me, her face just inches from mine. She kissed me again, this time on the mouth. I kissed her back.

"Is good?"

"Is very good," I said and kissed her again.

After, we were in her room, naked, empty Trojan wrappers scattered on the floor. She was on the bed. She rolled over on her belly. I caressed her fleshy bottom and said, "Tell me about Tiffany."

"Tiffany is very beautiful," she said and wiped her sweaty face with her hand.

"You're very beautiful, too."

She shook her head. "Tiffany is more beautiful. She make the music."

"Tell me about Kirk or Marcos or whatever else he calls himself."

She said with affection, "When Marcos very young, he very skinny and small. Boy beat him in school. Girl call him sissy. So Marcos exercise and become like macho man. Make boom-boom on everybody. Kirk Atlas!"

She suddenly got a burst of energy.

"Kirk!" she repeated. She jumped off the bed, slipped on her panties, a Yale sweatshirt, and white furry slippers. She kissed me and walked over to a white dresser. She came back with an envelope and put it in my hand. It was full of cash.

"Ten thousand dollar," she said.

"Ten thousand dollars? What's it for?"

"I buy you."

"You pay me?"

"Yes. I pay you."

"I'm flattered. I don't usually get paid for this."

"No. You stop find Tiffany."

I covered myself with a bedsheet.

"You want me *not* to look for Tiffany?"

"Yes."

"And you're willing to pay me ten thousand dollars?"

"Everything I have. Everything I save."

"You're willing to give me your body *and* your life savings?"

She lowered her head.

"Why?"

She looked up at me like an abandoned child. "Maybe you find Tiffany? Maybe you make her no come back?"

"What do you mean I find her and make her no come back?"

Pilar shrugged. "I no like Tiffany."

"Why?" I said. "What did she do to you?"

Pilar screwed up her face and crossed her arms. I recognized the look. Ramona had it. That was it for tonight. No more information.

"Listen," I said, rising. "Maybe this was a bad idea. I'm going home to my basement apartment in the Bronx now and forget I was crazy enough to even come here. You're a pretty girl. And you're young. And I drank too much Coca-Cola. But that excuse will only get me so far. You call me when you're ready to talk."

"No!" she said. Her face was panicked. She stripped off her sweatshirt and tried to push me flat on my back. She shook her head. "No more talk! No go! Kiss me!"

"I can't."

"Why no?"

"I wouldn't respect myself in the morning."

Her brown eyes got real sad and I felt regret right away.

I grabbed my pants and shoes and the mess I made, dropped the ten grand on the bed with my card, and moved quickly through Pilar's apartment. As I closed the front door, I could hear her weeping in familiar starts and stops. I thought of my mother answering the phone the night of my father's murder. It was that same quality of hurt in Pilar's crying.

Outside. Cold wind slapping my face. Pilar's building receding into the night. I walked quickly in the direction of my parked car wishing I had kissed Pilar goodbye. That's when I heard a woman scream: "Chico!"

I turned. I saw someone falling from the rooftop of Pilar's building. I ran back as fast as I could, got out my pocket flashlight, shot through the open mouth of an alley, down a short flight of steps, through a long narrow corridor, to where that "someone" had fallen.

"Pilar," was all I could say, careful not to step in the blood.

She was between the garbage cans, on her back, head busted open, bones shattered, one brown leg pulled under her body. Her Yale sweatshirt was torn where it probably snagged the fire escape on the way down. Her deep brown eyes were open in shock, a pool of blood circled her head like a furious halo. Her white furry slippers had come off and sat in a pool of red. Their little white hairs blew in the cold winter wind.

I walked, fast as I could, out of that alley. But before I made it, I looked up and I saw a dark silhouette up against the white moon, peeking over the ledge of the rooftop that Pilar had fallen from. The person was wearing a dark hat. I stopped, stepped back, pointed my flashlight. The dark outline vanished.

I ran and made it to the front door of the building, scanning the streets for that red Mustang and those two guys I had spotted earlier. Nothing. Nobody. I tried the door. Locked.

I checked my Timex. It was 2 A.M.

I flipped open my cell phone. I called the police and gave the dispatcher the details and the address.

"Yeah," I said, "she's dead."

THREE

I was part of an Astoria mob standing across the street from the crime scene. Police cars, fire trucks, ambulances, sirens, and badges had invaded the silence of early morning on Ditmars. I stood on the sunny sidewalk in the cold, collar up, head full of cotton. I puffed on a cigarette that I had bummed off a Pakistani man in the crowd and scanned the worried faces, looking for the Greek or the two thuggish guys with the red Mustang.

I saw Officer Jessica Torres signal for me from across the street. She ordered the crowd to stay where they were on the sidewalk. I stepped into the street and walked over.

"Looks like a jumper," she said, all brunette crew cut, broad backed and broad shouldered, pale chubby hands on her gun belt, leaning on one hip like a tough cowgirl, annoyed by my continued presence and questions. "We have your statement, Santana. Thank you. You can go home now."

I looked away from Officer Torres and saw a familiar figure in blue among a gaggle of New York's finest at the mouth of the alley where they found Pilar's body.

I tossed my cigarette. "Samantha!"

Samantha turned, looking over the heads of the other cops. She saw me and walked through the crowd. "Chico?

Samantha Rodriguez, petite, long black hair tied up on her head, lovely brown skin, Mexican-American from Queens, got a B.S. in criminal justice from John Jay, and then headed for the police academy. To save innocent lives. We had a thing once, years ago. I hadn't seen her since. It was quick and painful.

"You know this guy?" said Officer Torres.

"We went to John Jay together," Samantha said. "What happened, Santana?"

"She yells out. I turn. She's tumbling off the roof."

"You saw her jump?" said Samantha, both hands playing at the edge of her gunbelt.

"I saw her fall," I said. "And, as I was telling your compatriot here, I saw somebody else up on the roof."

"You saw her pushed?" asked Samantha.

"No," said Officer Torres. "He saw her fall and then he says he saw somebody up on the roof."

"Male or female?" said Samantha.

"It was dark," said Officer Torres, kicking a greasy paper plate off the sidewalk into the curb. "He don't know."

"I'm just saying that there was somebody else up there," I said.

"We got your statement," said Officer Torres, exasperated.

"What was the nature of your relationship?" Samantha asked, crossing her arms.

"Pilar was part of a case I'm working on," I said, stamping a foot down on my discarded cigarette. "I thought maybe she knew something about a girl I'm tracking. I was invited."

"What did you fight about again?" said Officer Torres and spit into the gutter.

"I didn't say I fought with her."

"You were with her," Torres said, fishing now, flipping open her notebook, maybe showing off for Samantha. "Why did you leave?"

"It was late," I said.

"Where were you going?" Torres said.

"Home."

"You slept with her, right?" Torres said.

"Yes," I said and looked at Samantha, who frowned.

"Do you usually sleep with leads?" said Torres, glancing at Samantha with blue accusing eyes.

"Only if they ask real nice," I said. "There was somebody on the roof."

"Okay," said Torres, flipping her notebook closed. "This isn't helping. We have your information. We'll call you if we need anything else, Santana."

"What about the two guys outside the building?"

"We'll ask around. Woulda made our job easier if you had gotten the plates."

"What about the Greek?"

"I said," snapped Torres, hand at the edge of her gun belt, "we'll ask around. Is there anything else you'd like to add before you go besides no information on anonymous Greeks you don't know the name of in Astoria?"

"I'm a bad swimmer?"

"We'll call you if we need you," said Torres. "I'm going back in. Coming, Sam?"

"I'll be with you in a minute," said Samantha.

Officer Torres smiled sarcastically at me, cocked her head to the left, said "Good night, Kojak," and sauntered away, like she had just shot down a local town drunk who was dumb and intoxicated enough to believe himself a faster draw.

"What's her *problema*?" I said.

"She's okay," said Samantha.

"I saw somebody."

"*Hombre*, you know the drill," said Samantha. "We'll run a checklist for signs of foul play. Questioning whoever needs to be questioned. Search the apartment and see if there's anything missing or funny."

"Something's funny all right."

Samantha Rodriguez took out a pen, grabbed my hand, and wrote her number on my palm. "Call me if you need someone to talk to."

I looked at the number as she held my fingers.

"Still drawing at the Metropolitan?" she asked.

"I don't draw anymore."

"How's Ramona?"

"We're not together."

She shook her head gently and said nothing.

I shook my head, too.

"Nicky?"

"Barcelona."

"*Bueno*," she said, all dark brown eyes and Mexican features. She released my fingers. "It's good to see you, Chico. Stop following strange girls home. We're not in college anymore. I'd kiss you, only my commanding officer is watching. Call me."

FOUR

Mimi's Cuchifrito was located on Brook Avenue in the South Bronx. I lied to myself that I was only going there to stand still a minute, catch my breath, gulp down a cup of strong Puerto Rican coffee, maybe a roll with butter. Bullshit. I sat at the counter with a copy of the *New York Post* and ordered two freshly battered and deep-fried potatoes and washed them down with two large cups of sugary iced coco juice.

Mimi's Cuchifrito ain't exactly known for its healthy eating. Sweet plantains, codfish, chopped beef, are all battered and deep fried. Even the menu is deep fried.

"Chico!" Mimi yelled, coming out of the kitchen, blowing me a kiss and wiping her fingers on her blue apron. *"Boricua!"*

Mimi was smart, proudly fat, an explosion of red hair and miles of cleavage, fifty-three years young. She was in blue jeans that were too tight and a low-cut orange blouse over enormous breasts. She wore too much makeup—eyeliner, lipstick, rouge, powder, perfume, and anything that she could spray or rub or apply without developing a fatal skin rash. Mimi was, besides my buddy Nicky Brown, the closest thing I had to family. Mimi never had children. She couldn't. I didn't have all the details. I didn't want them.

"Did you call Nicky?" she asked. This was her way of saying that she was worried about me.

"Not yet."

"*Momento,*" Mimi said.

She turned to the men who were playing dominoes at the opposite end of the counter, and delivered a joke in Spanish. Her small male audience laughed hard and loud and slapped their rough peasant hands on the slick white counter.

I tried to stuff down the last of my second *papa rellena*, when my belly began to ache. I looked up at the faded photo over the stack of white Styrofoam cups. It was an old childhood shot of Mimi, Nicky, and me outside a Times Square movie theater during Easter. I swore that Nicky, sporting an Afro and a brand-new lime green Easter sweater that matched my own (thanks to Mimi), was looking down at me, disappointed. Bad Chico.

I thought back to Nicky and his father, Carlos Brown, and the summer Nicky killed him.

Nicky was just going home to Summit Avenue for a visit, a simple South Bronx visit—that was all. He told me he greeted his neighbor Mrs. Hernandez, who was sitting on the stoop "drinkin' one of those Porto Rican sodas"—*Malta*—and watching over her three boys as they played stickball. He waved hello to her and the old Jewish landlord, Mr. Schwartz, who always seemed to be wearing the same brown vest, white T-shirt, and brown porkpie hat. Schwartz, the only Jew in the neighborhood, lived on the first floor with his fat wife, three German Shepherds, and a pretty sixteen-year-old daughter named Rachel. He was out walking his dogs—Cujo, Killer, and Sweetie—when Nicky went past them into his old building. Up the three flights of stairs Nicky went when he heard a scream that almost forced his heart out of his chest. The scream was ancient and familiar. It was his mother's scream.

Nicky grew up on Summit Avenue with this scream, with his father getting drunk and losing at numbers and crashing his rusted Pinto into every fence, tree, and mailbox in the neighborhood. Nicky's mother, Dorothy, fought back with tooth and nail and hammer if she had to, but always got worse than she gave. Nicky came into the world, he said, with "a slap in my face and a kick in my ass."

When Carlos lost his job driving a cab for Fat-Fat Taxi and his drinking and hitting got worse, Nicky's mom decided that it would be better for Nicky's health to go live at St. Mary's. That's how Nicky got there. Not 'cause his mom didn't love 'im but because she loved him and Carlos more than she loved herself. Some women are like that.

Nicky got to the top of the stairs and banged on the metal door. Carlos came out, face scratched, wearing a bright African dashiki with blood spatter. Nicky knew that the living room was full of velvet prints of African landscapes, of white hunters with guns taking down an elephant, of shirtless African men in white loincloths, and even a painting of Carlos himself as an African king. But all he could see then was the red blood on the dashiki. His mother's blood. And all his father could say was, "May I help you, nigger?"

And every ghost and scream and demon, every slap, every kick Nicky ever took from his father and witnessed his mother take, trembled and shook in the arms and shoulders and fists of a fifteen-year-old kid, already over six feet, almost two hundred pounds, muscular, who was training his body for the Golden Gloves championship.

Carlos was too drunk and high to realize that it wasn't the

six-year-old kid who stood at the door facing his abusive father that day. This kid was dangerous. Carlos stood there, beer in his hand, grinning with white teeth, and Dorothy's blood on his dashiki. And Nicky lost it.

When the police came, the Jewish landlord Mr. Schwartz told them a simple story, which his tenant Mrs. Hernandez also repeated. Carlos came back crazy from Vietnam. He was drunk and had gotten into a fight with his wife, Dorothy. After beating her bloody, still drunk, he fell down three flights of stairs, shattered both arms, legs, and spinal column, and broke his neck.

The police never came for Nicky, because Carlos was dead and no one missed him.

Case closed.

Nicky came back to St. Mary's that night, packed a bag, and hit the road. He ran off to Manhattan at first, lied about his age, found a job as a bouncer, then a security guard, then took the G.E.D. test and enrolled in John Jay College. The Golden Gloves never happened. Nicky "The Hammer" Brown never stepped into the ring again.

At St. Mary's Home for Boys in the Bronx, it was Nicky, four years older than me, who took me under his wing. It was Nicky who taught me how to punch, how to kick, to run, to learn, to hunger, to roll with the punches. It was Nicky who introduced me to John Coltrane and Charlie Chaplin, to Billie Holiday and the Marx Brothers, to Frank Sinatra and Red Foxx, Bessie Smith and Lenny Bruce. It was Nicky who got me, before he ran off to hitchhike through America, my first security job at the Metropolitan Museum, where I met Ramona in the African Art wing, where she sat reading *The Lover* in French. It was Nicky who had taken me into his apartment in Harlem when I left St. Mary's and had no place to live. It was Nicky who talked me into going to John Jay College.

After my father died and my mother lost it and dropped

off the face of the earth, before Ramona, it was Nicky. It was always Nicky. He was the only man I ever knew who I could forgive for trifling with the sixth commandment: Thou shalt not kill.

I looked over at Mimi and then at my soiled fingers caked with bright orange grease and food coloring.

Mimi walked back toward me and reached over the counter, grabbed my hands, and wiped my fingers with the end of her blue apron in a concerned and motherly fashion.

She smelled my fingers, raised an eyebrow and said, "Smoking?"

"Rough day."

Mimi was the only person who came visiting when I went under for six months. She came by with tins and plastic containers full of food and drink. For six months, with palm tree and coconut stories, almost every day, she came.

"Ramona?" asked Mimi, releasing my forgers and grabbing a rag hanging from her pocket.

"I don't want to talk about Ramona."

She began wiping the counter. "Advice?"

"Sure," I said.

"Follow your heart," she said.

"Your advice really helps me. You should be a detective."

"Really?"

"No."

"Chico!" She stopped wiping the counter. "Respect! You are a very bad boy."

"I try."

"Did I ever tell you about the time I was a little girl in San German and this flying saucer—"

"Yes."

"And the time Fajardo came home with a goat and—"

"You told me."

"And did I tell you, you need a haircut?"

27

"And new shoes."

She touched my hair. "I can cut it for you. I went to Wilfred Beauty Academy for two weeks, you know?"

"No *gracias*," I said.

"When are we going bowling?" Mimi asked.

"Soon," I said.

"What happen?" asked Mimi, grabbing my hand again and massaging my fingers.

"You know the rules," I said. "I don't ask what you put in your *mofongo*, you don't question me about my cases."

"Is it a girl?"

I hesitated, stared at her snub nose, wide mouth, freckled face, and eager eyes glowing under thick black eyelashes. "Let me ask you something."

"You're too young for me, Chico," she said, dropping my hand.

"Okay. That's disgusting," I groaned. "Check, please."

Mimi laughed loud, her belly and breasts shaking, grabbed my newspaper and slapped me on the head with it, and then picked up a ketchup bottle as if that was next.

I rubbed my forehead and said, "If I tell you about my case? Will you do something for me?"

"Yes," she said with a gap-toothed smile, dropped the paper and the ketchup and leaned over the counter.

"A girl is missing," I said in a whisper. "I have to find her."

"Why do you look for her?"

"It's my job."

"Is that all?"

"Another girl is dead," I said.

"Dead!" said Mimi, straightening up, her hand at her throat. "When? Where? Who?"

"Last night in Astoria. I think she was pushed off a roof."

"Chico! *Jesus!*" said Mimi and clapped her hands together with worry and crossed herself.

The dark Spanish men at the other end of the counter stopped chattering and turned to look at us. Mimi waved, signaling that everything was *bueno*. They went back to their arguing about money and poverty, American statehood versus independence for Puerto Rico, boxing and Yankee baseball. Mimi turned on the TV that sat on top of the soda cooler. She walked from behind the counter and sat on the stool beside me.

"If you want to help," I whispered, "I need you to stay calm."

Mimi nodded and leaned in, hands clasped together. "This girl who is dead, she is a bad girl?"

"I don't know yet," I said. "Do you want to help me?"

"Depends," Mimi said, leaning back on her stool.

"It's simple. I'm hired by Albert, you remember Albert from St. Mary's?"

"Alberto?" she said.

"Yeah," I said. "This creep Albert works for asked me to find a missing girl and I follow a second girl and my second girl gets dead."

"Que necesitas?"

"Do you know any Brazilians working in Astoria, Queens?"

"I know one girl," said Mimi. "Yolanda. She takes care of two boys in Astoria. But she lives over La Valencia Bakery across the street from here. Yolanda knows everybody."

Laughter burst from the men at the other end of the counter. We ignored it.

"Could you ask," I said, "if Yolanda or anybody she knows knew a Pilar Menendez who lived on Ditmars and worked as a waitress on a boat in City Island and was friends with a short, husky, bald Greek who loves drinking ouzo. And ask Yolanda if she might know or have ever heard of a girl named Tiffany or Olga or a guy named Irving. Chinese or Cuban or both."

Mimi wrote the names and details down on her check pad and said, "Why do I want to know this information?"

"Tell her that Pilar won some lottery money and we're trying to find any family she might have left behind in Astoria. Tell Yolanda there's a reward."

"Cuánto?"

"Fifty dollars."

Mimi made a face. "Yolanda has a little girl with asthma."

"Tell her it's negotiable," I said, rising.

Mimi blew me another kiss and said *bendición*. I got up, stretched, repeated *bendición*, and tried to drop a tip on the counter. Mimi sucked her teeth and handed it back. I never pay at Mimi's.

"See you soon," I said, pocketing the money.

"God willing," Mimi said. "God willing."

FIVE

Pelham Bay. Going home finally, I saw a familiar Mustang parked outside the two-family redbrick house across the street from mine. I walked past a leafless tree and went down into my basement studio apartment. The overhead light was knocked out, and the hall was dark. I stopped at my door when I heard a loud, angry voice thunder from inside:

"Hey, Salvatore! What the hell are you doing in there?"

I tried the doorknob. The door was unlocked.

I took a deep breath, pushed it open and calmly went in.

My stuff was scattered all over my apartment. A tall, skinny figure wearing a black leather trench coat turned. I saw the gun.

"Don't move!"

"Don't worry," I said, with my arms raised.

Private Investigator Oscar Pena. The only Puerto Rican kid I ever knew who grew up on Arthur Avenue, a tiny Italian section, a couple of blocks really, in the North Bronx. He was also the only Puerto Rican I knew who honestly *hated* Puerto Ricans and hated blacks *even more*. Oscar and I went to John Jay together, just like Officer Samantha Rodriguez. But our relationship had been even longer and more painful. Oscar came to my first criminal psychology class wearing a suede sports jacket, a tan cashmere overcoat, and a yellow ascot. It was summer. Right away, I hated this kid and he hated me right back.

Oscar Pena, blondish hair, pale face, heavy lidded eyes like a frog, was standing near my mattress on the concrete floor, pointing an enormous .357 Magnum.

"Yo, Salvatore!" yelled Oscar and banged on the door to my bathroom, directly behind him.

A putrid stink, a cross between sweat, rotten eggs, and raw sewage came into the room, as solid and real as me or Oscar. A smell that walked and talked and told stories about the Old Country. A Sicilian story, I thought, as I heard my toilet flush.

"Jesus," Oscar said, waving his left hand in front of his nose.

A hulking Salvatore Fiorelli, black beard, black hair, also wearing a black trench coat, and a Yankee baseball cap, came out of my tiny bathroom, and stood behind Oscar, blushing.

Sal was a good old Italian boy, also from Arthur Avenue, also went to John Jay. Oscar and Sal ran with a group called Talent Unlimited Investigations on Hunts Point.

It was them that night in Astoria, Oscar and Sal, creeping around, Sal leaning on the parked Mustang, Oscar pacing and pretending to be on his cell phone, both waiting and watching me and Pilar outside her building.

"Get his gun," said Oscar.

"I don't carry a gun," I said. I hate guns.

Sal walked toward me, got behind me, lifted my coat, and felt around.

"What?" I said, looking back at Sal and dropping my arms. "No roses? No candy? Just the old manhandle?"

"He's clean," Sal announced.

"Of course I'm clean," I said. "You never know when you'll be frisked in your own home and it's better to smell safe than sorry."

"Shut up, spic!" Oscar said, still pointing the .357 at me.

"Shut up yourself," I said. "Refresh my memory. Did I invite you two over for some of my delicious Bustelo coffee or is this just an ordinary home invasion?"

"We need ya to come with us, chief," Sal said.

"I would love to go riding around with you, *paisan*. Only I got a beauty salon appointment. I hear the Jheri-curl's coming back and I wanna be the first on line. Also, I get car sick when I'm not the driver."

"We'll roll down the windahs," said Sal and laughed.

Oscar stood there smirking and went into his coat pocket and pulled a yellow banana. He tossed it at me.

"Our anniversary," I said, catching the banana and looking Oscar in the eye. "I totally forgot, honey. I am so thoughtless. *Perdon.* Forgive me."

"For the trip," Oscar said. "I thought you might get hungry. Bananas, that is what monkeys eat, right, spico?

I peeled the banana, bit it, and chewed.

"Ah, just like Mami used to make."

"You gotta come wit us," Sal repeated.

"Can't do it, fellas," I said. "Wish I could go with you, though. Sounds fun. But I could maybe change my mind if you told me who we were going to see and why. And don't say Santa, because somebody told me just yesterday that he don't exist."

"We're not *asking* you to come with us, nigger," Oscar said. "We're telling you."

It was then I thought how some people might deserve to die.

Something heavy sat in my throat, in my tiny underground studio, flanked by two men with guns. I don't like having guns pointed at me. It makes me mad. I've never been shot, so the pain of being shot, like death, is an abstraction. And I'm not one of those people afraid of abstractions. Sure, I've seen guys shot. Shot good or shot dead. My old man was shot dead. But I am not afraid of and I am not impressed by guns. Especially not guns held by Oscar and Salvatore. And if I was gonna go anywhere, I wanted some information first.

So I sat down on my only chair, which was next to the refrigerator, and said, "Look, boys, you could both go home to Arthur Avenue, buy yourself some nice sausage or fresh pasta, cook, drink Chianti, and think about what you almost did here today. Or you could tell me who's knocking and why they're knocking and we can get going."

"You know," said Sal. "Pilar Menendez. The girl we saw you wit last night in Astoria."

"You're gonna give our employer what Pilar Menendez gave to you."

"I'm not even gonna touch that one," I said. "What is this about?"

"Don't play dumb."

"I'm not playing," I said. "Ask any of my old math teachers."

"Get up!" Oscar yelled.

"Now, now, Oscar," I said, looking him in those cold froggy eyes again. "Pilar Menendez was just a friend. I'm allowed to have friends. This relationship ain't gonna work if you keep trying to monopolize my time."

Oscar kicked my chair. I jumped up and almost belted 'im. Control, Chico. Play it cool and you may just get outta this one with no missing teeth or bullet holes.

"Be more polite, Oscar," said Salvatore. "Ya catch more flies wit sugar."

"This is no fly," said Oscar. "It's a cockroach."

"Tell me what this is about," I said. "Or get outta my apartment before I call the cops, have you arrested for breaking and entering, trespassing, and stinking up the joint without a license."

Oscar took off his coat. Under the black trench, he was wearing two gun holsters, one empty and the other bulging with a second gun, a Glock. He threw his trench and his guns down on my mattress and began rolling up his shirtsleeves.

"Okay, funny man," Oscar said. "We asked you nice to come with us. You brought this on yourself."

I almost laughed at the sight of Oscar's skinny arms as he took a weak and wobbly boxing stance, hands low, chin out. I could take Oscar out, no problem. I've had my share of fights in gyms and on street corners, been beaten black and blue, had my teeth rattled and chipped, seen my own blood on the sidewalks of the Bronx and beyond. I've given and I've gotten. But it was Salvatore had me worried, standing there like an Italian brick house. I took no pleasure in imagining his meat slab of a bicep clenched around my throat if I didn't work fast. I was feeling rusty. Neither my kicks nor my combinations were strong.

I raised my open hands. "I don't wanna fight, Oscar. Just tell me who you're working for and what they want and *then* we'll go. What's so hard?"

"Do you think it's that easy, spico?" Oscar said, coming forward. "It's not! I'm going to beat you silly, nigger! I'm going to smash that nigger face of yours! I've been waiting for this moment for years. I never liked you, spico, not in school, not now. I'm gonna break you in two."

Oscar let loose a soft but clean shot that missed and connected with my refrigerator door. He recovered quickly and came at me again. I deflected Oscar's punch with a sweep of my hand. His punch connected with the wall. I considered using a wrist-lock but he made me mad, so I knocked him off his feet with a good old-fashioned uppercut to the jaw instead. I felt his teeth shake as his body went soft and he hit the concrete floor like a dead stone.

Salvatore stepped between me and Oscar, yelling, "Okay, fellas!"

"No!" Oscar yelled back. "Lucky punch!"

"This guy gets any more lucky," Sal said, "you might wind up brain dead."

Oscar got up off the floor. He went to his trench coat on my mattress. He picked up his German Glock and pointed it at me.

"What the fuck, Oscar?" yelled Salvatore.

Oscar came at me, a murderous flash in his eyes. He pressed the gun into my chest and said, "One less black spic in the world."

"Oscar?" Salvatore yelled again. There was fear in his voice. "Don't bust my balls. Put da gun down."

Oscar just stood there, gun at my chest, trembling with rage, his eyes biting into my face, until finally I said, "Do it or drop the gun and let's get going. I wanna be back before *American Idol*."

Oscar pushed the gun into my chest.

"Fine. Do it."

"Shut da fuck up, Chico!" Salvatore yelled.

Oscar just stood there, gun in my chest. It was stupid to say "do it." I knew better than that. But I was angry. And anger can make you do stupid things. I thought about Nicky's father, Carlos. Anger can kill you. What the hell, Santana?

I looked at Oscar and said, "I'd like to cancel my last order."

Salvatore inched toward us, slow, like a feather trying to make its way through syrup. And slow he removed the gun from Oscar's hand and slow Oscar relaxed, and slow he dropped his arms, and slow everyone let out a breath of air, relieved. No one more than me.

"Let's motivate," Salvatore said, grabbing my arm. "*Basta!* No more dickin' around."

"Do I have time to change my underwear?" I said.

We walked out to Salvatore's rusty red Mustang and he unlocked it.

I felt a hand on my shoulder. I stopped. I turned.

Oscar paused, looked down at his shoes, sagged his head.

"Maybe Sal's right," Oscar said.

He put out his left hand. We shook and I turned again to get into the Mustang.

The last thing I remembered was Salvatore yelling, "C'mon, guys, hop in," when I felt the metal object hit the left side of my skull, a connection of such force that there was not only a shock of pain but an explosion that made the world go white and fall sideways.

And then everything went black and there was no pain, nothing, and I saw myself rising above the cold streets of Pelham Bay. And all my past, my old thoughts, my old problems and theories, my old ideas and that picture I had of myself as a failure in love and work and family, left me. Just a Bronx orphan kid, a wandering, basement-dwelling, chain-smoking, beer-guzzling, coffee-swilling detective with a dead junkie doctor for a father and nut-job for a mother. The marriage, the lying, the messing around, all of it, it all left me. And I felt as though I were flying upward, without fear, everything bad vanishing from my sight as I went up. . . .

SIX

I awoke in a large, cinder-block room with one small but thick and gated soundproof window and a metal chair. My head ached like a busted drum. They had taken my shoes and the room was freezing cold.

I got up and looked out the window and saw a sea of docked trucks being loaded and unloaded with bags and boxes and crates. The mechanical Goliaths that caught my eye were marked:

HMD

MEAT & DAIRY

I was being held prisoner in a locked room in some refrigerated warehouse in the Hunts Point Meat Market. As kids we used to come to the market to try and hustle chump change loading and unloading trucks before anybody asked how old we were and if we were in the union. If they found out you weren't in the union, it was no money for the movies that night.

I was still standing at the window staring at a white stretch limousine parked near the entrance to the market when the door to my prison was unlocked and locked again. I turned and saw a man standing with a little Asian girl at his side. The man wore a white silk suit, a red handkerchief in the pocket, and expensive shoes. He was holding an unlit cigar and a copy of *The Wall Street Journal*. He was tall and athletic with a pale face, dark goatee, and green eyes.

"Have a seat, young man," he said and pointed at the metal chair.

Sweet. A kidnapper and a gentleman.

"I'll stand," I said. "But thanks."

"Do you like children, Mr. Santana?" he said, patting the little girl's head.

"Only if by children, you mean my inner child," I said. "No. My wife's the one who likes kids."

"You're married?" he asked.

"Separated at the moment," I said. "You're the host. How do we do this dance?"

"Gingerly," he said. "My name is Hannibal Rivera. The Third. I am Marcos Rivera's father. You may know him as Kirk Atlas."

Hannibal Rivera the Third. He smiled proudly when he said it. Except for the dark goatee, he looked exactly like the passport photo I had of his brother Samuel Rivera. They could have been identical twins. The child with him was about eight or nine years old, a pretty little girl with large almond-shaped eyes and straight black hair. She wore little heels, black stockings, and a little black dress under her winter coat. Her lips were painted red, her cheeks rosy, and she filled the room with perfume. She didn't look like a child at all, but a child made to look like a woman. And we were nowhere near Halloween. The idea of what could be going on made me sick in my gut.

"This is my goddaughter," said Mr. Hannibal Rivera the Third, as he put his arm around the girl. "Her parents are old friends and good employees, Chinese, hard workers."

He bent down and whispered, "Go, Ting Ting," handed her a red lollipop, and motioned for her to sit on the metal chair. Ting Ting sat, staring at the floor, sucking on her lollipop.

"Hablas espanol?"

"Not really," I said. "I'm stuck with English. But if you talk real slow I can understand most of it—except for the nouns and the verbs."

"Do you play?"

"Excuse me?"

Rivera held up his newspaper. "The market."

"Not my racket," I said. "I'm more of a bowler."

I took a deep breath and went into my pitch-slash-bluff. "Okay, Mr. Rivera. I'll forget all about this. The break-in. The aggravated assault. The kidnapping. Your wearing white after Labor Day. If."

"If?"

"If," I repeated, "you answer some questions. I ask the questions. You answer them."

Mr. Rivera plopped his cigar into his mouth and talked while he chewed on it. "Pena and Fiorelli warned me that you were a bit unorthodox. So am I. But what if I told you to go to hell?"

"I have nothing against New Jersey."

Mr. Hannibal Rivera offered his hand. I took it. Rivera nodded and said, "You're the boss."

I doubted it.

"Why are we here?" I asked.

"Your friend Pilar."

"I just met her," I said. "What about her?"

"She's dead."

"I know."

"Did you know she was a blackmailer?"

"We didn't talk much about her hobbies."

"A week ago, Pilar came to us and told us that our son Marcos has an unhealthy obsession. Finding his cousin Tiffany. She also told us that she knew of a videotape that would be extremely detrimental to our family. Do you have the videotape? We can pay."

"We?" I said.

"My wife and I," he said. "Josephine. We are only trying to protect our son."

"Pilar was blackmailing you. Pilar is dead. So you're worried about Marcos, is that it?"

"By God," he said. "You are a detective."

"Don't be glib," I said. "That's my job. How does Marcos feel about all this? He didn't seem afraid of Pilar at all."

"He doesn't know about Pilar's videotape. My son is a fuck-up, Mr. Santana. Just an overfed college drop-out with a regular monthly allowance. A series of fortunate accidents have made him more independent than he deserves. His mother is worried. She makes me worry."

"So Marcos is a momma's boy?"

"My wife is a bit older than most women with sons his age. She's not well. She has not left the house in three years. First, this upsetting business with Tiffany and the videotape and now, Pilar, who had been working for him, who was blackmailing us, commits suicide in Astoria. My wife suffers. When she suffers, I suffer. I don't like suffering, Mr. Santana. It plays havoc with my golf swing."

I noticed that Hannibal Rivera wore no wedding band, and that the shade of skin on the wedding band finger was even with the rest of his hand.

Hannibal Rivera held up his hand. "Your staring is making me nervous, Mr. Santana."

Ting Ting made a whining noise and pointed.

Mr. Hannibal Rivera took the little girl by the hand and went to the thick window. He lifted her up so she could look out.

"Mr. Santana," Rivera said, holding the girl, arms trembling. "My wife has a weakness. An Achilles heel. She loves her son and I love my peace of mind. I want to keep this trouble with Marcos in the circle of close family and friends."

"What trouble?"

"Tiffany running off. Pilar. The videotape. The blackmail. This suicide in Queens."

Mr. Rivera put the girl down again. "We want Marcos protected from himself, quietly. After Pilar Menendez came to us with talk about some videotape, we hired Mr. Fiorelli and Mr. Pena to keep an eye on Marcos *and* Pilar."

"Where is Tiffany?"

"I have no idea," said Hannibal Rivera. "And, frankly, I don't care. The girl is a lunatic. Her father tells me she believes in fairies or some such nonsense."

"What was Pilar blackmailing you and your wife about? What was on the videotape?"

"You're terribly demanding," said Hannibal Rivera. "For a man with no shoes."

I looked down at my socks. He had a point.

"I didn't hire detectives to locate Tiffany, Mr. Santana, but to keep an eye on Marcos and Pilar and report back any sign of trouble. Suicide would go under the heading of trouble."

"I understand," I said. "So what do you want from me? Recommendation for a better detective agency?"

"No," Mr. Rivera said. "You work for Marcos."

"Seems like it."

"I would like you to come and work for me."

"What about your son?"

"You can still pretend to be working exclusively for Kirk Atlas."

"Sounds like a double cross," I said. "Why would I do that?"

"I thought perhaps you were, like Pilar, interested in bettering your financial future."

"Right now," I said, pointing at my socks, "I'm just interested in shoes. Black Rockports. Size twelve."

"I'm sorry about that," Mr. Rivera said. "My instructions were to bring you here for our little talk. I didn't ask for any unnecessary roughness. I was very clear about that."

"Why did your hired goons search my apartment?"

"They were looking for the VHS cassette."

"The one that Pilar was blackmailing you about?" I asked.

"Yes," he said. "I want you to stay close to Marcos and recover this VHS cassette if you should come across it. I'm willing to pay generously."

"Who has this tape?" I asked.

"We thought Pilar. Then we thought she may have given it to you. We don't know. But we do suspect that someone close to Marcos may be in possession of it."

"What's on this VHS cassette?"

He grinned at me. "I'd rather not talk about it."

"I'd rather not look for something you'd rather not talk about."

"It's of a sexual nature," said Mr. Rivera.

"How will I know if I find it?"

"The tape will be clearly marked 'Car.'"

"Car? Why?"

"I'm not sure," said Rivera. "It's an old tape. Black with a white label. We gave Pilar a ten-thousand-dollar down payment, but she never got a chance to turn over the tape."

"Is there any connection between this tape and Pilar's death?"

Hannibal Rivera coughed and cleared his throat. "Certainly not."

"Good," I said. "I don't need that kinda trouble."

"What kind of trouble?"

"The sort," I said, "where the person who pushes a girl off a roof tries to do an encore performance using me as a stand-in. How much you willing to pay?"

"If you find the tape," said Hannibal Rivera the Third, "and you return it, without reviewing it, on your word of honor, you will never have to work another day in your life."

"How much *exactly* are you willing to pay for my services in the present tense?"

"One thousand dollars a day."

"You have a fine sense of humor," I said. "But I got troubles, pain, and heartache that need more love than that."

"How much love?"

"Crazy love," I said. "I'm a doughnut and coffee man, but I've heard that caviar is quite tasty. I'd like to spoil myself."

"One thousand per day, plus expenses?"

The more I played Hannibal Rivera into believing I was just another greedy punk looking for a big payday and the more he kept upping my price, the more I knew that this wasn't just about a runaway niece, baby-sitting, and damage control for a wannabe celebrity.

"I like you," said Rivera.

"Yeah," I said. "That's been going around lately. I'm a real likeable guy. Especially when my belly's full of expensive caviar. But you keep making offers for the cheap kind. Just how much do you want to protect your son, Mr. Rivera? I'd be more than just eyes. I'd be eyes, ears, nose, and throat. That's not cheap."

"Understood."

"But first." I eyeballed him like I meant business. "My shoes."

Mr. Hannibal Rivera the Third guided me to the door. He knocked. The door was unlocked from the outside. A man dressed in a black chauffeur's uniform entered, and without words or eye contact, he handed me my shoes and walked out.

I slipped on my Rockports and waved goodbye to little Ting Ting. She smiled and waved, too. I'll be back for you, honey, don't you worry.

Mr. Hannibal Rivera went into his breast pocket and came out with a white envelope.

He handed it to me.

"I always like to know what kind of man I'm doing business with," he said. "Now I know."

When I looked inside the envelope, and counted, I almost self-combusted. Twenty-five thousand dollars.

SEVEN

It was bright, cold, and the wind was blowing as I wandered past cement trucks and scrap metal yards, the Bronx River on my right, seagulls cawing overhead. Except for a few cars and trucks, the streets were deserted. The infamous hookers of Hunts Point weren't out yet and I felt like a man on death row reprieved from some undeserved doom. I walked away from the Hunts Point Market, away from that cinder-block room, away from Hannibal Rivera the Third and Ting Ting.

I thought about Mr. Chang. What would Mr. Chang do about Hannibal Rivera and Ting Ting?

Bruce Lee was the man who introduced me to movie martial arts, Mr. Chang was the man who tried to teach it to me in real life. Mr. Chang owned Chang Sporting Goods on Fordham Road and Tiger Chang's above it. I hung around the store with Nicky, who was working there after school peddling sneakers and training in the studio on weekends. One day, when everybody was at lunch, just me and Mr. Chang in the store, three teenage punks strolled in and picked up baseball bats, one shouting, "My kung fu is stronger than your kung fu!" Mr. Chang came from behind the counter, arms folded, and smiled, calm as a tree trunk, motionless as a rock. This was a thin, short, fifty-year-old-man who looked thirty. He wore simple khaki pants and white dress shirts. He had glasses. Mr. Chang looked more like an accountant than like a man who swam in the ocean in December and broke bricks with a dirty look. After studying the suspiciously calm Mr. Chang and his tiny smile for a bit, one by one the three knuckleheads got scared and threw down the baseball bats, cursing, "Ah, fuck you, Ching Chong. Charlie Chan. Ching-Chong-King-Kong!" After they left, Mr. Chang just nodded and I put the baseball bats back in their stands. When Nicky found out what had happened, we secretly tracked the punks down and proved our kung fu was stronger. When we told Mr. Chang what we had done, he fired us both, saying only, "You have not heard me." Walking back to St. Mary's, Nicky could only shake his head. "Either he don't understand or we don't."

I'm still trying to figure out which. . . .

I felt for the twenty-five grand stuffed inside my coat pocket. Still there. I turned left on Edgewater Road. I had not slept in days and my head was sore and welted from that knock-knock joke Oscar told with the end of his gun. But it was lunchtime and I was still sober. Not a bad day, Santana, I thought, as I walked and started daydreaming about Ramona. I could probably find her among the stacks at her job in the Brooklyn Public Library. We could be happy again. Take her out to a movie. Coffee and flan after at Mimi's. Maybe think big and go off with her to the Dominican Republic. Haiti? No. Puerto Rico? No. Barcelona? The mountains and the ocean are so beautiful. That's what Nicky said.

No.

Humoring rich eccentric jerks. That's part of the job. I'm used to it. Helping out an old childhood friend. I stand by that. But when Pilar Menendez was killed, that changed everything. One minute, she's alive and warm in my arms. Next minute . . . That's when I knew I'd do whatever I had to do to make things right.

I flipped open my cell phone and made the call.

"Hello, boss lady," I said into the phone.

Joy made a growling noise. "About time."

Joy St. James had been one of the first black female detectives on the NYPD. When she retired, she became a professor at John Jay College, where I'd been her star pupil. But that was years ago. Joy owned and operated, along with her husband, Hank, a retired Irish homicide detective, St. James and Company, a private investigation group with close ties to law enforcement. I was, until six months ago, one of nine independent contractors with St. James and Company.

"Did you miss me?"

"Not really," she said. "Six months you been gone. What've you been up to?"

"Sitting around eating bon bons. Watching Oprah. You know. Working on myself."

"You fill out that application for the gun permit?"

"Yeah. Thanks. Guns are good. I got six. One a month. One more and I get a free toaster."

"Smart-ass."

I crossed at Longfellow Avenue under pale sunlight, wind blowing cold, and repeated my mantra. "I'm not law enforcement. I don't wanna be law enforcement. My job is to gather information or find people, not kill them. I hate guns."

"Well, the bad guys are rather fond of them, Santini. Remember what happened to you on that crazy mailman case?"

"Flesh wound. It was a letter opener."

"Twelve stitches in your chin ain't no flesh wound, Santuna."

I inhaled deeply, and the burn of fresh air in my chest traveled to my belly. "I need a small favor."

"You haven't been awake for the last six months, I hope? How's the insomnia?"

"What're you, my shrink? I'm working a case. Guy named Kirk Atlas. He's a wannabe Hollywood actor."

"Kirk Atlas? Sounds made up," said Joy.

"You think? His real name is Marcos Rivera. Same animal."

"How's it pay?"

"Money's good."

"What's his malfunction?"

"Missing girl. Dead girl. The usual."

"How do you meet these people?"

"I don't know. I guess it just comes natural."

I stopped at a lonely bodega for a pack of cigarettes and a cup of coffee. Marc Anthony sang *I Need to Know* on a small radio. I pointed at the Newports and a pot of freshly brewed beside it and the thin grocer poured. I dropped the money owed and went back out before the five spoons of sugar even settled at the bottom of my cup and Joy said: "When're you coming in?"

I sighed and walked. I could see people and traffic and civilization in the form of the Bruckner Expressway. "I need some help."

"I got a possible Westchester case if you're interested."

I sighed again.

"You'll never get rich turning down work outside New York City, Chico. There is life beyond Van Cortlandt Park, you know?"

"I wear a Timex. I light my cigarettes with a silver Zippo and my shoes are Rockport."

"You're a ballbuster."

"Takes one to know one."

I sipped my coffee.

"We got a nice Jamaican girl working the phones here on the weekends. I could put in a good word for you."

"Now you're my pimp?"

"Somebody's gotta take care of you, boy."

"Good luck. Listen—"

"Why didn't you at least show up at the Christmas party?"

"I don't like parties."

"Sometimes I wanna punch you in the head, Chico."

"Stop flirting."

At the green light on Garrison, finally surrounded by other living souls, I walked through the shadow of the Bruckner Expressway overpass, past the stopped traffic of cars, through a small crowd toward the Hunts Point train station.

"Is there anything you do like?" said Joy.

"I like to be left alone, mostly."

"Why do I even think about you?"

"Because you're secretly in love with me."

"Right. I love the idea of living in a basement in the Bronx, waiting for you to stop working long enough to notice I've left you. That must be it. Poor Ramona."

"Ouch."

"You can take it. Come back to work."

"I'll stop by soon," I said, walking. "Can you have Kelly do some criminal background checks on the computer for me?"

"What's wrong with *your* computer," she said.

I came to a full stop on the Hunts Point plaza, opposite a necklace of shops and storefronts running along the crowded streets of Southern Boulevard. "You know I don't own a computer."

"Time to join the twenty-first century, Porto Rico," said Joy. "Let me have it."

"Albert Garcia," I said. "Marcos Rivera aka Kirk Atlas.

Samuel Rivera. Tiffany Rivera. Olga Rivera, Hannibal Rivera the Third, and throw his wife Josephine on the grill too with some Pilar Menendez."

I finished my coffee. A bus rumbled by and the wind started to blow so cold it felt like the skin on my face was being peeled back. A tiny old woman cursed the weather in Spanish. An African man selling bootleg DVDs out of a blanket on the sidewalk agreed with her in French. Two burly red-faced men in thick winter coats were hustling street money on a numbers game they were running off a folding table. A Latino holy roller in a dark suit, across from the plaza, outside Kennedy Fried Chicken, announced to disinterested Southern Boulevard shoppers that Jesus Christ cured AIDS.

"Anything else, your highness?" asked Joy.

"I especially need anything and everything you can get on Tiffany Rivera. Criminal records, last known address, school records. Tiffany Rivera is the missing girl and Pilar Menendez is the dead one. So any orders of protection for Menendez would be great."

"What do you mean she's dead?"

"I think she was pushed off a roof. Long story. I will owe you big time."

I walked toward the entrance of the underground Hunts Point station.

"Okay. But don't make me come get you," said Joy. "I wanna see your brown butt in here asap."

"Joy?" I said, going down the stairs for my train back home to Pelham Bay.

"Yes, Chico?"

"We'll always have San Juan."

"*Sayonara*, Santuna."

"*La cucaracha*, Joy."

I hung up and considered going to see Albert or Kirk Atlas. Nah. I needed some rest.

Let the cops have this quarter. If they got nothing, I got next. Maybe by the time I woke up, Samantha or Mimi would have some news about the Greek.

I wanted to go home. Really. I did. But all I kept thinking about as I went down those concrete steps to my six-train platform, was a pool of blood and white furry slippers with their little white hairs blowing in the cold winter wind. Pilar.

EIGHT

Murder?" said Albert. Seven A.M. He was slumped in a battered brown armchair under a black-and-white movie poster—*Out of the Past*—in his cramped apartment on the Grand Concourse. The armchair was an island surrounded by a mess of milk crates full of old VHS cassettes and film scripts.

Albert shared the one-bedroom apartment on Grand Concourse with his grandfather, Uncle Dee. Albert worked as a waiter at the Chinatown Angel on Fordham Road. Uncle Dee worked as executive chef in the dining room at HMO Financial, owned and operated by the Rivera family. Albert and his grandfather did not just love movies; they had a fourteen-film-a-week habit. They were movie junkies, black-and-white, the hard stuff. Albert's grandfather was in love with old films like *Marty, Harvey,* and *It's a Wonderful Life.* Albert was more about *The Maltese Falcon, Double Indemnity,* and *The Big Sleep.* Albert was a thirty-seven-year-old City College film student by day, a waiter by night, a wannabe movie director 24/7. Albert Garcia was an interesting and complicated cat.

I was sipping on a cold bottle of Bahia like beer had just been invented, looking through the milk crates for any tape marked "Car." I complimented Albert on his amazing film collection. I wondered aloud if I could look around a bit and maybe borrow something. He said he'd love to loan me any movie I wanted. *Marty* played on the TV as I leisurely searched the milk crates and talked to my old bud about my theory of murder.

"Was Tiffany's life in danger when she ran away?" I asked. "Was she a danger to herself?"

"No," said Albert.

"Is she a drug addict? A thief? Did she steal something or kill somebody?"

"None of the above," Albert said. "She's a good citizen, healthy, sane, eighteen years old, Julliard student, musical prodigy, beautiful, and smart as a whip."

"All right already," I said. "She's smart. God bless her. But is she or isn't she in danger?"

"No," said Albert.

"So lemme get this straight," I said. "You guys sent me to track a girl who doesn't want to be tracked. Who is not a teenage runaway, a drug addict, a thief, or a killer. Who has money. Who writes to say she's safe. Who is no danger to herself or others and I just happen to stumble into a murder?"

"C'mon, Chico," said Albert, still wearing his red polyester pajamas. "Accident. Suicide. Yeah. But murder? Jesus!"

"I saw two suspicious thugs outside Pilar's building. The next thing I know she's doing a Mark Spitz from the rooftop. I saw somebody up there."

"Who?"

"I don't know. It was dark."

"It was dark. Maybe it was your eyes playing tricks on you."

"Maybe," I said, examining a cassette. "Tell me more about your Kirk Atlas."

"I know that kid since forever," Albert said. "He owns the Chinatown Angel. He's my boss. He's my writer, my actor, my producer. I don't like it. I'm shooting a science fiction flick for God's sake. I wanna make crime pictures, heist movies, things like that. But beggars can't be choosers."

"I thought Kirk Atlas was your buddy?"

"Buddy?" Albert said in disgust. "The kid's a shark. There isn't one sincere bone in his body. Kirk's the kinda guy who laughs twice at a joke. Once when everybody's watching and then later in the week when he finally gets it. But he wouldn't kill anybody. Especially not Pilar. I wouldn't call it love. But they had a thing."

"Plenty of guys," I said, "kill girls they have a *thing* with. Tell me more, Albert. A girl is dead."

"Goddamit, Chico!" Albert yelled and jumped out of the brown armchair. "You don't think I know that Pilar's dead? It's a suicide. Everybody's messed up over it. My girlfriend Olga collapsed when she heard. Marcos sends Pilar home every night by cab. Why are you complicating this? Why did you have to drive her home?"

"I had a hunch."

"I bet you did," he said, fiddling with a framed movie poster on the wall. "Do you usually keep hunches in your pants?"

"Be nice," I said, leaning on a milk crate and looking around the room.

"Aw, c'mon, Chico," said Albert, waving his arms. "I knew Pilar. She was a pretty young thing who wasn't afraid to use what God gave her. Don't tell me you went home with her in the best interests of your client."

"I was looking for clues," I said. I didn't think it was too smart to tell Albert about Hannibal Rivera the Third, or that I suspected he was holding something back from me.

"You were looking for clues," Albert said. "And you thought the clues were in Pilar's brassier? Don't lie to me, Chico. I don't have a vagina."

"We're talking about murder, not lust."

"Murder? Pilar slipped and fell from her roof. Or she jumped. She's dead. It was a freak accident or an intentional suicide. That's all. That's the conclusion the police came to. I knew Pilar, you didn't. The girl was depressed, on a cocktail of Prozac and who knows what else? Always threatening to kill herself after some big fight with Kirk. You're just lucky the police didn't think you did something to her. Am I wrong?"

I stood up.

"Did you find anything you like?"

"Nah," I said. "Nothing I haven't already seen. Who is Irving?"

Albert looked annoyed by my question and shook his head. "Everything looks suspicious if you think about it long and hard enough, Chico."

"Who is Irving?" I repeated.

"Irving is a friend," said Albert. "We used to all hang out at Kirk's parties. Me, Olga, Tiffany, Irving, and Pilar. So what?"

"Do you know a Greek in Astoria that was also friends with Pilar?"

"No," said Albert. "I don't hang in Astoria. And Irving doesn't know where Tiffany is. He's harmless. Don't think so much, Chico. Concentrate on one case and one case only. Just do this job for Atlas. Keep following Samuel. Find Tiffany. And try to control your urges. Help me. Don't work against me."

"Where'd you go after you left Atlas that night?"

"Here. Watching movies. Olga was with me. She was studying. I fell asleep. I drank too much. Why?"

"No reason," I said. "Can I talk to Olga?"

"No," Albert said. "I don't want Olga involved. She and Tiffany don't get along. This thing with Pilar has knocked her on her ass. She's staying with her aunt Josephine. I can hardly get in there. It's like Fort Knox. She's got school, exams, constant pressure from her mother and father. I'm trying to explain this to you in a clear way, Chico. You don't get it."

"Explain it slower," I said.

"My grandfather busted his ass to pay for these four years of college while I worked part time at the restaurant. Paid for every short film I shot. He's expecting great things from me. He lost my mother. He lost my grandmother. I'm all he's got. I'm not gonna let 'im down. I'm not gonna break his heart. He doesn't deserve that."

"I look forward to meeting him," I said.

I remembered a summer morning, many years ago, outside on the stone stairway to St. Mary's. Twelve of us kids back then called ourselves the Dirty Dozen. It was Nicky, Rob, Gabriel, Leroy, Bryan, Tito, Fitzroy, Michael, Terry, Joey, Albert, and me. We were religious kids, good kids.

There were only eleven of us that day on the steps in blue blazers and striped ties, arguing about where to go after Father Gregory's Mass.

Sister Irene had come down earlier with some bad news and some good news. The bad news had been that Albert Garcia was gone. The good news was that Albert's long-lost grandfather from El Salvador and another man in a gold Cadillac had come to reclaim him.

We were all glad for Albert. Of course, that meant there were only eleven kids left in our gang. We had to keep the name, though; the Dirty Eleven just didn't sound as good.

"You'll love Uncle Dee," said Albert. "You'll see."

"Where is he?"

"Atlantic City," said Albert. "Getting his gamble on." He looked away at the TV. "I'm just a simple guy trying to make a film."

He fierce eyes were glowing. His black hair was thick, oily, and standing on his head as if electrified.

"I work," Albert said, "I shoot my film. I come home and eat Chinese take-out and then go up on the roof and whisper and sometimes yell to nobody and everybody on Grand Concourse: I'm not a waiter! I'm a filmmaker!"

"Anybody ever answer back?"

"Yeah," Albert said, disgusted. "Kirk Atlas."

"So he's not that bad?"

Albert shook his head. "Desperate times, *amigo*. Like I said, beggars can't be choosers. He's got money. I need money. But don't let my ass-kissing fool you. The kid's a punk. Take my word. But he's no killer."

"Why did you ask for my help if Atlas is such a punk?"

"He wanted you to help him. He's like a child. He meets you. You're a private eye. He gets it into his head he needs a private eye. Night we met, I could tell you didn't like Atlas. I know you. You're honest. Like Nicky. You don't like a guy, you don't waste your time."

Albert sat on the edge of the brown armchair and pleaded. "You gotta understand, Chico, *this* is gonna be my first full-length film, even if it is science fiction. Kirk's giving me an opportunity, and I'm helping him look for Tiffany and I'm helping you get some money in your pocket so you can get that wife of yours back."

"She's not like that," I said. "You've never met her. My wife didn't throw me out because of money."

"That's what you think," said Albert.

I shook my head. "This whole case stinks."

60

"Chico," said Albert. "I'm not gonna twist your arm. Give Atlas back his money. I don't blame you. We're still friends. No hard feelings."

Albert put out his hand as if to shake. I ignored it. I sipped some more Bahia.

"What if I can't find this Tiffany?"

"Who cares?" said Albert, dropping his hand. "You still get paid, Chico. I do my part. You do your part. That's the deal. That's business. Kirk ain't much of a human being but he's a businessman."

"So even if I don't find the girl, Atlas still gives you the money to finish your movie?"

"Man, we're almost finished with the movie," Albert said. "We only have a few scenes left to shoot. Then we edit. Submit to film festivals. Get it sold. After that, I'm free."

"And you don't want anything to stop that from happening?"

"Sacrifice, Chico. That's what this is about. *Sacrificio.*"

In my coat pocket I carried a paperback, *Driving Lessons,* written by Ramona Guzman Balaguer. My Ramona. It was about a half-Dominican, half-Haitian librarian and her crazy ten-year marriage to a private investigator who was obsessed with his father's murder. Fiction. Right. The word sacrifice turns up a lot in that book.

"If this movie's any good," Albert said, "I could be on my way."

"On your way where?"

"Anyplace but here," said Albert, and stretched his arms out.

I started walking across the room to get a better look at something.

Tacked on the wall, under a real but dusty Uzi machine gun and a movie poster for *Farewell, My Lovely*, was a photograph of the Willis Avenue Bridge marked:

"What are these about?" I said, pointing.

"The Uzi is a leftover from my grandfather's days as a cop in El Salvador," said Albert. He pointed at the Willis Avenue Bridge photo. "I swim like a brick. Worse comes to worse, I can always jump. Just like Pilar."

"Cheerful," I said. "I hope that's a really bad joke."

"Of course," said Albert, with a sardonic smile. "That would be littering."

I glanced at the Uzi. "Gun work?"

"No," said Albert. "It's an old piece of junk. But it looks badass on the wall like that, don't you think?"

"What's your grandfather's real name?"

"Daniel," said Albert. "Daniel Diego. But everybody calls him Uncle Dee, a nickname he got in El Salvador as a child on account of being such a quiet and serious kid. It stuck. Don't let his taste in movies fool you, he hates people."

"You ever get to meet your grandmother?"

"She died in El Salvador."

"Your mother?"

"I found out that my mother and father died in a fire. Get this, it was here in the Bronx. I was there."

"You were there?" I said.

"No memory," Albert said, knocking on his head. "Like some kind of post-traumatic stress. What you don't know can't hurt you."

Then he looked sad and stared at Ernest Borgnine on the TV again. "He was even uglier than me, and he made it."

Tears welled up in Albert's eyes.

"Robert Rodriguez. Quentin Tarantino. John Singleton. Steven Soderbergh. David Lynch. Cronenberg. The Coen

Brothers. Spike Lee. Screw them all. Help me, Chico. Just follow Samuel Rivera. Help me."

I nodded. On the outside. On the inside, I thought about Pilar and that last kiss we never had.

I looked back at the small black Uzi again and saw that there was a quote taped to the side of the machine gun: *"Believe! Have faith! Make film! Kill if you have to!"*

Like I said, Albert was a complicated and interesting cat. Looking at that busted Uzi on the wall, I couldn't help but wonder just how much more interesting he could get.

NINE

The newswoman on the giant TV said that it now took over one hundred million dollars to run for president in the United States. Atlas told me that he thought about running for president. He also told me that he thought about winning an Academy Award or maybe producing pornography. He had set aside the photos of the pretty actresses with big boobs who auditioned for his low-budget movie *Doomsday,* just in case the porno thing came to fruition. He considered all of these things, winning an Academy Award, running for president, and making porno with equal seriousness.

"Samuel Rivera," I said, "has a mistress. More than one, but no sign of Tiffany."

Loaded with countless cigarettes and coffee and a little sleep, I was standing next to Kirk Atlas, winter sun beating at the tall window of his luxurious penthouse apartment in SoHo, looking out at the Hudson.

"What do you want to do?" said Atlas.

"I'd like to take a look at Tiffany's apartment for one," I said. "I'd also like to get in closer to Samuel, see where that leads."

"Done," said Atlas. "Olga's staying at my mother's, she'll never have to know. And fuck Albert. You're the detective. I'll get the keys. My family owns the building. I'll think about the Samuel thing."

"Do you know a guy named Irving?" I asked, feeling lucky.

"Irving?" said Atlas. "He doesn't know anything. I already asked him."

"Mind if I ask him?" I said.

"Dude," said Atlas, "don't waste my money."

No luck. Don't push it, Santana.

I had spent endless hours, on different occasions, in restaurants, spas, and private clubs confirming the fact that Samuel Rivera was not in contact with his daughter Tiffany. And I paid a hundred dollars at one particular Midtown hotel to take a gander at the computers. Samuel Rivera checked in once a month with a different woman. Not his wife. Not Tiffany.

I had even gone to Julliard, located and questioned some of Tiffany's classmates and music teachers. I told them I was a musician, a saxophonist, and that I had a gig at the Knitting Factory downtown and needed a violinist for a mixed media thing based on the music in the movie *The Taking of Pelham One Two Three*. (Which was actually one of the many "cultural events" Ramona had dragged me to see last year.) Nothing. Tiffany Rivera had taken a leave of absence from Julliard. Her last known address was the Arcadia West where she'd lived with her sister, Olga.

Meanwhile, Pilar's case had been deemed a suicide and Kelly called back from St. James and Company to say she had conducted criminal history checks on my people. Except for disorderly conduct charges against Pilar Menendez, during an arrest at a protest march for immigration rights, they were all clean.

"Awful what happened to Pilar," I said.

"I told her," said Atlas, "stop going on that roof when you lock yourself out. Just call the landlord. She wouldn't listen."

"Albert thinks she killed herself."

"That's what the police think, too," said Atlas. "I think she fell. I'm gonna have her body flown back to Brazil after the funeral."

Kirk Atlas was curiously satisfied that his servant and lover had met with an unfortunate accident. Open and shut.

"Yeah," said Atlas. "I told the cops she probably went out—" Atlas paused. "*After* you left."

He gave me a wink and a congratulatory slap on the shoulder as if to say *boys will be boys* and continued, "Maybe Pilar went out in search of dog food for the Chihuahua. She stupidly forgot her keys, and locked herself out because of the automatic lock on her door. She did it at least once a week. She went out on the roof to make her way down through the fire escape like she always did and slipped somehow and fell."

Yeah, and the Pope celebrates Kwanza.

I watched his face for sadness. Nothing. Atlas smirked at me. It was the smirk of a kid used to getting his way, the smirk of a bully. But would he hurt Pilar Menendez? Would he kill Pilar if she tried to block his search for his cousin Tiffany?

I spent years at St. Mary's Home for Boys with kids just like Atlas. I had fought boys and half-grown men with that same smirk. I had loosened their teeth and blackened their eyes, almost killed one once when I was fourteen. I wanted to crack that smirk off his face. But I remembered the short stack of thousand-dollar bills in my basement studio and my anger went soft. Listen, I'm not rich. I'm poor, been poor all my life. Who was I to sniff at twenty-five thousand dollars? A poor man can't afford to swim in booze and women and greasy food, cigarettes, and self-pity forever, no matter how big a demon he's trying to drown. Believe me, I tried. I'd let Albert and Kirk Atlas think they were calling the shots, for the sake of gathering information, for Pilar. I knew this in my gut, it was no suicide, it was no accident. I didn't care what Albert or Atlas or the police said. The way Pilar called out to me before she fell says she didn't jump. "Chico!"

"I don't mean to rush you," I said, checking my watch. "But I got things to see and people to do. Can I have the dog?"

I never thought I'd ever be rescuing Pilar Menendez's Chihuahua, but there I was. When Atlas reported that he was taking Pilar's dog to the ASPCA in the morning and there was a chance that they could put it to sleep, taking it home until I could find somebody to adopt it was the least I could do.

"Take it easy," said Atlas. "You'll get the dog. Hang out a bit. You just got here."

Kirk Atlas, wearing a creamy white terry-cloth robe that looked soft as pudding, shook his head and said, "You have no idea, Chico. How hard my life is. Money, money, money. Even in my sleep."

Poor, rich Kirk Atlas. All that money. Somebody get me my saxophone.

Atlas checked his reflection in the tall window.

"Don't envy me, Chico, that's all I'm saying. Thank God you're poor."

"*Gracias a Dios*," I said. "Where is the dog, anyway?"

He ignored my question. "You don't know the kinds of trouble I have."

I looked around the penthouse with its freshly polished

floors, oak bar, and leather sofas. A swollen leather armchair sat on Persian rugs in front of a healthy collection of guns in a glass case. There was a drafting desk, a chair beside a new computer, tripods, microphones, an enormous DVD collection, and a digital video camera worth over ninety thousand dollars (according to Atlas) in a corner of the cavernous living room. Over the computer was a makeshift sign.

BIG BOOT PRODUCTIONS

I looked back at Atlas and said, "I can only imagine your troubles."

He nodded.

"Fuck it!" said Atlas. "You gotta milk this world. And you gotta be willing to pay the price for the milk, right?"

Atlas locked those cold green eyes on my face, and said, "I'm just like you, Chico. Man of action. I might even make a good P.I. myself. What do you think? I mean, from what you know about me so far?"

"Sure," I said. "Why not?"

Atlas beamed at me like I'd just handed him an award. Kirk Atlas. Short but handsome, prematurely balding maybe, prematurely rich, in need of love and acceptance.

I checked my watch again. "I should get going."

"Take a look at this first," Atlas said and handed me his film script.

I took the fat manuscript, 120 white pages bound in a black hardcover with a white label:

DOOMSDAY
Story and Screenplay by Kirk Atlas

I thumbed through it. "You wrote this?"

"Sure. I bought a book."

"A book?"

"Yeah. I bought a book. I sat up one night and finished the script."

"In one night?"

"I can do anything," Atlas said.

I checked my watch again. "I really should get going."

"Read the screenplay."

Pilar was dead and Kirk Atlas wanted to talk about screenplays.

"You gotta read it," he said. Then he proceeded to tell me the story himself. "Our hero, me, lands on an abandoned planet, but little does he know, there are two other inhabitants of the planet. A woman and a creature, part male, part snake. The creature steals the hero's alien woman for procreation purposes. Hero must fight to get his alien woman back and survive attacks by the creature. The fate of a new world depends on which of the two get the chick."

I thumbed through the screenplay.

"What do you think?"

"It's interesting," I said. "I guess. I'm just a simple private investigator."

I thumbed through the screenplay some more. Atlas had written his script, added plenty of make-out scenes with BEAUTIFUL ALIEN WOMAN and included his character, HERO SCIENTIST, on every page.

"Also," Atlas said, "I'm playing the Hero Scientist and the Creature."

Naturally.

I wanted to open the window and toss the script into the Hudson or force-feed Atlas the pages but he'd probably just say that it tasted good but needed a little more Kirk Atlas.

"Yeah," Atlas said. "Peter Sellers and Alec Guinness played

multiple roles all the time. Look at Mike Myers and Eddie Murphy. I'm the American dream, baby."

I stared at the creature.

Atlas snatched up an Iron Man DVD. "A film based on a comic book, a kid's story made over a billion dollars world-wide. I told Albert let's stop screwing around here. No more idealistic speeches. Let's make a movie. Let's get rich."

"You're already rich," I said.

"I'm not rich," Atlas said. "Four hundred billion dollars. That's rich."

Atlas went into a drawer and came out with some bills. He counted them and placed them on the drafting table. Two thousand dollars.

I looked at the bills. I picked them up. He smiled. "For your troubles."

I turned and saw a girl who looked a lot like Pilar Menendez, only younger, entering now, in a tight white uniform, carrying a silver tray of bacon, eggs, and sausage.

Atlas sat down like a king on a red leather sofa.

"Renata?" moaned Atlas. "Headache."

I checked my watch and cleared my throat. Atlas looked up at Renata and said, "Chico's impatient. He has to go get his legs waxed. Bring it."

She put the tray down on his lap and exited again.

"Renata, Renata, Renata," Atlas chanted. "Shameless Renata of Brasilia."

He scooped up a forkful of eggs and shoved them into his mouth.

"You know what I love about her?"

"Personality?" I said.

"No," Atlas laughed. "There's something brutal in her touch, something like revenge. And I love it, I love my new punishment."

"Way too much information."

"Don't tell me you're still a Catholic?" Atlas said.

"No. But I try to be decent whenever I can squeeze it in. Also, I have a mean wafer habit but that's another story."

"I borrowed her from my mother the morning when Pilar didn't show up. It's like I hit the jackpot. Three times before nine A.M. Apparently, Renata needs it nonstop."

Kirk Atlas was in lust and he felt the need to share this with me.

"Must be nice for you," I said.

Pilar Menendez was freshly dead and Atlas had already replaced her. Ah, loyalty. Atlas stood up on the couch and studied himself in the living room mirror that stretched from the floor to the ceiling. He admired his shaved head, his short but muscular physique.

"The low-carb, high-protein diet is working," he said. "The body is good, don't you think?"

Before I could say anything Atlas hit the wood floor, and did twenty quick push-ups.

The phone rang. Atlas ran to it and pressed speaker phone.

"Yo!"

A frail girlish voice said, "Why do you answer like that? Did you get the invitations for Pilar's funeral?"

"I'm having an important meeting with my agent, Ma." Atlas winked at me. "I got the funeral invitations. They're beautiful. Let me call you back."

"You always say that and you never do," Atlas's mother complained.

"Don't start."

"I love you," she said.

"Hanging up now, Ma." Atlas pressed a button and the line went dead.

Then I heard a small dog barking and looked up and saw

Renata enter with two pills, bottled water, and Pilar Menendez's Chihuahua, Baby.

"Thank you, Pilar," said Atlas, taking the pills. "I mean, Renata."

Renata gave Atlas an angry look and handed me the dog's leash and stormed out.

"Thanks for taking Pilar's mutt," said Atlas. "I can't. Condo rules. You understand."

I looked down at the Chihuahua. He looked up at me, shivering the way they do and barking. That's when I spotted a framed photo of Tiffany Rivera on a short table. She was wearing a fancy pink dress and stomping her black combat boots while confidently playing a violin in the living room of some ritzy apartment. A short man with a big belly, in an expensive double-breasted black suit, no necktie, black hair, fifties, husky, stood to her left, smiling proudly.

"Who's the guy in the photo with Tiffany?" I asked and pointed.

"My uncle Benjamin," said Atlas.

Then his face lit up. "Dude, I just got a more brilliant idea. You want to get in close to my uncle Samuel? I'll get you in close."

"How close?"

"As close as possible without your cover being blown."

"What cover?"

"Deep cover," said Atlas. "You can go undercover, dude. I can get you a job."

"What kinda job?"

"What do you know about international finance?"

"Just what I learned on Wall Street."

"The stock exchange?"

"The movie," I said. "Oliver Stone."

Kirk Atlas pulled a cigar from his big pocket, lit it, and puffed thoughtfully, "How do you feel about food service?"

"Well, I like the food part. Not so sure about the service. Why?"

"There's a position open in the executive dining room at HMD."

"How do you know that?"

"I go there for free lunch when I'm in the city," said Atlas. "I was there when the last waiter quit to go back home to El Salvador. I suspect you'd be a good waiter, Chico."

"Thanks," I said.

TEN

Mimi had found the Greek. It was night and we were sitting in Mimi's Cuchifrito sipping her homemade coquito. I was still wearing a tuxedo, not because I liked to play dress up, but because I had spent all day posing as an executive dining room waiter at HMD Financial where Samuel Rivera worked.

HMD Financial had its headquarters on 43rd Street. It was the banking arm of Hannibal International Meat and Dairy, which had farms in Mexico, Central and South America, the Caribbean, and Florida. There were three Rivera brothers: Hannibal Rivera III, Samuel Rivera, and Benjamin Rivera. Samuel Rivera was co-owner of the whole operation and vice president at HMD. His older brother, Hannibal, was the president. The middle brother, Benjamin, was the wild one, slumming in the sixties, hooked on fast girls and strong drugs.

Benjamin Rivera overdosed a couple of months back. Overdosed on heroin. It happens.

Anyway, I loved coquito. The rum and sweet milk never failed to take me back to those days on Brook when I would sneak sips from unguarded plastic cups at Mom and Pop's regular Friday night house parties, where the local folks, their friends, folks who worked in the factories and made the Bronx run, danced as if today was all that existed, as if today was nothing but sweetness. It was a time after the Bronx stopped burning, before the factories shut down, before all the work got sent overseas, before crack cocaine, before my father died. It was one of the best times I've known.

"His name is George," said Yolanda. Yolanda was the nanny in Astoria who lived over La Valencia Bakery. She sat on a stool on my right in large gold hoop earrings. She was about twenty-six. Dominican. Her face was dark like a soft brown leaf. Her hair was short and she had no trouble filling out her tight blue jeans and tight gold-colored blouse. No trouble at all. But I wasn't looking for any trouble. I needed a name.

"George Theodorus," said Yolanda. "He owns the Theodorus Taverna on Broadway and Thirty-first Street. He is a *loco* who spends a lot of time with neighborhood *borachos* and teenagers talking about nothing."

"I met George the night Pilar died," I said. "He was a little tipsy. And carrying a jug of ouzo."

"*Sí!*" said Yolanda, crossing her legs and adjusting the strap on one of her gold heels. "That is George. Always with his ouzo."

"How well did you know Pilar?" I asked.

"I don't know Pilar," said Yolanda.

"She knows a girl from Costa Rica," said Mimi, seated on my left, "who knows a girl from Colombia who knows a girl from Brazil who knows Pilar."

"Of course," I said, looking at Yolanda.

"George," said Yolanda, "is good friends with Pilar's land-lord. His name is Nikos."

Yolanda bit her thick bottom lip, handed me her nanny card with a long gold fingernail, and said, "If you need any-thing else, you call me. Any time."

I smiled and Yolanda stared at me and smiled back. And then Mimi cleared her throat and I helped Yolanda put on her gold-colored winter coat and grab her gold-colored purse off the counter.

Mimi cleared her throat again and made a face at me. She signaled not-so-discreetly by rubbing her fingers together as Yolanda stood there blinking at me.

"Oh," I said. "The reward."

I took out a hundred-dollar bill and handed it to Yolanda.

Yolanda frowned. "Mimi said two hundred."

"Right," I said and shot Mimi a look. Mimi, who under-stood the price of doing business and sharing the wealth, just smiled big. I handed Yolanda one hundred more and headed for the door behind her as she made her way home across the street to her husband and daughter over La Valencia Bakery.

"Where are you going, Chico?" asked Mimi.

"I'm off to see a Greek in Astoria."

"Wait!" she said, and grabbed her keys and winter coat and snapped off the lights.

"Where are you going?" I asked.

"I go with you," said Mimi. "I can help you, Chico. Yolanda told me *todo* about this George Theodorus. You will need me."

"Need you?" I said. "Why would I need you?"

Theodorus Taverna in Astoria was full of Greek men mostly, smoking and drinking, playing chess and talking. A waitress with hairy forearms and a bit of a mustache was collecting dirty coffee cups and smoking a Marlboro. The man behind the counter was the same potbellied Greek all right, still short, still bald, still wearing what looked like the same short-sleeved shirt and black slacks he was wearing that night we met.

George Theodorus gave me a look that said he didn't know me and didn't wanna know me.

"Can I help you?" he said.

"We met," I said. "That night with Pilar. You were picking up some ouzo. Remember?"

George Theodorus seemed to remember and shot me a dirty look and then he saw Mimi behind me with her red mane and cleavage and his look changed. He came from behind the counter and greeted me with a big bear hug like he'd known me for years. "Pilar," he said. "My poor Pilar."

Then George turned to Mimi. He grabbed her hand and kissed it and then kissed both her cheeks and said, "And who is this beautiful young red-headed Helen? From what Troy did you escape?"

Mimi giggled like she was the popular cheerleader in high school meeting the football star for the first time. George invited us to sit, to eat, to whatever we wanted or needed. We were his guests. We were welcomed. The cash register, perhaps?

Okay. Maybe Mimi was right. Maybe I did need her.

We went and sat at a small table in the back, under a giant fresco of the Parthenon in ancient Greece and a signed ancient publicity photo of the actress Anna Magnani. Maria Callas sang *Pagliacci*. George brought us cups of espresso and plates of stuffed grape leaves, feta cheese, and olives and insisted on telling Mimi about his world travels. Finally, after half an hour of this, I said, "I want to be honest with you, George. I'm not just a friend of Pilar's. I'm a private investigator, investigating the disappearance of a girl named Tiffany

Rivera. I think that Pilar's death smells fishy. Can you get me into her apartment for a look around?"

"What do you think, George?" asked Mimi.

George nodded thoughtfully for a long time, staring at me and then at Mimi. Then he made a call to his friend Nikos, Pilar's landlord, another bachelor who made ouzo in his basement and who George had been visiting for his monthly supply the night I bumped into him with Pilar.

We went back to Pilar's building on Ditmars. George's friend Nikos, who greeted us wearing a cheap three-piece suit, a striped tie, and a comb-over, kept smiling at Mimi after kissing her repeatedly on both cheeks like a man in the desert kissing a bucket of fresh water. Nikos called me a capitalist tool, politically ignorant, bourgeois, and an anarchist, and then gave me permission to check Pilar's apartment. I checked the stairs and the roof first, looking for some sign of foul play that the cops might have missed. Nothing. Nikos let us into Pilar's apartment.

I found no videotape marked "Car."

"What are you looking for, Chico?" Mimi said.

"I don't know."

That's when I saw the poem on the altar again, "Mad Girl's Love Song" by Sylvia Plath. I also found a folded piece of paper. It was some kind of title page.

Trilogy of Terror
by Irving Goldberg Jones

Later, George and Mimi and I walked and went and sat in Athens Park before a statue of Socrates. Nikos wanted to come but George said that he needed to talk to me and Mimi alone. As we sat, sandwiched between a children's playground and a basketball court, George told us that he would stay up with Pilar and Irving for many nights in this park or at the café, sharing the joys of poetry and philosophy and writing and ouzo and arguing the meaning of life and love. He smiled shyly at Mimi when he said love. He became almost like a second father to them, he said.

"What do you know about Tiffany and Olga Rivera?" I asked.

"Olga?" George said. "I never met the girl. But Pilar and Irving told me that she was a lawyer who wanted to be a writer. Irving helped her sign up for a writing class at Hunter College, where his father teaches, behind her parents' backs. Her parents would have stopped her if they knew, said Irving. It was bad enough she was dating some filmmaker."

"Albert?" I said.

"Yes!" said George and slapped my leg too hard. "That's his name. Never met him either. Olga, Tiffany, Albert, Marcos, I know the names. They were Pilar and Irving's Manhattan friends. They never came to Queens. And Tiffany? One of the things I know about that girl is that Irving was nuts for her and that she was the reason Irving and Pilar stopped talking."

"What happen?" said Mimi.

George continued, looking only at Mimi now. "One night here after they came back from the city, after some film, *Metropolis,* I think, Pilar and Irving had a big fight."

"About what?" I asked.

"About a story that Irving wrote," said George. "Pilar went home crying. That night, Irving sat right here and confessed to me that they knew something about Tiffany, who comes from a very powerful and dirty family. Something about a murder."

Mimi crossed herself. *"Dios mio!"*

George looked at Mimi intensely. "Murder! My soul wept

for that poor boy. Just nineteen years old and a beautiful boy with a beautiful soul in love with the common good and what has he gotten himself mixed up in?"

"*Pobrecito!*" said Mimi.

"Irving talked," said George, "about feeling divided and torn. And he wept and talked about loyalty and telling the truth and how guilty he felt, and how he cried, like Orpheus losing his love he cried. He was in hell. The morning after, he denied the whole thing. Claimed he was drunk. Blamed it on the ouzo. But he wasn't just drunk."

"About how long has it been since you saw Irving last?" I asked.

George was staring in Mimi's eyes and Mimi said, "How long?"

"About two months." George said, eyes on Mimi. "You can't bullshit a Greek, Mimi. In six days the Greeks created civilization. On the seventh day we created bullshit."

"No bullshit!" Mimi agreed.

"Exactly," said George. "You are from my generation, Mimi. You know."

Mimi gave me an *I-told-you-so* look. "I know."

"And Irving knew," said George. "Irving and Pilar knew something about this Tiffany and a murder and now Pilar is dead."

"Who do you think may have wanted Pilar dead?" I asked.

"The person who pulls all the strings," George said and looked over his shoulder. "Don't need a reason."

"Who pulls the strings?" asked Mimi.

"Pilar knew too much," George whispered. "Somebody wanted it covered up, just like Kennedy."

"Okay," I said. "Who?"

"Who has million-dollar companies on the stock market? Who owns apartment buildings in New York and property all over? Who travels the world and eats in expensive restaurants every night?"

"The Candy Man?"

"Chico!" snapped Mimi.

"Rivera," said George.

"Which Rivera?" I asked.

"Pick one," said George. "The whole barrel is rotten. Find Irving. He knows what happened to Pilar. He knows that the Rivera family is somehow responsible. Find the story."

I pulled out the title page that I found at Pilar's. "This story? 'Trilogy of Terror?'"

George shrugged and looked around and took Mimi's hand, "We're probably all in danger. They're probably watching us now."

Mimi jumped up and looked around nervously. "Chico! *Vámonos!*"

"No!" said George, also jumping up. "Wait, Mimi!"

"No wait!" said Mimi, walking away. "Watching us? No! You wait!"

So much for the Puerto Rican Agatha Christie.

I grabbed George by the arm: "Did you actually see this story that Irving wrote?"

"No," said George.

"Do you know where I can find Irving?"

"HMD," said George and quickly told me that Irving Goldberg Jones was an English major at Columbia University where Olga Rivera was a student. Irving lived on the Lower East Side with his mother and worked as a messenger at HMD Financial, owned and operated by the Rivera family, where Olga helped him get a part-time job.

I was posing as a waiter at HMD Financial and Irving Goldberg Jones was right under my nose all along.

"Chico!" yelled Mimi, standing at the entrance to the park. "*Vámonos!*"

"I'd like to talk to Irving."

"Irving will not talk to you," said George.

"Maybe you could talk to him for me? Introduce us?"

"Irving stopped talking to me," said George, heading toward Mimi, "after I told him that he had to tell the police if he knew anything criminal about this Tiffany. You're a cop. Irving hates cops."

"I'm not a cop," I said. "I'm a private investigator. We don't look as good in uniform and we're a little more bitter—served best with a white zinfandel."

George put his hand over his heart. "Pilar. She was a real good soul, you know? Clean. You too, Chico. And Mimi. Especially Mimi. I'm Greek. Greeks can tell."

"A clean soul. Is that a good thing?"

"Real good," George said. "If this Tiffany or any of her family did something to Pilar, I want you to get them."

"Most definitely," I said.

I shook George's hand as we walked out of the park toward Mimi, and George said, "Trust no one," as Mimi walked briskly before us toward my Charger repeating, "Chico! Let's go! *Vámonos!*"

ELEVEN

Murder. Murder. Murder. I couldn't sleep. I opened my eyes, and there were tears, and that same fucking lump in my throat. I got to my feet, went over to the kitchenette, opened the refrigerator, grabbed a beer that I had picked up earlier at the local bodega, popped it, and drank deep. I popped another one and drank that one, too. Then a third. It was starting again. The slipping back. As the light of the refrigerator cut through the darkness, the theme of my old life became visible in my basement apartment. I was alone. I had no one to count on and no one counted on me.

I lit a cigarette and looked around my one room. Everything had been scattered around by Oscar and Sal; my files, storage boxes, surveillance equipment, amateur boxing trophies, amateur martial arts trophies, amateur bowling trophies, my mother's rosary, old Curtis Blow and Grandmaster Flash tapes, old comic books, drawing pads, colored pencils, a baseball autographed by New York Yankee Roberto Clemente, and books Ramona had given me. I was gonna read them all some day. I picked up an old copy of the *Daily News*. I stared at the old advertisement I'd been saving:

Bronx Office Space
Available immediately in beautiful building on
149th Street and 3rd Avenue

Oh, I had plans.

I threw the paper down and grabbed my once favorite coffee cup, embossed with HAMLET in red letters. Another gift from Ramona from the times we had gone to see free Shakespeare in Central Park.

I picked out the signed copy of her paperback novel, *Driving Lessons*. Ramona—hazel eyes, fleshy lips, kinky reddish hair—smiled all sultry on the book's back cover. Before she had kicked me out of our rent-controlled Park Slope apartment six months ago, Ramona had accused me of suffering from serious trust issues because of the murder of my father and the loss of my mother when I was a kid growing up in the South Bronx. Things I could easily face in therapy, she said, if I stopped trying so hard to be a tough guy. Right. But that wasn't why she threw me out. It was the drinking and the smoking and the women.

Okay.

Maybe it was just the women.

I picked up the file on my father's murder, Adam Santana. They found my father, doctor to the poor and misbegotten, dead in his South Bronx medical office on Longwood Avenue with seven bullets in his back. There were crime scene photos, police reports, medical reports, forensic reports, ballistic reports, blueprints, fingerprints, footprints, facts, names, words, Savage Nomads, Red Skulls, Black Panthers, Young Lords,

Los Macheteros, everything and nothing. Words on white paper. Words, words, words. Facts, all disconnected. I had gotten this material with the help of Joy St. James and her police connections.

I picked up the missing person reports on my mother, Gloria Santana. I had everything I needed to get started, to solve my father's murder and track down my mother. I could hear Nicky Brown's voice saying, "So when are you gonna get started, baby? Today is today."

I picked up a framed wedding photo from the floor: Ramona in a beautiful white silk wedding dress, being embraced by me in a black suit, kissing at the columned entrance to The New York Public Library. Married in a Catholic church. The intimate wedding, down the aisle, ceremony and reception, twenty-five guests. Our song was Nat King Cole's "Unforgettable."

I put the photo down and went into the bathroom to splash cold water on my face. I stood wet at the bathroom mirror. Ramona's faded note was still taped to the middle of the glass: *I feel so lonely with you.*

I thought about Hannibal Rivera's twenty-five thousand dollars in the sock under my bed. I felt the lump in my throat. It was the same lump, the same burn in my eyes and chest. The lump felt new, as if I was reading Ramona's note for the first time.

I feel so lonely with you. It was the cruelest thing you could say to the person you claimed to love and cherish forever. Even if it was true.

That same Friday night, showered, cologned, mouthwashed, and aftershaved, I went looking for Ramona again in Park Slope, Brooklyn. Maybe it was the money. A little more money might make all the difference, I thought.

I drove from the Bronx to Brooklyn. It was 1 A.M. when I parked near Grand Army Plaza and got out of the Charger and walked toward Prospect Park. It was freezing and dark. The Brooklyn library stood majestic in the distance and a cold wind blew, as if to say, "It's over, Chico. Go away." I walked beside the park, shivering.

I walked for blocks until I could see Smiles Pizza and looked up at my old apartment at the top of the three-story brownstone. I quickly crossed the street and ran up the steps. I rang the bell. No answer. I almost yelled out, *Ramona!* But I didn't. I just kept on ringing. No answer. No luck. I used my old keys to enter the building, walked up to the third floor, and rang the bell at the door. The bell gave a small tinkle and I whispered, "Mona?"

I tried my old keys again, but found the locks had been changed.

Then the door opened and I saw her. She was wearing a nightgown and slippers in the shape of cats. Her face was brown and her thick, kinky reddish hair fell down about her shoulders.

"Hello, Mrs. Chico," I said.

"Are you insane?"

"I'm a detective," I said. "Of course I'm insane. What's your excuse?"

"I'm a writer," she said. "And at six in the morning I have to be at the library, where I have a job, where I pretend to be as sane as everybody else so I can pay my bills. So whatever this is, I can't."

I put on my best sad face. Ramona frowned but stepped aside and I walked into my old apartment and scanned the room. Everything, except the red rocking chair, was either gone or packed in brown moving boxes. The African masks were off the red walls and rugs were off the wood floors. The tall red bookshelf that used to be filled with the books of Zora

Neale Hurston and Virginia Woolf and Nella Larson and Marguerite Duras were bare. The Earth, Wind, and Fire albums were packed away with the Nina Simone, jazz, blues, and classical CDs, the Miles Davis print, and the balls of colorful yarn and knitting needles. The green houseplants that had covered every windowsill and the three stacks of *New Yorker* magazines that used to sit on the coffee table beside the French-English and Spanish-English dictionaries were gone. The only other object in the room not in a box or wrapped in crumpled sheets from the *New York Times* was a new manuscript.

The Detective
by Ramona Guzman Balaguer

Fiction again. Damn writers. They needed stories. Their story. Your story. That's what writers did. They stole. You're just giving her more material, Chico. What're you doing here? What're you thinking? This is nuts.

The two fat Siamese cats, Pushkin and Alexandre, scampered into the living room. Pushkin came brave and running, greeting my leg with head butting, body caresses, and purrs as if to say, "Wa'sup, long time no see, bro."

Alexandre, as usual, stopped, looked up at me with those wide and petrified blue eyes, and shot back out of the room, as if his tail had been set on fire. After ten years, Alexandre still didn't like me.

"Are you drunk?" Ramona asked,

"No."

"What's wrong?"

"Nothing."

"What're you doing here?"

I forced a smile. "I live here?"

Ramona did not smile.

"I have a case. My own case. I wanted to talk. Didn't know where else to go. A girl is dead. Just twenty-two years old."

"Did you sleep with her yet?"

"That's a rotten thing to say."

Ramona looked away. "How are you?"

"I'm fine," I said, the lump in my throat.

"Really?"

"Roof over my head, job, plenty of Irish Spring soap."

"Good."

"Jesus, it's good to see you."

"We have to make this quick. I have a used book sale at the library in the morning and a signing Monday night and I'm moving."

"Why?"

"I can't live here anymore," she said. "Too many old ghosts."

"It's rent-controlled."

"You want it?"

"No," I said.

Suddenly I grabbed her and kissed her. I couldn't help myself. She smelled of mango and coconut shampoo. I pulled her close and ran my hands along her thighs, grabbed her bottom, thick and trembling under my touch, her heavy breasts against me, and she didn't resist. She touched and kissed me and pulled at the waistband of my pants. Then she stopped.

"Wait."

"What's wrong?"

Ramona was silent but I knew.

She sat on a large brown moving box. "I can't."

I sat down on the red rocking chair next to her in sudden exhaustion. A chill came over me. My teeth chattered and all my limbs were shaking.

Ramona groaned and repeated, "I can't."

I leaned back in the rocking chair. "What is it you once loved about me?"

"You were a free spirit, Mr. Ramona."

"So why did you stop loving me, Mrs. Chico?"

"You were too free, Mr. Ramona."

"At least I'm consistent. Gimme a second chance, *mamita*."

"You never should've slept with those girls. You never should've done that."

"I was wrong. I'm changing. I'm making some real money on this case."

I dug into my coat pocket to show her the two grand I had recently gotten from Atlas. Ramona looked away.

"What's wrong?"

"Nothing. *Nada*. You shouldn't be walking around with that much money in your pocket. And you should go."

She wanted change, and I wouldn't change, and now I'm back and I'm changing, and I got money, too. Why is this so hard?

Ramona sighed deeply. "I've had enough, Chico. I've had enough struggle with you. *Oye*, ten years is enough."

"I have money."

"It's not the money. It's you."

I got up and moved toward Ramona.

I placed my hand gently on Ramona's breast.

Ramona put her hand over mine and said, "What're you doing little pig?"

"Doing what little pigs do."

"That's all you want, isn't it?"

"No. I'd also like some corn bread."

"Well," Ramona said, taking my hand away. "I don't want it anymore. Not with you. I can't."

"You can."

"I don't want to."

I pulled the Zippo lighter out of my pocket and began to fiddle with it.

"If you've changed, why do you still have a lighter?"

"I do a lot of reading in bed?" I gave Ramona a guilty look.

"So who killed your girl?"

"I don't know, yet," I said.

She bent over an open box and tried to hand me a stack of battered old books.

"I don't want your old books."

"You hungry?"

I looked at her from head to toe. "Very."

Ramona shook her head as if to say that I was hopeless and went to the kitchen to cut me up some of her sweet homemade corn bread. I watched her fleshy legs moving across the kitchen. The two silver cat bowls were still on the floor. The refrigerator still supported a gang of magnets—Human Rights Watch, United Homeless Organization, Meals on Wheels, and my mother's old *sofrito* recipe, written in my mother's hand:

Cut green peppers, orange peppers, garlic, onions, olives and other ingredients into small pieces. Place ingredients in blender. Fill blender with half an inch of water. Put blender on CHOP. Place into small plastic containers. Keep what you are going to use in fridge. Freeze the rest for the future.

For the future. Poor *mami*, I thought, and then I imagined Ramona as a child growing up in Santo Domingo, and I remembered the kisses we shared that first night on the Columbia campus (on the steps of the Loeb Library) and the love and the sex and how we promised it would never end. And now Ramona placed my sweet corn bread and two cold beers, Sam Adams, on the kitchen table as Billie Holiday sang, ". . . He beats me too."

And we sat under a framed print of Frida Kahlo's two

nude women in a forest and everything felt unbearably sad and lost.

"Listen," I said, fighting that stupid lump in my throat again by changing tracks. "Do you still know that girl who works in administration at Columbia?"

"Woman," snapped Ramona.

"Woman," I repeated. "Do you still know that woman who works in administration at Columbia?"

"Cynthia?"

"Yeah," I said. "Could you have Cynthia check and see if she can dig up anything written by a student there named Irving Goldberg Jones?"

"Oh my God!" said Ramona, her eyes wide, jaw dropped.

"What?"

"Is that why you're here, Chico? You need help with your case?"

"No," I said. "Of course not. Never mind."

But the truth was that she was partly wrong and partly right. Killing two birds with one *piedra*. That was my modus operandi. After ten years, Ramona knew exactly how I rolled.

She shook her head and said, "Hopeless."

And, later, alone, outside Ramona's, standing on the stoop, looking off at the trees of Prospect Park, I lit up a cigarette. I took the smoke into my mouth and I inhaled as deeply as I could, and it hurt, it hurt like a boy shot in an argument over dice, it hurt like a woman attacked in a park, it hurt like a dead man on the stairs. It hurt something like home.

TWELVE

W e're dropping Samuel Rivera for now." It was Saturday and I sat in Kirk Atlas's Hummer 2, a bloated white whale of a car with tinted glass windows. We drove across the Willis Avenue Bridge into the Bronx.

"Do you know how many male chauvinists it takes to screw in a light bulb?" Kirk asked, not responding to my statement, since every minute of the day was just another excuse for the Kirk Atlas Show. And away we go. . . .

"How many?"

"None," he said. "Let the bitch work in the dark."

Atlas laughed like I was the one telling the joke and he had heard it for the first time.

"That's a good one," Atlas said.

"Yeah," I said. "Good one."

Detecting crime, like life, is a chess game. Okay, checkers. I don't know how to play chess. But in either game, at some point, you gotta make your big moves. So far, I was making small moves. Going forward, becoming one of the guys in Atlas's book, trying on his beliefs, opinions, ideas, jokes, no matter how putrid.

Being a private investigator sometimes means you gotta play against your better self if that's what it takes, charge into your opponents' vulnerability, revealing compassion for them even if you have none, jive if you got to. Jive's a big seller. Jive gets you information, confidence, confession.

You play to come out of every rap session even closer to the suspect than when you came in. You could lose, make a false move; a little too much jive could wipe you off the board. But there's no other way sometimes.

The funny thing was that Kirk Atlas wasn't a murder suspect in my mind—he was just my egotistical client—but damn if his father Hannibal with his "Car" VHS cassette didn't seem like a good suspect.

"I want to look at a kid, a part-time messenger at HMD."

"Who?" asked Atlas.

"Irving Goldberg Jones," I said.

"Again with Irving?" said Atlas. "I told you already. He's a waste. He's a *socialist poet,* for God's sake."

"A socialist poet?" I said. "Sounds contagious. I have reason to believe that this kid Irving knows where Tiffany is. I need you to trust me and take my word for it. I need you to put in a call to your inside man at HMD. Have me transferred from the dining room to the mail room so I can have some intimate chats with this Irving Goldberg Jones."

"But why? Where are you getting your info from?"

"I'm telling you I think he knows where Tiffany is. I might catch them together."

Atlas looked at me skeptically. Then I heard the joy in his voice. "Deep cover?"

"Yeah," I said. "Deep cover."

"Fine," said Atlas. "Brilliant!"

"What are you going to tell them at HMD about my transfer on Monday?"

"I'll tell them you're allergic to butter," Atlas said. "Who gives a fuck?"

"I do," I said. "People talk. Tell you what, I'll get myself fired."

"Why fired? Why not just have you transferred?"

"I need Irving to trust me. I wanna build sympathy with the socialist poet community at HMD."

"You'll need a reason for them to fire you."

"I'll think of something. You just have your man call the executive dining room on Monday. Have them call around seven A.M. with a job opening in the mail room. I'll do the rest."

"You still wanna check Tiffany's apartment tonight?"

"Yeah," I said.

"Olga's still at my mother's," said Atlas. "Uncle Dee suspect anything at HMD?"

Uncle Dee was a good guy. I felt bad lying to him.

"As far as Uncle Dee knows," I told Atlas, "I'm just Albert's old childhood friend and a professional waiter."

"Okay," said Atlas, driving, one hand on the steering wheel. "The key will be waiting for you tonight at the Arcadia West. Monday, you work on Irving. And if you find Tiffany soon, I'll get you gigs in Los Angeles."

"Los Angeles?" I asked.

"Dude," said Atlas, after checking his teeth in the rearview. "I already talked to some people about you. People with big money and big problems. People who like privacy. If you do good on this Tiffany thing, sky's the limit."

"That's pretty high," I said.

Atlas spit out the window of the moving Hummer 2. I gave him a disgusted look. He smiled.

The Arcadia West, a luxury building over thirty stories, complete with crystal chandeliers, was just behind Lincoln Center and across from a housing project. It was freezing outside. I entered at a large back door marked EMPLOYEES and approached this white guy, an iron-faced guard in a uniform and matching hat, sitting at a desk.

"Morning," I said. "I was told to report here. I work for Marcos Rivera. My name is Chico Santana."

The guard looked at his visitor list and then at me with a scowl and puckered lips.

"Identification and sign in," said the guard.

I flashed my driver's license and signed the smudged and tattered white sheet of paper filled with rows of names and destinations attached to a brown clipboard.

"Take the elevator to the basement."

I walked to a freight elevator. In the basement, I was greeted by a tall, skinny, black kid with curly hair that glistened with gobs of gel. He was wearing a clean gray maintenance uniform a size too big for him.

"Watchu want?"

"I'm here to pick up some keys," I said. "I work for Marcos Rivera."

The kid smirked.

"Go to the back. Into the laundry room. That's where they keep the maintenance office."

I pointed down the hall. "Back there?"

"Yeah, genius. Back there."

I stared at the kid. The world is ruined by killers and creeps.

I walked into a large, brightly lit room filled with washing machines. There was a tiny office in the corner of the room marked MAINTENANCE. I went inside.

It was empty except for some folding chairs, one desk, and a wastepaper basket. An old radio played Frank Sinatra: "I can't give you anything but love, baby."

A fat man, another white dude, entered the room. He was wearing a shirt and tie with Wrangler jeans, and a Mets baseball cap. The fat man sat down at the desk. Holding his belly. He looked at me and said, "Who the hell are you?"

"Chico Santana."

The fat man studied my face. "You the one Kirk Atlas called about?"

"Yeah."

"You an actor, too?"

"No. But I dance a mean Bachata."

The fat man frowned. "What did you do before you worked for Marcos as a messenger?"

"Me?"

"No. The guy sittin' next to you."

"Waiter."

"You used to work as a waiter?"

"Variety is the spice of life," I said.

"How old are you? Twenty?"

"Much older."

"Bullshit."

I handed him my driver's license. The fat man checked it and said, "Baby-faced killer, huh?"

"Something like that."

"So you work for Atlas?"

I nodded.

"The big shot!"

"Right," I said. "The big shot."

"So whatchu doin' down here?"

"What goes up must come down," I said. "I'm just here to check out an apartment."

The fat man gave me a skeptical look, laughed. "Right. Well, I don't need any more troublemakers down here. Are you a troublemaker?"

"No," I said. "Can I have those keys now?"

The fat man smiled. "Why don't you just sit your black ass down till I tell you what's what? I'm the boss down here. I don't need you. You need me. Understand?"

I glared at him.

"Down here, tough guy, I'm Kirk Atlas," said the fat man. "I run the company. I'm the big shot. Sit!"

It was zero below outside and midnight and I wasn't about to drive all the way back to the Bronx empty-handed. I swallowed hard and sat.

The fat man held up my driver's license. "That's better."

I didn't know what kind of power trip he had on his menu but I had a job to do.

"First things first." The fat man grinned and yelled, "Malik!"

The skinny black kid with too much gel in his hair entered on cue.

"What's up, Danny?"

Danny, the fat man, placed one of the folding chairs in the middle of the room under the naked overhead bulb. He looked at me. "Go ahead, pretty boy."

"Go ahead?" I said. "Pretty boy?"

Malik, the skinny kid looked at me and laughed.

"You need the keys?"

"Yeah," I said.

The shit life puts you through.

"So stand on the chair, dummy," said Malik.

I said with gritted teeth, "C'mon, brother, gimme a break."

"I ain't your brother," Malik said.

Danny the fat man said, "It's like a rite a' passage. Everybody passes through here does it. Right, Malik?"

Malik nodded.

I got up on the wobbly chair.

Malik looked up at me. "Sing!"

I looked down at Malik. "'Scuse me?"

"Sing!"

"What should I sing?"

Malik smiled from ear to ear. "I'm a Little Teapot."

Slowly I sang like I was playing Amateur Night at the Apollo:

> "I'm a little teapot, short and stout.
>   Here is my handle.
>   Here is my spout."

Danny and Malik laughed, bent over and backslapping. I saw somebody out of the corner of my eye, come in through the door of the small office . . . applauding.

I turned my head. "Albert?"

Albert Garcia stared up at me, holding a Nikon camera, and snapping photos of my finest hour. Behind him were two maintenance men in gray uniforms, eyes searching. The shorter of the two also looked up at me, wearing an evil grin and a name tag over his heart.

I looked at his name tag: JOSÉ. He had blondish hair, thick and heavy with hair product, combed back from his pale white face, heavy lidded eyes like a frog. No, his name was not José. I know this guy and he's no José.

Private Investigator Oscar Pena.

Standing at Oscar's side was Salvatore Fiorelli, also wearing a maintenance uniform. Danny the fat man clapped me on the back and said, "I didn't think you'd actually do it, kid!"

Malik doubled over with laughter. "Rite of passage! That's a good one, Danny!"

"Okay, okay," Albert said. "That's enough, ladies."

The maintenance men, including Oscar and Sal, filed out of the room. Albert closed the door behind him.

"What the hell is this about?"

"Easy." Albert laughed. I need a soundtrack for *Doomsday*. You got a great singing voice. You're hired."

"Is this Tiffany's building?"

"Yeah," Albert said. "And Olga's."

"Is this about Olga?" I asked, jumping down off the folding chair.

"No," said Albert. "We were shooting some stuff in Central Park and Marcos told me about you coming here tonight and going to see Irving in the HMD mail room on Monday. Even after I told you that Irving and Olga don't know anything. I thought it was funny. You're stubborn. I brought you into this thing, remember? I know you."

I nodded.

But I didn't know what to think or who to trust.

"You don't want me to search Tiffany's apartment?" I asked. "You don't want me to find Tiffany?"

"I don't care," said Albert. "I'm not trying to mess up your search, man. I'm serious. This was just a joke. We're friends, Chico. No matter what happens, okay?"

"Sure," I said.

"Tell you what. I'm gonna go shoot some photos to use in *Doomsday* tomorrow. I want you to come along. A walkabout. Like in the old days. You want to see the apartment?"

Albert went into his coat pocket. "You need anything else? Call me. I'm your friend, not Atlas. Remember that."

He tossed me some keys, and said, "See how easy?" The back of the key chain in the shape of a musical note was inscribed:

There is no war in poetry.
Love, Irving

Upstairs in Olga and Tiffany's apartment, I was as giddy as a diabetic set loose in a candy store. I checked both bedrooms. Olga's bedroom was neat and tidy. Two bookshelves. One filled with poetry. The other filled with books on law and political science. Tiffany's bedroom was empty. The walls were a pale pinkish color with white trim. It looked like the inside of a birthday cake. There were angels painted on the ceiling. I went through Tiffany's empty drawers, searched her empty shelves, her desk, her closets, looking all over for a clue, anything, something mistakenly thrown away, left behind that might tell me something about her or Olga or Irving or their relationship. Something that might help me figure out what happened to Pilar. All I found was some Zoloft prescribed to Olga and an opened book in Olga's bedroom that was sitting on top of her comforter, Sun Tzu's "The Art Of War." I flipped it over and read a sentence underlined recently in red ink: *Make them mutually suspicious so that they drift apart.*

THIRTEEN

Sunday afternoon we met in Greenwich Village. Albert shot bars and clubs and pool halls and teenagers in black with vampire teeth and platform shoes and NYU students and drunks in love with liquor. A walkabout. Like in the old days. We went through Stuyvesant Town to Lexington to Broadway. At the Flatiron Building, Albert talked about the one billion gallons of water pumped every day into New York. But I was looking for another kind of information.

"Fascinating," I said sarcastically as we passed under steel and glass, culminating in the 1,250 feet of the Empire State Building.

"No need to get nasty, Chico."

"Sorry, bro."

I relaxed a bit as we trekked from the concrete lions perched outside the 42nd Street library, to the ever-flashing lights of Times Square and Broadway, to the multileveled Museum of Modern Art, to Central Park.

Central Park was an endless frigid gray of naked trees and fields and paths. We walked to the Bethesda Fountain and watched the water just like when we were kids.

Albert lit a joint and inhaled and said, "We should move to Texas!"

Then he talked about our mutual love of movies and the possibility of my helping him write and shoot a screenplay idea he called *Killer's Way*. He talked about replacing "that treacherous Serb of a cinematographer from SVA" with me. Albert would teach me everything he knew about camera setups. I would follow Albert's directions, point and shoot, point and shoot.

"How hard could it be?" said Albert, puffing on his joint.

"How much you paying?" I asked.

"You would work for free," said Albert. "You're an amateur."

"Sounds about right," I said.

"If you can solve crimes," Albert said, "why not shoot a crime picture?"

"I know it's been a bad week," I said. "But you're starting to babble."

We walked some more through Central Park and Albert shot photos sitting on rocks and on benches and in empty children's playgrounds. We walked through hidden woods and streams and curving paths and Albert spread his arms and started running, yelling, "I am Spartacus!"

I ran, too. Like two fucking kids we were.

As the sun went down, Albert stopped shooting and we went bowling for a couple of frames at the Port Authority bowling alley and then we doubled back to a Times Square movie theater and caught a crime picture.

Afterward, outside the theater, Albert hummed Nancy Sinatra's "These Boots Were Made for Walking" and said, "Kubrick woulda done it better."

"Uh-huh."

"You know what?"

"What?" I asked.

"You and me, Chico. We're both guys who've been knocked around. Nothing handed to us. Scraping from the bottom. We have to work harder and longer to get what we deserve out of life."

"What do you deserve?" I asked.

"Everything," Albert said. "Everything."

Merrily we went to my favorite old dive bar, Rudy's, on 8th Avenue. The bar, dark and fairly empty, smelled of beer and hot dogs. Sitting on a wooden stool, before a bowl of shelled peanuts, I finally said, "Pilar and Olga and Irving. They were close friends, huh?"

"They had a lot in common," said Albert. "Depression. They talked about it all the time. I ain't exactly Mr. Shits and Giggles myself. But it was like a little club they had. That's why Pilar's jumping is no big shocker."

"A suicide club?"

"No," Albert said, shelling a peanut. "Not that psycho. Irving and Olga met in a political science class at Columbia. Then they started hanging around with Pilar after Irving recruited her at one of the world-famous Kirk Atlas parties. Poetry. And social justice. After that, Pilar and Olga and Irving got real close. Then we all started hanging out together for a bit. Until Benjamin died and Tiffany ran off and Olga got mad at Pilar who was mad at Irving and everybody went their separate ways."

The bartender came over with a pitcher of cold draft beer, two glasses, and two hot dogs, set them down in front of us, and walked away.

I poured myself a glass and one for Albert. "Why didn't you

tell me about Irving working at HMD when I asked you about him?"

"Guess I didn't think of it," said Albert, biting into his first hot dog.

"You forgive me, sweetheart?"

"Yeah," I said. "Sure, honey."

After too many beers and bad jokes and Johnny Cash songs on the juke, we headed out of the bar.

"Oh," said Albert. "One more thing. You'll be going into HMD and talking to Irving, who is big on conspiracy theories, so better you hear it from me instead of him. Not that I ever liked your being at HMD with my grandfather in the first place but the man with the gold makes the rules and that man ain't me."

"All your grandfather knows," I said, "is that we knew each other at St. Mary's."

"Don't get paranoid," said Albert. "But Benjamin Rivera overdosed two months ago around the same time Tiffany disappeared. Overdosed on heroin. And Irving seemed to think that Benjamin's overdose was not accidental, that Benjamin Rivera had been murdered for insurance or for property or for stock shares in HMD. That it wasn't an overdose. That it wasn't an accident. That's what he told Olga. That it was murder. The boy is cuckoo."

"Do you know anything about some story that Irving may have written about Tiffany?"

"No," said Albert. "What story?"

I studied his face to see if he was bullshitting me. Nothing. His confusion was genuine.

"What story?" repeated Albert.

"I don't know yet," I said. "Probably nothing."

Either way, Hannibal Rivera the Third and Kirk Atlas made for some very *interesting* employers.

HMD Financial. Forty-third Street. Six A.M. Monday morning. At Fifth Avenue, I entered the bank's Art Deco lobby, nodded at a friendly guard, flashed my I.D., took the elevator to the seventh floor, and opened the door to the brightly lit kitchen.

"Cancel my account!" Uncle Dee yelled and threw the invoices he was holding on the stainless steel counter. He slammed down the phone and took a slug of rum from his silver flask.

"In the old days, Chico, at this time, I would be making love on silk sheets with a beautiful woman in some exotic part of the world."

"Those were the days, huh?"

Uncle Dee smiled and nodded, then frowned. "Mr. Samuel Rivera forgot to say good morning again."

"Jerk!" I reached up and removed the basket from the regular coffee machine.

Uncle Dee pointed at the ceiling, "He comes down here and complains about our running out of trout last week for that Hong Kong meeting. Doesn't even say good morning or *holá* or anything. Just complains and goes back out."

"You don't need Samuel Rivera's *holá*."

"We all need the *holá*. It's common human decency, Chico. It's not much, but it's minimum."

We are all at war, and Uncle Dee thinks a hello across enemy lines is a white flag that says it's okay, you can rest here.

"Ah!" Uncle Dee remembered something and made an impolite gesture at the ceiling. "Samuel Rivera complained about my omelet!"

"No!"

"Yes!"

Uncle Dee's Spanish omelet was made with fresh ingredients only, always the best. He was gifted in the art of cooking, but the omelet was his secret weapon. It was spiced and seasoned just right, with an equal distribution of extra ingredients, white onion, green onion, finely chopped tomato, and some El Salvadorian ingredients he would not name. To question the quality of Uncle Dee's omelet was to question Uncle Dee's right to exist.

There were no words in English or Spanish for this kind of insult. And when there is no consolation in words, men like Uncle Dee do one of four things: they fight, they make love, they drink, or they work. It was time to work, so Uncle Dee began to crack his eggs, chop his vegetables, grease his pans, and start his fires.

Inspired by Dee's work antidote, I left the kitchen and entered the executive dining room. I lined the credenza along the oak-wood walls with cereal boxes, milk, sugar, and seven bowls. I counted and placed seven spoons, seven forks, seven butter knives, seven cloth napkins, seven linen mats and seven coffee cups at seven spots on a long mahogany table.

I almost forgot that I was a private investigator and not a professional waiter. Almost.

Soon seven executives shuffled into the HMD dining room wearing their plastered-on smiles and business suits. I stood at my place beside the glass door, leaning slightly against the wall, with two coffee pots.

Samuel Rivera, wearing glasses and a dark pinstriped banker's suit and tie, said, "Hannibal has to start pulling his weight."

Somebody else said, "What do you propose?"

"I don't know," said Rivera. "But he can't just keep sailing the world on *La Nina*. A different port every night and when he's in town he does nothing but drive around the city in his limousine. I mean, if you were President of this company and you did that, what would happen? Just think about it. He's the eldest. He's supposed to be the responsible one."

Eyebrows were raised around the room, tiny smirks.

"I don't know about you," Rivera said, looking around the room. "But I couldn't do that. A man needs to work."

Another suit said, "I might be able to force myself. Floating around the Mediterranean doesn't sound so bad."

Two suits smiled.

Mr. Rivera frowned.

"No. You're right, Sam," another executive said. "It would be tedious after a while."

Samuel sat at the head of the long mahogany table, then the rest of them sat. At forty-six, Samuel was vice-president of HMD and the youngest man in the room. Add a goatee and a dollop of transparent evil and you'd swear you were looking at Hannibal Rivera the Third. The other men at the table were in their late fifties or early sixties. They sat mostly in silence, under the bright and colorful Picasso prints, as I went around the table with the two coffee pots. It was time to get myself fired.

I stopped at Mr. Rivera. "Coffee?"

As usual, Rivera didn't look up at me. But this time, instead of pouring coffee, I turned his coffee cup over, and walked away.

"Waiter!" Rivera pointed at his empty cup. "You didn't give me any coffee."

"You didn't ask for any," I said.

Everyone looked at me, shocked. Rivera stared, as though a *chupacabra* had landed a spaceship in the middle of my forehead.

"Yes, sir," I said and made a frustrated sound, blowing air like an angry trumpet. I shook my head, went back, and turned the cup over again.

Without taking his eyes off my face, Rivera said, "What's on the menu for lunch?"

"What?"

"Fish! What is the fish of the day?"

I stared at Mr. Rivera, blank and dumb, like somebody else had had to tie my shoes that morning.

Rivera, arms crossed executioner style, said, "You don't know what the fish of the day is?"

"I can check, sir."

"Do you at least know where you are?"

"I can check on that, too, sir."

"Never mind."

As I poured his coffee, Rivera whispered *idiota* and shook his head.

"Jesus Christ!"

He jumped up out of his leather chair, wiping hot coffee off his hand and trousers.

I looked at him all sheeplike. "Oops?"

"What the hell is wrong with you?"

"I'm sorry."

"Yes, you are!"

Rivera stormed out of the dining room and into the kitchen. This was it.

I went and stood outside the dining room in the bank's Art Deco hall. I heard angry voices coming from the kitchen.

Uncle Dee was saying, "If you fired everybody in New York who didn't do his job without a few mistakes, the city would stop. The mail wouldn't get delivered. The garbage wouldn't get picked up. The trains and cabs wouldn't move. Show me the man who does his job without errors, perfectly!"

"Nonetheless," Samuel Rivera said.

I pressed my ear closer to the wooden door. Rivera talked about my "lack of professionalism."

"I don't want to see his face."

"So that's it," Uncle Dee said. "You're going to fire him for having a bad morning?"

"Please, Daniel!"

Uncle Dee said, "What? We're not castrated enough for

you? If nothing else, we have a right to work and live and die with our pride. If he goes, I go!"

"Shhh," Rivera said. "Uncle. This isn't about you. Shhh."

The voices faded into a whisper and soon they stopped. Footsteps. A slam. I heard someone coming toward the wooden door. I pulled back.

Uncle Dee stuck his head out and said, "Chico, can I see you in the kitchen?"

Uncle Dee was sweating as I put my coffee pots down near the sink. He sighed. "Could you sit?"

"Aw, shit."

I dropped my head as if the shame of being fired were killing me.

"Look, you know how things are now. I'll probably be next."

"You have almost twenty years," I said. "They won't fire a man with almost twenty years on the job."

"You think so?"

"Twenty years is a long time."

Uncle Dee made the sign of the cross. "God willing."

"I'll go clean out my locker."

I put out my hand for Uncle Dee to shake.

Uncle Dee screwed up his face. "C'mere!"

He grabbed me and hugged me, and slapped my back.

"You'll be okay," he said. "You're from the Bronx. You're a soldier. I can tell."

The phone rang. Uncle Dee excused himself to go answer. I checked my Timex; 7 A.M. I walked real slow along the marble floor toward the locker room.

"Chico! It's a miracle!"

I turned and saw Uncle Dee, beaming. "I just got a call. There's a position open in the mail room. They wanted to know if I knew somebody. Rivera never goes down there. The job is yours if you want it."

FOURTEEN

Irving Goldberg Jones was sitting on the tattered couch in the HMD mail room, staring at the TV he had just popped a DVD into.

Irving Goldberg Jones was a romantic kid in glasses, a student at Columbia University, a writer, a poet, a self-described socialist, half black, half Jewish, tall, beanpole thin. His face was the color of coffee with extra milk. His hair was a long kinky Afro, a cross between Einstein and Buckwheat from the *Little Rascals*. He was wearing black jeans, black shoes, and a black Che Guevara T-shirt. Nineteen. Just a kid.

An old couple had appeared on the TV screen. They were in the office of a company with technology that allowed them to transfer the brains of the old into bodies of the young. The old couple was poor and couldn't afford two operations. Only one could be young again. The other would have to wait and grow old and perhaps die before the younger of the two could work to save up enough money for a second operation. In the end, they left, still old, walking together. They were dying. But they were peaceful, happy, together and holding hands. It was enough. An action which never ceased to make Irving sigh with longing, though he'd played that *Twilight Zone* episode a million times in the mail room before.

I turned away from the TV and faced Irving and saw that he had a fresh black eye.

"What happened to your eye?"

Irving gripped the messenger bag he was holding on his lap.

"Some fascist cop clocked me," he said.

"Why?"

Irving explained that he had been punched in the face by a cop outside Macy's who he was trying to stop from choking a shoplifter.

"The cop slammed the woman against a wall," Irving said. "And threw her on the ground. For shoplifting a pair of winter gloves."

"Damn," I said. "I hate abusive cops."

Irving grunted but said nothing else. All day. Nothing. Not a word. This was gonna be harder than I thought.

The following day. I was wearing a Pancho Villa T-shirt. On the back of the shirt was a quote: IT IS BETTER TO DIE ON YOUR FEET THAN TO LIVE ON YOUR KNEES.

Amen.

Irving and I had not become fast friends after I started my messenger job at HMD like I had planned. Every chance I got I acted like I hated everybody and everything (like I said, he was a poet) but Irving didn't line up. As far as Irving knew I was just another surly New York messenger with a Kryptonite lock and a bad attitude that got me "transferred" from my job as a waiter in the executive dining room to the mail room. But it wasn't working. And I needed to seal the deal.

I moved along 42nd Street on my bike as the road bent and dipped and turned and sloped upward again and strangely, surprisingly, I found I liked it, the details of the city as it passed before my eyes.

Being a bike messenger was systematic and predictable, as natural as eating or sleeping. From one drop to the next I went, from the East to the West to the North to the South of Manhattan, parking my bike, chaining it to a meter, a gate, a tree, making my drop, and going again past the tall concrete and steel behemoths of Midtown, the hidden nooks, the tiny parks, riding with subways rumbling below, beside cars and buses and taxicabs, past pedestrians at yellow, red, green lights, until I felt I really was seeing the city for the first time, finding it all shockingly busy, the crowds, the buildings of glass, stone and brick, the statues of city founders, heroes, politicians, millionaires, billionaires, grifters, scoundrels, thieves.

I almost felt like riding forever, no end in sight, casting off and abandoning my old life, cold winter wind on my face, rolling up Times Square and out of New York City.

Then I caught sight of him: Irving Goldberg Jones riding along on his bike, and I knew exactly what I had to do. Build a connection where none existed. Joy St. James called it my specialty.

"Watch out!"

I hit the brakes suddenly and my packages went flying.

I had stopped short in front of Jones. He looked at me with startled eyes and said, "You came outta nowhere."

I got off my bike and parked it up against the curb. Irving got off his bike, too, helped me pick up my packages and added, "Nice T-shirt."

I snatched up my strategically dropped book, *Leaves of Grass*. Irving's eyes lit up as he took it from me.

"Do you like poetry?" Irving asked.

I touched my chest as if his question went into my heart like a thunderbolt, as if I wanted to jump around and testify, to bang a tambourine, to commit a thousand sins.

"I love poetry."

Irving's eyebrows rose and a giant smile took over his face.

Soon we were talking about poetry and Irving was inviting me to a reading and we laughed about our *close call.*

Yeah.

It's what I do.

That night I stood in Irving's bedroom in the cluttered apartment on Delancey Street in the Lower East Side that he shared with his mother. On the walls were colorful paintings of workers at the Fulton Fish Market and Katz's Delicatessen. Sculptures and poems in frames and materials for homemade candles and handmade soaps were scattered around the room along with protest signs that read NO WAR, NUCLEAR WAR KILLS CHILDREN and PEACE NOW.

In shelves and on the floor and on the bed in Irving's room were countless books of poetry. Tacked on the wall, over his desk, was a news clipping about Hugo Chavez of Venezuela with three question marks.

Irving Goldberg Jones searched for some misplaced poems, mad Afro shooting this way and that, with mustard on his chin, chewing on half a lettuce, tomato, and Swiss cheese sandwich and chugging a Dr. Brown's Cream Soda. He put down his half-eaten sandwich and soda. He scooped up some pages, sat across from me, and nervously rattled three small stones in his hand as he read.

"What's with the rocks?" I asked.

"I got one from a visit to Wounded Knee," said Irving, without looking up from his poems. "Another from a visit to an abandoned Virginian slave auction site, and another from Dachau."

"Okay," I said.

A bit creepy but okay.

"I'll throw them away," he said, "when there's nothing left to fight for in the world, when all people are free."

Just then the door opened and a wild-eyed white woman in paint-smeared overalls, carrying a paintbrush, rushed into the room and yelled at Irving, "You tell Walter Jones, your father, when you see him tonight, that he is an ass!"

"Why don't you tell him yourself?"

The wild-eyed woman's jaw dropped.

Irving turned to me and said, "She's in a mood today."

"Your father," Ruth Goldberg said, undaunted, waving her paintbrush. "You know what he did? That schmuck?"

"Mom," Irving said, pointing at me. "My friend Chico is still here."

Ruth nodded and said, "Hello, friend," and went back to Irving. "Do you know what your father did?"

Irving rolled his eyes. "No. And I don't care."

"Feh!" said Ruth. "Screw him and screw you!"

Irving looked innocently at his mother, pointed at himself and said, "Why screw me? What did I do?"

"Don't defend that man! I carried you in my belly for nine months! Don't you dare defend that man to me!"

"I'm not defending him." Irving threw his arms up. "I didn't say anything!"

Ruth raised her hands to heaven. "One of these days I will crush that man with my own two hands!"

Irving shook his head. "Why do you two even speak? Why do you meet for coffee? Why do you go to the theater? Why do you cook him dinner every couple of weeks?

Ruth looked at her son. "You don't understand anything about love!"

And as quickly as Ruth Goldberg entered the room, she disappeared with a door slam.

A couple of hours later I was sitting in a joint called The Nuyorican Poets Cafe with my new best friend Irving Goldberg Jones and his father, Professor Walter Jones.

"What did you think?" Irving said, as his father placed Irving's poems down on the café table.

"It's poetry," said Professor Jones. "I guess."

"What's wrong with it?" Irving asked.

"Well. Your first poem is called 'Nobody Loves You Poet.' I mean, really. Your poems are a little self-indulgent, son."

Professor Walter Jones, a thin black man in his sixties with thick glasses and a short gray Afro, a professor of political science at Hunter College, tugged at the worn sleeves of his shabby tweed jacket and adjusted his bow tie. Laughter and smoke spilled down from the balcony just above our heads as Willie Colón's trombone wailed.

"Why are you judging?" Irving yelled.

"It's my job to make judgments," said his father.

"I asked you to read my poems. Not to judge."

"I'm not a writer," said Irving's father. "What do I know?"

"That's true," Irving said. "You're not a poet."

"But I will say this," said Mr. Jones. "I found these poems all a bit indiscreet."

"It's poetry," Irving said. "They're supposed to be indiscreet."

"Perhaps," said Mr. Jones. "But you only seem to write about things that happen to you. What happened in your childhood, your friends, things about your mother's days with me in East Germany. Things I've told you in private."

"So?"

"I would be more comfortable," said Mr. Jones. "If you used your imagination."

"That's the most ridiculous thing I've ever heard," said Irving.

"Well, I don't read poetry. So maybe I'm not the man to ask," said Mr. Jones.

"No advice?" Irving asked. "Nothing constructive to say?"

Irving's father looked at him and said, "Don't quit your day job."

I gave Irving a sympathetic look and gave his back a consoling pat.

"Thanks, Chico," said Irving.

"Look," Professor Jones said to his son. "You'll take your trip to Cuba and you'll come back and you'll go for your master's in education and you'll teach. Teaching is a good profession."

"I want to write."

Professor Jones removed his glasses, looked his son in the eye, and said, "You're not serious."

"I am."

"Don't be a putz, Irving!"

"I think," I said, "his wanting to be a poet is a noble thing."

Irving gave me a look that said he would follow me into hell wearing a hat made of candlewax and an outfit dipped in kerosene. The boy was mine. All I had to do now was ask. If he knew where Tiffany was, he was gonna tell me.

More laughter and cold wind blew into the café when an old friend of mine danced in like a hurricane on five-inch heels, leading a tiny crowd of howling Brazilians. She was all hips and dark cleavage stuffed into a familiar short white winter coat. Pilar's coat. She saw us and floated across the room like a cloud and settled down at our table. Tipsy and reeking of rum, makeup, and perfume, she kissed both my cheeks as if I were some long-lost love.

121

Renata said, "Chico!"

"You know Renata?" asked Irving.

"I know heem," she said. "How are you, Chico?"

"I'm good. I don't need much."

She grinned. "You no look happy to see me?"

"No. I am. Very happy."

"Well," Professor Jones said. "It's been groovy. I have a plane for New Orleans to catch." He grabbed his small beat-up suitcase, stood up, and put on his trench coat. He nodded at Renata. He slapped my shoulder and said, "A T-shirt is not politics." Then he looked at his son and said, "Get a haircut," grabbed his fedora, and exited the café.

Irving sat there staring at the empty place where his father had sat.

"Larkin was right on," Irving said. "They fuck you up, your mum and dad."

He looked at me and he shook his head. "Sometimes I could kill 'im."

"No," Renata said. "You both good people. You no mean."

"Yes, I do. I do mean."

Professor Jones leaving gave me some breathing room for when Irving turned back to me and said, "So how do you know Renata?"

"Marcos," said Renata, ratting me out.

"I met Renata," I said, taking her hand and squeezing, "at a small gathering in SoHo.

"Kirk Atlas," Irving said. "Is that how you got the job in the executive dining room and then in the mail room? Marcos is a friend of yours?"

Renata looked at me, all mischievous.

"I wouldn't say a friend."

"What then?"

"Old business associate," I lied. "He owed me a job."

"So after they fired you in the dining room Kirk hooked

you up in the mail room? You must have some juice with him."

"I do. I won't lie. It pays to know the right people."

"Shoot," Irving said. "How do you think I got my job?"

"Olga," Renata said and looked at my face for a reaction. Jesus. She's playin' me.

"Olga?" I said.

"Yeah," said Irving. "My friend Olga Rivera got me my job in the HMD mail room. Did you know Pilar?"

"We met."

"Renata is now living in Pilar's old apartment," said Irving. Renata grinned at me. It was not a nice grin.

"I met Renata a couple of days ago," said Irving, "looking into what happened with Pilar."

Irving took a giant pause. "Pilar is dead, you know?"

"Yeah," I said. "I know."

"I didn't believe it when I heard," said Irving. "I had to go check myself. That's how I met Renata." He shook his head suspiciously and said, "Waitaminute? Do you know Tiffany?"

I looked over and I saw that Renata was sitting there, staring at me intensely now, tapping her beer bottle with long red fingernails, nodding her head and grinning.

"I don't know her," I said. "But I do hear she plays a mean violin."

"Yeah," Irving said, still looking at me suspiciously. "Who'd you hear that from? Kirk?"

"Yeah." I checked my Timex watch. "So when is this poetry thing supposed to be starting?"

Later, because of Renata's little game, it wasn't easy getting anything out of Irving again. So when he told me that he was a lightweight when it came to drinking I got him drunk on beer and rum after he read a sad poem called "The Last Samba," dedicated to Pilar Menendez, his parents, and an unrequited love, Tiffany.

When he blacked out around 3 A.M. on a couch on the second floor of the café, Renata long gone, I made my escape, but not before turning out Irving's pockets and not without a short story I found in those pockets, a story I read on the No. 6 train back to Pelham.

FIFTEEN

Trilogy of Terror: Chinatown Angel
by Irving Goldberg Jones

Two-thirty A.M. Most of New York City is asleep. It's
time.

You stand tired and cold under a black winter sky
on a street corner in Chinatown. You wear a dark hat,
coat, and gloves.

The street is deserted. You feel invisible as a taxi
passes and hate rumbles in your belly. You look down
at your hands. They're shaking. You're alone.

You see that bastard inside the restaurant, dressed
in his usual soup-stained button-down shirt, white
apron, and black trousers. Brooks Brothers. Who wears
Brooks Brothers to work in a restaurant? Your head
aches.

He has ruined you, everything you are. Though your heart pounds and your knees tremble, you know it has to be done. You knock on the glass door.

He opens the door, clutching a brittle vinyl record.

He's a big-bellied bear, hair still black and thick, still handsome, still burning the midnight oil, an insomniac, a businessman, the owner of a luxury condo in SoHo, a yacht, a gold Cadillac. Oh, and the Chinatown Angel restaurant! The smug bastard.

He scowls. His eyes are hard, unforgiving, like yours.

"Forget something?"

"I wanted to talk."

He steps toward you.

He stands silent for a few minutes, holding that damn record, looking at your outstretched hand. Finally, he shakes his head, puts out his hand, and smiles back. "I'm glad you've come to your senses."

You watch as something seeps into his eyes, a hint of loneliness, a gleam of wanting to be understood or forgiven or both.

"Would you like a drink?" he asks.

You follow him, into the kitchen with its harsh and unforgiving fluorescent lights. As he walks you feel inside your right pocket for the small black bag with its rubber tubing and syringe. Then you feel in your left pocket for the gun. A .22 with a mother-of-pearl handle. Ready. A little liquid courage and that will be the end.

On a chrome counter in the middle of the room sit three dirty plates, empty coffee cups, drained shot glasses, gambling chips, and a deck of cards with nude models from the fifties. The remnants of the last poker game he will ever enjoy.

From a vintage record player in a corner of the room comes Jimi Hendrix's electric guitar. *Purple Haze.*

He points with thick fingers. "I love this riff."

He goes to the liquor closet and comes back with a new bottle of Jack Daniel's. He gets two clean glasses, opens the bottle, and pours. He looks at you and smiles. "Peace pipe."

He throws back his drink in one gulp and signals for you to do the same. He pours two more. You slam them back and he pours again.

He plays records for you as you drink: Bob Dylan, Janis Joplin, The Rolling Stones. He hums and taps along, happy when he plays his music. He thinks his money makes him immune.

He pulls two cigars and a gold-plated lighter out of a pocket in the white apron tied around his waist. He lights and puffs. Smoke floats past you in lazy rings. He grins, warm and sweet, and hands you one. "You see, we don't have to be enemies."

He doesn't know how much you hate him. You always did. Maybe it was all just a matter of time. He sees the unlit cigar in your right hand and in your left hand, a gun.

He flicks some cigar ash on the floor.

"You want money?"

"No," you say. "I'm going to kill you."

He slams back another drink. "Am I that bad?" he asks.

"Let your life be your judge," you answer.

He shakes his head. "That was many years ago. I was sick and suffering. Whatever I did wrong, I made up for it."

"You can't make up for all the evil things you've done."

His eyes dart about the kitchen from the stoves to the freezers to the sinks and back to the gun again, searching for a way out, always looking for an angle, even now, especially now.

"I can't turn back time. I can't undo the past. I can't fix that."

His face is a blank mask, vacant of emotion, eyes like concrete, a cool stillness running from his brow to his chin. "You're not going to kill me."

"Roll up your sleeve."

You take the small black bag out of your coat pocket and toss it on the chrome counter.

He closes his eyes. He understands.

"You only have two choices."

You raise the gun and stalk toward him. You point the gun at his head. You hold the gun steady. "Door number one."

You point at the small black bag. "Or door number two."

You grip the gun even tighter. The bastard opens his eyes and throws up his hands.

"This isn't you. You're not a killer!"

"Roll it up!"

He lets out a breath of air from deep inside his gut. He sits still and silent for a few minutes and you watch as a tear streams slowly down his cheek. He looks up, eyes open, directly into the harsh light of the fluorescents.

He does not move and when he does, he does something you do not expect. He slaps his own face in a rage, again and again and again. He is not as free of the past as he thinks. He is not innocent. He is not immune. He is filthy man trying to escape responsibility. He must be punished.

"Enough!" he says. He is finished, red-faced, breathing hard, bloody-lipped, but calm.

"Enough."

He rolls up the sleeve of his left arm, revealing the tattoo of a naked Chinese girl with angel wings and an apple in her mouth enveloped by a green snake.

He takes the small black bag and expertly removes the rubber tubing and the syringe. He fills the needle. Before he hits the vein he looks up at you. There's no horror in his eyes, no fear, not anymore. The bastard is smug, even now!

He plunges the needle into his arm, injects himself and says, "That'll teach me."

His eyes close and he begins to rock back and forth. The lethal dose of heroin is taking effect. He is dying. It's over.

His eyes shoot open.

You point the gun.

He laughs. "You want this to look like I overdosed here by accident. You can't shoot me! You can't even afford a scuffle."

He stands up. You stand up. He totters from left to right, filled with the drug.

He moves back and stumbles over his chair. He goes down on the floor and lies there, looking up at you with defeated eyes. Then he hacks and coughs and spits and flails his arms and legs, gasping for air. He rolls over on his back, choking and cursing.

The dose of heroin is in his veins, the demon of permanent sleep at work, perpetual midnight falling. Not so smug anymore. Let the good people live. Let him be dead and rotting, a guilty thing on the floor of the kitchen.

You stand and watch him, lying there on the floor, slumped under the chrome counter. His green eyes close.

You look at him and you know the bastard's dead and there is a release of everything, of years and decades of anxiety and hate. You know it won't be long before they find the body and lower it into a grave and shovel it out of the world. They'll play Hendrix at the funeral.

You look down at your hands. They're no longer shaking.

SIXTEEN

I drove into Manhattan along 135th Street and Lenox past the Schomburg Center. Before she met me, Ramona had fallen in love (in her bookish imagination) with Arturo A. Schomburg, a black Puerto Rican scholar. A black Puerto Rican named Schomburg? Tell me about it. An egghead with the largest collection of books on anything and everything African. Ramona had been researching materials for her master's when she fell in love with the idea of the dude, who was long dead by 1960. She had a picture of Arturo pasted to our bedroom mirror. It was the first time I found myself jealous of a dead guy. It wouldn't be the last.

I turned left at 124th street and parked my car outside the offices of St. James and Company. It was housed in a three-story brownstone.

I entered the lobby with its dark oak walls, swiped in at the electronic door, and said hello to Kelly Diaz, the office manager, who lived with her kid and a husband in Sugar Hill. Kelly Diaz was twenty-five, a big-boned, big-breasted, Colombian girl with short purple hair. She stopped typing at her computer and came out of her large office area, a converted kitchen and living room. "Welcome back, handsome," she said, kissing my cheek and pressing her hand against my chest.

"Sometimes you give me ideas," I said.

"Wanna share?"

I stared into Kelly's big blues. "I would, but you're married. And I got many bad men to catch before I sleep."

I went past Kelly up the staircase to the second floor.

As I entered the second-floor office, Joy looked up at me and slid a folder across her glass desk. Her office was down to bare essentials: two chairs, a file cabinet, and fresh flowers.

Hank was standing by an open window eating a jelly doughnut. He had a red Irish face, thinning brown hair, and brown eyes.

There was this about him, too: the man was as honest as the day was hard. In the eighties, when Hank was still a homicide detective, he tracked the murders of two Puerto Rican teens to a couple of members of the NYPD, named names, and sent some rotten apples to court for indictments. The case never made it to trial, and that was the end of his police career.

I looked back at Joy.

"Hello, boss lady," I said.

"You remember Chico," Joy said, glancing at Hank.

"How are you, buddy?"

"Hank served as head of the research team on your Benjamin Rivera request," Joy said.

"You need any information, leads, permits, Hank Murphy's your man."

Hank bit into his jelly doughnut. It dripped red filling onto his white shirt and Joy's spotless glass desk.

Hank excused himself and went out.

"You know, I asked for that Benjamin Rivera info a while ago, Joy. You guys sure took your time. What's up with that?"

"Sorry it took so long, sir. You know, it's that little obstacle we like to call paying customers."

"Paying customers get served first?" I said. "Where's the love?"

"My mama didn't raise me right," said Joy.

"You need Jesus," I said.

"I got Jesus. Who you got?"

"Richard Pryor?"

"Sit your brown butt down and start reading."

"You talk about my butt a lot," I said. "I'm starting to feel objectified." I grabbed the report and sat down.

"What's it look like?" she asked.

"Looks like I got pulled into waters I can't swim."

"Money still good?"

"Great. Can't live without it. But too many people are trying to play me. I got a roof-jumping waitress, a socialist poet, and a dead junkie millionaire."

"Why are you helping this Kirk Atlas, anyway?"

"I told you. Albert. He's a filmmaker."

"I thought he worked in a restaurant."

"He does. Albert's one of those guys who doesn't want to work in a restaurant all his life."

"Ah," Joy said, wiping her desk. "I get it. This Albert Garcia has dreams. Goals. Aspirations."

"Exactly."

"Boy, I told you to stay away from people like that."

"You know me. I'm hard-headed."

"So what about this Kirk Atlas?"

"Kirk Atlas? He's an ass. But he's a rich ass. And, according to Albert, he's about to become a famous ass. He's agreed to help Albert with his first film if Albert helps him find this Tiffany Rivera. That's where I came in."

"Okay," Hank said, entering, his face glowing. "What did I miss?"

"Not much," said Joy.

"Did you read my report?" said Hank.

"Not yet. Did you guys get my fax?"

"Yeah," said Hank, holding up a copy of Irving's "Chinatown Angel" story.

"You wanna hear what I got?"

I leaned back in my chair. "Bring it on."

"Benjamin Rivera," Hank began, proudly flipping open his report, "fifty years old at time of death, five-foot-six, 250-pounds, middle son of the late Hannibal Rivera the Second, who inherited one of the largest privately owned agricultural concerns in the Caribbean."

Joy said nothing and kept looking out the open window.

"Benjamin Rivera got a law degree from La Plata University but apparently never took the bar exam or worked as a lawyer."

"One less lawyer," Joy said. "Tragedy."

"It gets better," said Hank, his eyes lighting up like a schoolgirl's at a prom. "He spent two years in a psych hospital in Upstate New York. It was discovered that he had embezzled one point two million dollars with the help of an accountant at HMD Financial. Benjamin was involuntarily committed by his brothers, Hannibal and Samuel, and then cut out of his inheritance from the family's businesses. He was arrested twice for running a prostitution and drug ring from his apartment in a building that his family owned in the Bronx."

"What about his death?" I asked.

"Oh, it was an open and shut case, apparently. The medical examiner's office determined that the cause of death was a drug overdose. They found reasonable traces of antidepressants in his blood and unreasonable amounts of alcohol and heroin. The examiner wrote that the dose of heroin Benjamin Rivera took was so large that he might as well have injected himself with poison in the Chinatown Angel."

"What was Benjamin Rivera doing in the Chinatown Angel?"

"He owned the place," Hank said, riffling through his report again. "He bought it over twenty years ago from a Mr. Andrew Kwan. It used to be in Chinatown before Andrew Kwan moved it to the Bronx."

"So Benjamin Rivera owned the new and improved Chinatown Angel?"

"That's right."

"But I thought you said Benjamin Rivera was completely disinherited?"

"Well," said Hank. "Not *completely*. Benjamin Rivera got himself into rehab, got clean, got some family assistance, and all was forgiven; bygones were bygones."

"The comeback kid," I said. "Anything else?"

"He had ham for dinner," said Hank.

"Any signs of foul play?" I said. "Besides the ham, I mean."

"No. The place was clean. No signs of forced entry. No physical trauma to the body. No signs of struggle at all. They found five hundred dollars in cash in his wallet and a locked safe full of more cash."

"Where exactly was the old Chinatown Angel?" I asked.

"Mott Street," said Hank, handing me a slip of paper. "It's called the Wing Wok Restaurant now."

One of the details that I underlined in Irving's story was his taking the Chinatown Angel out of the Bronx. Maybe it was nothing.

Or maybe, bingo was his name-o.

"Anything else I need to know?" I asked Hank.

"Rivera's niece found the body."

"His niece? Tiffany?"

"No," Hank leafed through his report. "His body was found at around two A.M. by Olga Rivera."

SEVENTEEN

It was freezing as I walked through Chinatown with its red and gold dragons, past shops with Chinese vendors setting up to sell roots and fish and herbs, TVs and cell phones and stereos. I walked up Canal toward the Manhattan Bridge gateway, turned right at Mott Street, and went into the Wing Wok Restaurant—formerly known as the Chinatown Angel.

I sat at the counter as I had done for two days in a row. Mr. Wing and his waiters had claimed they had never heard of Tiffany or the Chinatown Angel. I ordered tea and a warm bun, waiting for someone to appear. Who? I didn't know. But I would when I saw them.

The restaurant was still mostly empty when she entered.

She wore a pink winter coat, pink hat, pink snow boots and a pink Powerpuff Girls backpack. She carried a violin case plastered with cartoon angels.

Her blue jeans were tight on her tall, slender, shapely figure. Bright and smiling, she entered and I could smell her as she came toward me, confident as a young panther, all lilac perfume and promise. She wore a Mickey Mouse watch and a silver bracelet with an angel's head hanging from it.

Her hair was no longer dyed blond. It was black and silky and down to her hips almost. Her face was all high cheekbones and flawless skin, and almond-shaped eyes filled with green lightning. I'd been thinking Tiffany's green eyes were contact lenses. They weren't. They were the real deal.

"Hello, angel."

"Hello, Mr. Santana," she said.

She knew who I was.

I felt something stir in my chest as Tiffany removed her pink coat and hat and I saw her wrapped like a gift in a tight T-shirt, a row of letters across her breasts: BORN TO RUN.

"I want you to listen to me, Mr. Santana. I know you work for my cousin Marcos."

I glanced around. "How did you know?"

"A friend called and said that you were looking for me, suggested that I move out of Chinatown as soon as possible."

"So this *friend* knew where you were all along?"

"Please go away. I can pay."

"Not that easy."

Tiffany touched my hand and said, "Don't be mean to me."

I melted. I melted and eased off like some chump.

Compose yourself, Santana.

"Do you have any idea what you'd be doing to me?" she asked. "If I had to leave Chinatown? Do you have any idea?"

"I don't get ideas," I said. "I had one once. It was small and had a little bell. It broke. It was my last one."

She made a quizzical face. "Are you a detective or a comedian?"

"I'm a detective by profession. I only dabble in comedy. It's a defense mechanism. But my *real* passion is interior design."

"I see," she said, and smiled.

"I can put on my deadly serious face if you'd like."

"No," she said. "Life is already too deadly serious."

"I second that emotion."

"I just want to be left alone," she said. "Will you please help me?"

Isn't that the way it always starts, Chico?

Later, we walked, arm in arm, along Mott Street. Her idea. She wanted to explain why I should leave her alone, happy and undisturbed in Chinatown. She said that she wouldn't let me go until I was convinced that letting her be was the right thing to do. She dragged me inside a store filled with giant golden Buddha statues, candles, bowls filled with cooking oil, and oranges, and little yellow slips of paper.

"Are you happy, Chico?"

"I'm not miserable. You?"

"I'm trying to be happy," she said. "The longer I live in Chinatown, the more I see how easy it is to stay afraid. Sometimes fear looks like protection. Sometimes fear feels like home. Some people never leave it."

"Is that why you left home? To get away from fear?"

"Yes."

I stared at the fat Buddha statue. We went back out and walked along Canal.

"The morning I decided to run away," Tiffany said, "I woke up without much hope in humanity, my family, New York, Julliard. It all seemed so pointless, you know? All that money. All those opportunities. All that potential. For what? Everybody's miserable. And it all ends so soon. Is it any wonder Pilar Menendez killed herself?"

"You know about that?"

"Yes."

"How did you feel about Pilar?"

She said: "I'm sorry Pilar is dead. It made me sad when I heard she killed herself. I know my sister Olga was close to her. I'm sure she's suffering."

"Pilar didn't seem to like you much."

"Oh," said Tiffany. "Pilar was like a lot of girls. You should've seen the way she looked at me sometimes. You either love me or hate me. I used to care about stuff like that. Since I've been in Chinatown, since I ran away from my family, here among working people, my spirits have lifted and hope has come back and I don't care about girls hating me. I feel sorry for them."

"Good for you."

"I'm happy," she said. "Can *you* say that? Forget me. Forget you ever saw me. I know you were paid to find me, but you seem like a good man. I hear you're a beautiful person."

"You've heard too much about me," I said. "What's the name of your crystal ball?"

She grabbed my hand and traced what she called my "life line" and said, "Do you understand what bliss is?"

"A breakfast cereal? A floor cleanser?"

"No, Chico. Be serious now." She talked like she knew me. "I'm following my happiness. My bliss."

"Is *bliss* another way of saying *Irving*?"

"No! Irving and I are just friends."

"He's in love with you. I've heard his poetry. It's bad but maybe his love is good."

"My music is my whole world now. My one and *only* love."

"So there isn't any guy in the picture?"

She paused and pushed a lock of dark hair back from her face. "No."

"How about a girl?"

"No," she huffed. "I'm not a lesbian if that's what you mean."

"Take it easy," I said. "Some of my best lesbian friends are lesbians."

"I'm not a lesbian," she huffed again. "I like boys."

"Okay, okay, Miss Hetero-Cuban-Chinese-American. Slow your egg roll."

"I'm not going back," Tiffany said. "If my mother and father find out I'm here, they'll make me come back. Please don't make me."

"If your mother and father don't support your being here, how do you support yourself?"

"I teach violin."

We stopped again on the short stoop outside the Wing Wok Restaurant.

"Would you like to come up?"

"Okay," I said. "But no funny business."

"I'll try to control myself," she said.

Just as she said that, a girl in brown khakis and a brown winter coat appeared out of nowhere. Short. Skinny as the drawing of a stick figure. Big glasses. Boy's haircut. She charged over and suddenly SMACKED! Tiffany harder than I had ever seen any human being smacked and ran off.

"Hey!" I yelled.

"No," said Tiffany. "Let her go."

"Who the hell was that?"

"My sister," she said, in a distressed voice. "Olga."

So that was Olga.

"What was that about?"

"She hates me," said Tiffany. But her face was not sad. She smiled. It was as if she deserved the slap and the slap had helped her. "She really hates me."

———

We went into the four-story building and stopped at a green door on the third floor.

"Shoes," she said.

I took off my Rockports and entered the apartment. It was a one-bedroom that smelled like dumplings.

"I saw this apartment," Tiffany said, switching on the lights, "and I knew I had to have it. People here live in their own world. They work and never notice me. They couldn't care less. No pressure. To play Carnegie or marry a rich handsome man. Nothing. I am nobody here. I like being nobody. The Wing Wok is not The Lodge in East Hampton, but it's good food. I'm learning Cantonese and Mandarin. Life is simple here. My parents probably think this is a phase I'm going through. Especially my father. It's not. I have found my life. My place. I'm alive here."

I looked around the living room. A big pink sofa occupied almost the whole of one wall. The kitchen area was filled with postcards. The apartment walls were covered with cartoon clouds and angels, pink and brown cherubs with wings, playing violins, smiling cheerfully, on fat white clouds.

Beneath two tall windows was a golden cage filled with screeching birds.

"Aren't they beautiful?" Tiffany said.

She walked over and pushed a tiny metal gate in the cage. The colorful birds poured out into the room. They flew and feathered their way too close to my face, flashes of green and yellow and blue. I guarded my eyes as they went screeching by like colored lights and perched on dark spots throughout the room or flew away crying into rooms not visible. And when the storm of feathers and high-pitched screams finally died down and something near silence ruled the room once more, all I could say was, "Jesus!"

"Birds are the closest thing we have to angels." Tiffany Rivera, with her birds in a room of white clouds and angels, stood and looked at me innocently.

"What's up with your sister Olga?"

"You remind me of her."

"I love being compared to someone's sister. Makes me feel manly."

"No," she laughed. "Olga is very sad inside, like you."

"What do you know about me?"

"I see your eyes."

"Don't believe every eye you read. Is that why Olga slapped the crap out of you just now? To express her sadness?"

Tiffany ignored me and took off her coat and sat at a wooden table stocked with an electric rice cooker, little crystal angels, and a gun. Over the table, there were three framed Hollywood movie posters, one from the late thirties, featuring a Chinese-American actress called Anna May Wong in *King of Chinatown*, and *Charlie's Angels* with Lucy Liu, and *Wings of Desire* by Wim Wenders.

"You like movies?" I asked.

"Yeah," she said and looked up at the posters. "Doesn't everybody?"

"I do," I said. "I don't know about everybody. Where'd you get those?"

"My sister's boyfriend Albert gave me those," she said and picked up a little crystal angel.

"All three?"

"Yes," she said. She didn't look at me. She ran her fingers along the smooth surface of the crystal angel.

"Those framed movie posters aren't cheap," I said. "Not on a Bronx waiter's salary."

She looked at me, slightly annoyed.

"He gave the posters to you before or after you ran away?"

She paused. She placed the crystal angel down on the rice cooker. "Before."

"He must really like you. You like Albert?"

143

"Yes," she said and crossed her arms. "He's smart and talented and hardworking and dedicated and he's good to Olga."

"Were you close?"

"To my sister?"

"Albert."

She began removing her short pink socks. "I'm close to all of my friends and *some* family," she said. "It's through relationships that we grow. I put myself close to people so that I can learn."

"What happened with Olga?"

"I don't want to talk about it. It's depressing."

"I'll let you cry on my shoulder."

She rubbed her pretty feet as if warming them from the cold. "I get goose bumps when I meet a new friend," she said. "Are we friends?"

"Depends," I said. "What's the job description?"

"Friends are conversation. Conversation is energy. Friends also protect each other's solitude."

"So I become your friend. I keep my mouth shut about where you are?"

She shot me a dazzling smile.

"What about Olga," I said. "She knows where you are."

"She won't tell Marcos or my parents," said Tiffany and stretched out her long arms. "She doesn't want me back. I didn't get much sleep last night. I was playing violin at this café in Williamsburg so late, I stayed with a girlfriend. I never made it home."

"Girlfriend. Huh?"

"You have lesbians on the brain."

"I wish," I said. "Tell me about Hannibal Rivera. Tell me about your aunt Josephine."

"Tell me about Hannibal Rivera," Tiffany repeated. "Tell me about your aunt Josephine. What is it with you?"

"I'm a detective on a case, Tiffany. I'm not just hanging out."

She got all huffy again, jumped up and went to the refrigerator. She grabbed some leftover dumplings, two bottles of Tsingtao beer, and slammed the items down on the table with two sets of chopsticks.

Her silly Mickey Mouse watch glistened as she worked her chopsticks and ate the dumplings. I picked up a little crystal angel.

"Traditionally," said Tiffany, "an angel is like a middleman between God and us. But an angel is really just a voice inside. A light. They're guides. That's why you shouldn't hate anyone. You never know who your angel might be."

"Uh-huh," I said.

"Laugh if you want," she said. "But angels are incredibly powerful and always come through when you ask them for help. Sometimes not in the way you expect, but in the end you realize it was for your own good."

Her face was glowing. And I got it. What they saw in her. Tiffany Rivera was captivating. It wasn't just the fact that she was a looker. On top of that was the fact that she talked to you as if she had known you for years and she trusted you and she touched you when she spoke like it was the most natural thing to do and it *felt* natural. And she asked you questions and she listened as if the answers were the most important thing in the world. She made you feel with her eyes alone that she was in your corner and you should be in hers. She smiled more than she frowned and she laughed more than she pouted. She was happy. She *looked* happy. Like she had a secret for happiness and she was more than willing to share if you hung around long enough.

"And this?"

I held up the gun. It was a .22 with a mother-of-pearl handle. Just like the gun in Irving's "Chinatown Angel" story.

"It's not loaded," she said. "I have a license. Marcos gave that to me for my birthday. I'm finally going to get rid of it. Do you want it?"

"No," I said, grabbed a dumpling and plopped it in my mouth. "What's up with your parents?"

"They want me to be pretty," she said, "playing pretty music until I find a pretty rich husband and make pretty grandchildren. They don't think I'm humble enough. I disgrace the family. Well, I'm not the only one. I write them postcards saying I'm safe. They seem satisfied with that so far. But if they knew where I was, they would have to drag me back just for show. They're not really big on being parents."

"You big on being a daughter?"

"No. Everyone's always pretending to be happy in my family. I grew up with these aggressive and obnoxious kids, private schools, cocktail parties, expensive dresses. They kept trying to get us to fit in, me and my sister Olga. We didn't fit. My parents always reminded us that we were lucky. How bad things were in Cuba and China. We were lucky and we should be happy. But we weren't. I'm not a little girl anymore, Chico. I'm not totally innocent, only babies are totally innocent. But I'm a good person. I've never tried to hurt anyone on purpose. Maybe I stumbled into things. But that's it. Never intentional. Just clumsy. You see that, don't you?"

She grabbed my hand. "Come with me."

"Where to?"

She jumped up and repeated, "Come!"

I followed, or was dragged, by Tiffany to the mouth of a hall that led toward what looked like a sunny bedroom at the end of it.

Here we go again, Santana.

She looked at me with a sweet smile.

"It's not what you think," she said.

It's not?

She touched my face with a tender palm and said, "I want to play my violin for you. The sunlight is beautiful in there."

Violin in the bedroom? That's a first.

"Will you tell me about your sister Olga and Pilar and your uncle Benjamin Rivera?"

"I will tell you everything I know," she said. "And we'll be friends. Let me get out my violin. You wait for me in there."

I stepped past Tiffany and went toward the bright room.

I saw him in the room as soon as I hit the door. I faced the tall, skinny young man with an Afro wearing a black coat over black jeans and a black shirt. He was on the pink bed a few feet away from Tiffany's bedroom door.

Irving Goldberg Jones stank of liquor and melancholy.

"Renata told me everything," he said.

Game over. Busted. But why? Why was Renata screwing over Atlas and ratting me out like this? Maybe Atlas calling her "Pilar" got to her. Was she, like Pilar, in love with him? I should have had no doubt about that question when she looked me in the eye with spite that night at the poetry club, slammed back her beer, curtsied, and danced away from our table.

Irving started rattling his stones and shook his head, staring at me. "I thought you were okay."

"What do you think now?"

"I think you're a liar. And liars can't be trusted."

"What're you gonna do about it?"

Irving stood up and came toward me. "If I wasn't a pacifist, I'd punch you right in the nose."

"If you weren't a pacifist," I said, "I'd punch you back."

Irving spit at my feet.

"Classy," I said. "Where'd you get that *Chinatown Angel* story, Irving?"

He bit his lip and shook his head.

"We could do sign language?" I said. "Charades?"

"I thought you were a good guy," Irving said. "You were just after Tiffany all along. You were with Pilar the night she died. Tiffany didn't kill Benjamin. If that's what you think."

I didn't believe that Tiffany killed her uncle Benjamin. From what I knew about her and her birds and her angel talk so far, I didn't believe she was capable of killing anybody.

"Who killed Benjamin?"

"I did," Irving said.

His eyes were intense and pleading, pleading for me to believe him. For a moment I almost did. But something was missing.

"Why did you kill Pilar?"

"What are you talking about?" Irving said. "Pilar killed herself."

He reached into his coat and pulled out some crumpled pages.

"Renata told me about you looking for Tiffany. When I found my story missing, I called around. You were searching Pilar's apartment. George Theodorus told you about my drunken talk. About Tiffany and a murder. I knew you had my story. I knew you'd show up here."

He threw some pages at my feet. I saw a cover page: *The Trilogy of Terror: Benjamin.*

"I killed Benjamin," he said.

Tiffany, breathing hard as if she had been running, holding her violin, jumped into the room and screamed: "Irving, what're you doing!"

"I did it," Irving said. "I killed Benjamin."

"What?"

"I did it for you, Tiffany," said Irving. "I know what Benjamin did to you."

"What're you talking about, Irving? What did Benjamin do to me?"

148

"I called the police," Irving said. "I told them everything. I confessed. I love you. I love you. I love you."

Then there was weeping. Then my wheels turning and police sirens in the distance coming closer and Tiffany whispering over and over again as the horrible truth of what Irving was confessing hit her and Irving went down slowly to his knees: "Aw, Irving. Aw, Irving. Aw . . ."

I was standing out on Mott Street with the rest of the gawkers, mostly Chinese, some European tourists clicking away when the police arrived, sirens blaring after getting a call from Irving Goldberg Jones that there was a killer with a gun in an apartment over the Wing Wok who wanted to confess about a murder. Detectives asking questions, investigating, coming up with obvious conclusions, asked me what had happened. I shrugged, gave up my identification and my statement, everything I knew about Tiffany and Irving. I didn't give them Irving's stories. I would. Later. Tiffany was nowhere in sight. The last time I saw her she said that she was going into the Wing Wok Restaurant to make a phone call. I went inside to look for her. *Born to run . . .*

EIGHTEEN

Trilogy of Terror: Benjamin
By Irving Goldberg Jones

Benjamin came into the restaurant and found her on the floor in piles of white sugar.

"What are you doing?"

She looked up at him. His handsome face hovered over a white shirt. With a joyous expression on her face, she stood up, "I'm making sugar castles," she said. "I'm a princess!"

He stepped closer. The first slap knocked the girl into the counter. The second slap knocked her off her feet.

"Up!" he said.

The girl stood up, face wet with tears.

He said, "Come with me!"

He dragged the girl into the kitchen. He turned on the light.

It had never happened in the kitchen.

He is angry.

"Over!" he said.

The girl bent over a wooden chair as he grabbed a metal spatula off a shelf. He roughly undid the girl's belt and pulled down her pants. The girl thought about her favorite books.

The first blow from the metal spatula came hard and stinging. The next brought tears to the girl's eyes. The third, she wanted to scream. At the seventh blow, heart racing, the girl felt something between her legs, which felt much worse than the physical pain.

"Disgusting," he said, grabbing between the girls legs, groping. "Disgusting girl!"

Then came another blow and another and another.

He, sweating, exhausted, moaned, "Up!"

The girl pulled up her pants.

"What you did was bad," he said not looking at the girl.

"What you did was bad. Do you understand?"

The girl nodded, gasping for air, trying to hold back her tears.

"Say, 'I understand.'"

"I understand."

"I am saving you from being a bad girl."

The girl nodded.

"Say 'yes'!"

"Yes."

"What did you think you were doing out there?"

"I was playing," the girl said.

"Who said you could do that?"

"I don't know." The girl finally broke down, sobbing,

gasping and gulping for air. "I just did. I was just playing."

"That's not a good way to play," he said. "I have to clean that mess up. I have a bad back. I work hard all week. Who takes you to the circus and the movies and the beach? Your mother and father don't do that. I do. They're too busy to trouble with you. They don't care. Who loves you the most?"

"You do."

"And how do you repay me?"

"I make you suffer."

"You make me suffer! Yes. And that's not right. Why do you do this to me? Don't you love me?"

The girl lowered her head, kept her eyes on her pink gym shoes. "I love you."

"And if you tell anyone about this, what will happen?"

"You won't love me anymore," the girl said.

"I won't love you anymore. No more circus. No more movies. No more beach. Understand?"

A voice came from outside the kitchen. "Butterfly!"

The girl looked up at Benjamin.

"Kiss," he said.

The girl stood up on her toes, he bent down, and she kissed him quickly on the lips. He straightened up and looked away from the girl. "Go!"

"Butterfly! Where are you?"

She ran out of the kitchen, past the stainless steel kitchen door, and saw her mother wearing pearls and a dark suit with a white silk blouse, weighted down with shopping bags from Bloomingdale's.

"Hey!"

She bowed her head and her mother said, "What's wrong?"

She did not look up at her mother and said, "Nothing."

"You're crying."

She said, "I'm okay."

"What were you doing back there?"

"Nothing."

"It's late," her mother said. "How was the circus?"

She shrugged and said, "I don't know."

Her mother touched her face. "What are you crying about?"

"Love."

"What about love?"

"Love is bad."

"Who told you that?"

She shrugged. Her mother bent down to meet her eyes. She was elegant in black. She had long dark hair, a lovely face, and large dark eyes.

Her mother's family had traveled from Beijing to Britain to Cuba and finally to the States, in the years between 1930 and 1945. Her mother was determined not to become a workhorse in her father's restaurant supply company or what's-her-name in accounting. She worked her way up from Chinatown and finally settled into the bank, married the boss, and established new connections for him in China, Japan, Korea, and Vietnam. Her mother was no housewife—she was a career woman who took two slivers of her vacation time at the bank to recover from giving birth to her two girls. Her mother called her a butterfly. Her mother was not a butterfly. She was a dragon in a world of butterflies. He would never do that thing he did to her mother.

Her mother said, "Whoever told you that is wrong. Love is good. Love is always good. If it's not good, it's not love. One day, when you grow up, you will meet some nice boy, and you will see."

The girl looked out into the dark streets. "Will you love me no matter what I do?"

"No matter what you do," her mother said. "I will forgive you. You're my daughter. You're my butterfly."

"Am I your favorite one," she said.

Her mother let out a small laugh.

"You are a smart girl," her mother said, stooped in the open doorway lit by moonlight. "But there's things that you don't understand yet. Things that will become clearer as you get older. Just know this, your mother loves you no matter what."

"Can we go to the park tomorrow? Just you and me?"

"I have to work."

"You always work."

Her mother frowned.

"Come here."

Her mother opened her arms wide and took her in and hugged her, "Everything is fine."

As she walked quickly out of the restaurant with her mother, past the empty booths, she watched the checker board tiles of the restaurant drift past her pink feet.

"Everything is fine."

NINETEEN

I was in bed with Officer Samantha Rodriguez (off duty), who told me that the mother-of-pearl-handled gun in China-town was registered legally to Tiffany Rivera. Apparently, Irving had keys to both her new and former apartment at the Arcadia West. He said he had "borrowed" Tiffany's gun two months ago to commit the murder of Benjamin Rivera. Police were still investigating his confession. I had officially turned in my resignation at the HMD mail room. Meanwhile, Irving sat in Rikers. Murder charges pending.

I picked up Irving's stories, glanced at them, then stared at the wall.

"What're you thinking about?" Samantha asked.

"The third story in Irving's *Trilogy of Terror.*"

"That story again?"

"It's not just a story," I said. "It's a trilogy. That means there's one more out there. And they're not just stories."

"Why are we here?" she asked, covering her nakedness with my bedsheet.

"I'm going to start my own detective agency. I'm working on my ties to the law."

"We could've just had coffee, you know?"

"I'm trying to cut back."

I only felt a little guilty about Samantha. After some José Cuervo and serious acrobatics of the flesh, she was there beside me in bed naked. Her, trying to tell me about growing up in Mexico, of her dream of owning a small house in Astoria one day, filled with children, and starting her own clothing store in Forest Hills. Me, thinking about Ramona, talking about Pilar Menendez and Irving Goldberg Jones. I studied the "Chinatown Angel" story as the radio played music on La Mega.

"Stupid kid."

"*Que?*"

"Irving Goldberg Jones," I said. "The *Trilogy* stories are real. How real is the only question."

"How do you know he didn't just make them up?"

"The kid has no imagination," I said. "His own father said so. He's a pacifist with magic rocks in his pocket. I don't think he's capable of murder. And his old man said he only writes about things that happen to him or stuff that people tell him. But why write down a murder? Why take that chance?"

"Some men enjoy playing with fire," said Samantha. "It makes them feel dangerous."

"Benjamin Rivera overdosed two months ago. About the same time that Tiffany Rivera disappeared. And then Irving confesses to killing Benjamin Rivera. Why would Irving kill Benjamin? To play savior? Or to cover something up?"

"Like what?"

"That Tiffany killed her uncle Benjamin for molesting her."

Samantha took Irving's "Chinatown Angel" story from me.

"You ever kill anybody?" I asked.

"No," said Samantha, scanning the pages. "You?"

"Not yet," I said. "Nasty business."

"You want to?"

"Never," I said. "You?"

"*Nunca*. I pray never. But if I have to."

"Sure," I said. "If you have to."

Then Samantha said, after studying Irving's pages, "This isn't what a heroin overdose looks like."

"What?"

"This Irving kid described the death in his story as sudden. Heroin overdose is not sudden."

"So?"

"Irving Goldberg Jones didn't know what a heroin overdose looked like."

"Poetic license?" I said.

"Or maybe he wasn't there. He just made up the parts they didn't tell him."

I snatched up some pages. "That's it. Irving got these stories from someone else. He wasn't there. Someone told him how Benjamin died. Someone told him about Tiffany being molested."

"Who?"

"I don't know," I said. "Finding Tiffany again might take forever. I go straight at Olga, that might tick Albert off. Could shut me down. No way Irving is going to talk to me, either. Too soon. Would you think me less of a man if I told you that I didn't know what to do next?"

Samantha kissed my mouth and she got up, beautifully naked. She grabbed her little *Our Lady of Guadalupe* pendant from the top of my dresser and played with her hair.

"Does this mean we're gonna get married?" she asked.

"Do you want to get married?"

"Maybe when you're officially divorced, I'll answer that question."

She got dressed and said from the front door, "Call me when you're finished unpacking your old baggage. We'll have a proper date."

Then she turned and said, "If you really believe that girl Pilar was killed and you still want to go after it, go after it hard and soon before they bury her and that Goldberg kid for a murder he didn't commit."

That same morning I was outside in front of the house, walking the Chihuahua and smoking a cigarette, considering my next move. That damn dog ate good. I bought fresh turkey and chicken slices from the local butcher. Boo. That was the new name I had given him because he was always trembling. He would have that name until I could find someone to take 'im off my hands. After that they could call him Spanky for all I cared.

I hated Chihuahuas less since Boo had been rooming with me. His eyes looked less angry and more wet and sad and his legs seemed perfect for the size of his poor big head. He had this habit of staring with those deep black peepers when I drank too much beer or chain-smoked while watching TV after midnight as if he was saying, "Take it easy, *primo*."

And he would follow me to the front door every morning, looking up at me very intense and concerned. I could almost hear him say, "Easy does it."

And he'd be waiting for me at the door when I got back to Pelham, eyes popping, tail wagging, "Where ya been, *esay*? Where ya been?"

We had only had one fight, after a walk in Pelham Park. He came into the basement and started wiping his ass on the carpet, dragging himself across the room by his front paws, ass down, wiping himself clean on my floor. That night he ate dog food. Dry.

But mostly we got along like white on rice. I'd pop a beer and sit on my bed and tell the dog about my day, how the Rivera case was going, and he'd lie at my side, looking up, listening like he understood English or something.

Now, I'm not nuts. Not yet. I know Boo don't understand, but it's nice anyway, having another warm-blooded creature to come home and spill your guts to, even if he is the devil's spawn, even if he doesn't understand English. Some nights he'd whimper a lot and lean into me as I slept and he'd wake me up. But I never got mad on account of I knew he was crying for Pilar and I knew what that was like, to miss somebody in the night.

Hell, most marriages were worth no more than the relationship I had with that dog. Half were worth even less.

That's what I was thinking, standing outside my house with that damn dog, when Salvatore Fiorelli's red Mustang came speeding down the block. I braced myself as Salvatore came hulking toward me outta the car, holding a ringing cell phone. He handed it to me. I flipped it open, and said, "Yeah?"

"Terrible. Just terrible what happened in Chinatown."

It was Hannibal Rivera the Third.

"I'm glad you called. I don't believe Irving Goldberg Jones murdered your brother the way he said."

Hannibal Rivera the Third took a long pause. "The police are looking into it, Tiffany is safely at home."

"She's home again?" I asked, surprised.

"Yes," said Hannibal Rivera. "Tiffany is home. Her father is ecstatic. Her mother is pleased. Marcos is behaving rationally again. Case closed."

"I think Irving Goldberg Jones is innocent. I think your brother's killer is still out there. I think your brother's killing is related to the death of Pilar Menendez."

Hannibal Rivera hesitated.

"Mr. Rivera," I said. "You had two brothers, right?"

"Yes. Two."

"I have one brother," I said. I thought of Nicky. "Do you love your brothers, Mr. Rivera?"

"Of course."

"Well," I said. "If I had two brothers and thought someone killed one of them, I wouldn't be able to simply forget about it, because I had one left."

"Some investments," said Hannibal Rivera, "will only procure diminishing returns. A smart investor knows when it's time to divest. Wouldn't you agree?"

I didn't answer. "Your silence is making me nervous, Mr. Santana."

I glanced at Salvatore Fiorelli, who waited impatiently for the cell phone. "I doubt it."

"The next thing you'll be asking me is where I was the night of my brother's death."

"Where were you the night of your brother's death?"

Mr. Hannibal Rivera forced a mechanical laugh, "I was at my club in Old Westbury, eating steak, after a long hard day of golf. You can call if you'd like. It's over, Chico. Mr. Fiorelli has been instructed to give you a check. That should wrap things up between us."

"What about Marcos?"

"I want you to forget about Marcos," he said. "Let the police investigate Benjamin's death and that unfortunate incident in Chinatown. You call Marcos and say your final goodbyes."

"What should I tell 'im?" I said.

"Tiffany is back home. He no longer needs your services."

"He's gonna miss me," I said. "I'm real good company."

"Tell him you have cramps, gout, diarrhea. I don't give a damn, sir, what you tell him. It's time to go back to your life and forget the name Rivera, Chico. Spend your money wisely and never let my name, my family name, or the name of my son drop from your lips again. Our business is done."

"Mr. Rivera? What about the VHS cassette?"

There was a dial tone. He had hung up.

I looked at Salvatore. "Good luck, chief," he said and handed me a white envelope. He walked away toward the Mustang, motor running, waiting. After he drove off, I opened up the fat envelope from Hannibal Rivera III. It contained more cash: seventy-five thousand dollars.

TWENTY

I was treating myself to one last greasy meal at Mimi's Cuchifrito. I had enough money to live comfortably with Ramona until I found a new career. And for a minute there, I felt free. It wouldn't last.

Screw it. Maybe it would last.

I could retire for good from St. James and Company, forget about the Kirk Atlas case and the idea that Pilar was pushed and Irving was innocent, and most of all get Ramona back. I mean, Irving was emotionally unstable and Pilar was suicidal. Everybody said so. I had nothing that said otherwise. Nothing solid. Nothing that points or convicts. Right? Chico Santana and Company. I could change. I could get out. I could start my own thing, a new thing that included more sleep, no smoking, no drinking, no women except for my wife, and better eating habits, since I could now afford better food. That's what I was thinking when I took out my cell phone and dialed.

Someone picked up and groaned, "Don't you bring me no bad news."

Nicky Brown. I only called Nicky when my back was against it. Irving was in Rikers Island prison and refused to see me. Atlas wasn't returning my calls. Even Albert wasn't returning my calls and when he finally did once all he wanted to talk about was how much trouble Atlas was giving him on *Doomsday* and the next time we were gonna do a walkabout. When, Albert? Soon, Chico. I'll call you back. But he didn't want to talk about Tiffany or Pilar or Irving or Benjamin and please, please, please, stay away from Olga. It was over. Tiffany was home. Benjamin Rivera's killer was caught. Pilar Menendez was a suicide. The case was over, Chico. It's done. Dropped. Finito. I accepted it. I was out but I had an itch in the back of my brain that needed scratching. Nicky was a natural-born scratcher.

"How are you, brother?"

"Guess what?" said Nicky. "I'm getting married."

"What?"

"Long story long," said Nicky. "I was eatin' every day at this little bar in Madrid. It was this tiny place where I drank beer—Señor Pacheco's. Señor Pacheco told me there was this American girl who could get me cheap rail tickets to Barcelona. She ran a little travel agency outta her apartment. So I went to see her. She was a reddish brown black girl. I just stood there and looked at her and she looked back at me, not mean but real confident. After I bought my ticket she starts talking to me about the difference between being black in Europe and being black in America and about her favorite architect—Gaudi. We just keep talkin' and talkin'. She tells me her old man's a cop in Arizona. I tell her I'm from the Bronx and she tells me she has a grandfather in the Bronx. Next day, I'm still there. Next thing I know, she closes shop, we're off to Barcelona together, staying in a *pension*, just a room across from a Catholic church, taking pictures of all the Gaudi buildings in town. After a while it's like we've known each other forever. We'd sit in the plaza and drink coffee with the street musicians or out by the bay watching the boats, drinking wine. It got to the point I thought I'd never get back to America. She had this dog she found with a curled tail, called it Desperado. We took it everywhere. She's like Ramona, man, she understands Italian and Spanish and she's reading me passages from this novel called *The Leopard*. In Italian. Her last name is Johnson, some of her people are *supposedly* black Cherokees from Oklahoma and North Carolina and Mississippi. And she might even be related to Robert Johnson, who you know sings my favorite blues song of all time—"Rambling." Her name is Willow M. Johnson. Get this, the M is for Mankiller. It's her Indian name, baby. Her mama gave it to her. *Mankiller*. And don't talk to her about the Lone Ranger or you gonna go seven days and seven nights without sleep."

Nicky laughed loud and deep as only Nicky Brown could. "Where are you, anyway?"

"The gym," I said.

"How is Mimi?"

Mimi set down a plate of *bacalaito* and poured me a cup of that cold sweet coco. I could almost feel the fried and battered codfish sitting like a salty stone in a chamber of my greedy heart.

"She's good," I said. "I won't tell her it's you or she'll snatch the phone."

"Who is it?" said Mimi.

"Cable company."

Mimi frowned. She knew I was lying.

"You know me, Chico," Nicky continued. "I'm a wanderer. But get this, Willow's grandfather died, and he left her that apartment, a co-op, in, of all places, Parkchester in the Bronx. These Johnsons are everywhere, man, Arkansas, Chicago, New

York, Los Angeles, Detroit. I told her all about you and how we grew up in the Bronx. Don't let anybody tell you it's not a small world. And for some reason, Chico, we got to talking about the possibility of moving in together, me getting a real job, and her teaching in the public schools. Chico, I don't know why, and it still sounds crazy when I say it, but I asked her to marry me. It's insane. I know. I don't know why."

"I know why," I said.

"Why?"

"You're in love, you idiot."

"Can you believe it," Nicky laughed. "I'm getting married, Chico! Nicky Brown is settlin' down."

"Congratulations. I'm happy for you, bro. I really am."

Nicky was the coolest man I had ever known. He traced his cool back to two facts: he loved people and he never wanted what he didn't have. He just loved learning and traveling. And he was mysterious, too. He would call me from Yemen one month and six months later from Zaire and he would never quite tell me how he got the money for all the traveling he did, odd jobs here and there was all he'd cop to, and soon I stopped asking. Mysterious. But now, I heard it in his voice. He was just like the rest of us mortals. Nicky Brown wanted something. And I wondered if that would change him.

"How's Mona?" he asked.

"Don't ask."

"How's Mona?"

"I might be getting her back," I said. "Maybe."

"Hey, man! Good for you."

"Come on," I said. "You said she had me whipped. Bossing me around. Telling me what to do. How to live. How to be. Her rules. Her way. When she tossed me out you said 'Good for you! You're free.'"

"Yeah," said Nicky. "But you don't wanna be free."

I swigged my coco and washed the taste of Ramona's memory down. "I need to talk about this case I was working on."

"What's up?"

"A client gave me seventy-five thousand dollars to drop it."

"That's good money," Nicky said. "Brother gotta eat."

"All I know for sure is a girl fell off a roof in Astoria and she wasn't alone when it happened. Anyway, nobody's interested and I've got some money to make a new start with Ramona. I shouldn't even be talking to you. I should be opening up a checking account."

"Money's important," Nicky said.

"Money's important," I repeated.

"And if there is a killer on the loose," Nicky said, "and nobody cares, what can you do about it?"

"Yeah."

"How you sleeping at night?"

"I don't sleep at night."

"Exactly," Nicky said. "You did your best and maybe now it's time to walk with the cash and get some sleep and let Chico do Chico."

"I have thousands of reasons that say *walk.*"

"What more do you need?"

"I live in New York, one of the most expensive cities in the world. I could fight."

"You could fight and continue your investigation and waste months, maybe years, that you could use to get Ramona back. So why even think about fighting? Deposit the cash and walk away. What's the problem?"

"Two people are dead and one possibly innocent kid's in prison."

Nicky cleared his throat, "Are you getting mushy in your old age?"

"A rich guy named Benjamin Rivera died of an overdose two months ago. His niece Tiffany runs away. I'm hired by this cat calls himself Kirk Atlas through Albert Garcia. You remember Albert, from St. Mary's."

"Little Albert?"

"Yeah," I said. "Little Albert. Then a girl named Pilar Menendez, just twenty-two years old, offers me money to keep Tiffany disappeared and then she's pushed from her roof. A kid named Irving Goldberg Jones writes a story called "Chinatown Angel," which talks about a guy being forced to overdose on heroin, and then Irving confesses he actually did what his story said. Nineteen-years old, arrested in Chinatown for something I suspect he didn't do. Then there's this sex tape allegedly floating around and I think it might just connect everything together. Or not."

"Sounds complicated. Walk."

"But it's not that easy for me. You know why, Nicky. I'm not gonna bullshit you. It sticks to me. Every murder case. It always feels personal. Also there's this little girl named Ting Ting. She's in trouble."

"What kinda trouble?" Nicky asked. His voice grew deep and dangerous.

"Bad trouble."

"A child?"

"Yeah," I said. "Who am I kidding, Nicky? I can't let go of this case. Pilar was murdered and I'm the only witness and this Irving kid is sitting in jail, probably innocent and covering up for somebody. I couldn't live with myself if I walked away now. It's like giving up. It's like giving in to the killers. Letting them get away with it."

"So let it be written, so let it be done," Nicky said through the cell loud and clear. "I now declare the case reopened. How may I be of assistance?"

TWENTY-ONE

First move. I followed her from her building in Manhattan to the Bronx. My goal was to make friendly and relax her and get her talking. Did I suspect that she killed her uncle Benjamin? No. Why would Irving take the fall for *her*? But why did she slap Tiffany in Chinatown? And who killed her friend Pilar? And where was the third story in Irving's trilogy? I called Ramona. Her friend Cynthia couldn't find it in any of the literary rags at Columbia.

Irving was still on Rikers Island, pointing fingers at himself. Tiffany made herself scarce again. Pilar was dead. Olga was the key.

It was almost closing time and the moon sat like a dead eye, white and wide and open, over the shops of Fordham Road in the Bronx.

I pushed open the glass door of the Chinatown Angel.

Inside it was empty, except for one last table, two beat cops in blue uniform, wearing Glocks at their side.

The Chinatown Angel was warm and clean, with black and white checkerboard floors, pink booths and black tables. A small radio played. I recognized Mozart's Piano Quartet in E-flat. Ramona would have been proud. My nostrils filled with the scent of brewed tea and fried egg rolls.

The glass door was marked.

WARNING!
Premises Under Surveillance

The tape!

Hannibal Rivera the Third said he wanted me to keep my eye open for a sex tape. But it wasn't a sex tape. It was a surveillance camera videotape.

It wasn't marked *Car*. It was C-A-R: Chinatown Angel Restaurant.

I stood in the doorway and called Hank. "What was the status of the surveillance cameras at the Chinatown Angel the night of Benjamin Rivera's death?"

Hank yawned. "Kinda late. Huh, buddy?"

"Hank, please."

Hank went off to look at the files. He came back on. "The machine was empty."

"What kind of machine?" I asked.

"What do you mean?"

"Old or new?"

I heard some papers being riffled. "It was one of those old VHS recorders," said Hank. "Says here the cameras had been off. Forensics found no tape but no strange prints on the equipment, either."

I entered the restaurant and sat in a corner booth.

Albert saw me and scowled with fierce eyes. Then he seemed

to catch himself. He smiled with those crooked teeth and walked toward me with ice water in one hand and a plastic menu in the other. He placed the glass of water on the table.

"Looks like you're the last customer." Albert handed me the menu. "What can I help you with?"

I held up the menu. "For an appetizer, I'll start with friendship. Main course, I'll have nothing but friendship."

"If you're looking for a friend," said Albert, "you're in the right place. We call him General Chow. He makes chicken."

Albert sat and removed one black shoe. He rubbed his tired foot through the white sock. He went into his pocket, popped an aspirin, drank my water, and said, "What are you doing here?"

I looked at Albert and made a happy face.

"*Oye*, listen, I busted my *cojones* trying to find Tiffany. I'm just glad it's over."

The two cops, without dropping any cash on the table, put their blue hats on and got up to leave.

"Night, Rodney," Albert said, rising. "Night, Wilfredo."

"You mean, good morning," one of the cops said, exiting. "Thanks for the food, Al."

"No problem," Albert said, bouncing to the kitchen, yelling something in what sounded like really bad Chinese.

"*Jeen-tyenn*, ladies," said Albert. "Today."

Albert stood back as a small crew of three Chinese girls in black skirts and red jackets rushed into the room from the kitchen, laughing and swearing.

One girl carried a plastic tub filled with clean silverware still hot and wet. One carried steaming metal teapots and empty sugar bowls. One carried glasses and white stem vases.

There was a crash.

"Oh, shit!"

Albert looked at me. "You wanna meet Olga? She got here just a few minutes before you walked in."

"Small world," I said. "Where is she?"

Albert pointed and I could only see the top of her hair as she bent over behind the counter.

She came up and waved at me, holding what was left of the soy sauce bottle she had just dropped and shattered. She had a Cuban face with a great big splash of Chinese features. The same Olga Rivera who slapped Tiffany silly in Chinatown. Olga with her boy's haircut and thick glasses over her almond-shaped eyes.

"*Hun bow-chyen,*" Olga said, lowering her eyes. "I'm sorry."

Olga ran off into the kitchen to get a mop as the three waitresses shook their heads.

I looked at Albert and said, "Why is Olga here?"

Albert shrugged, "She's like you, she wants to be near me all the time now. Got real depressed about Pilar and now Irving. Not every day the police find a friend of hers plastered in a dirty alley in Astoria, another in her runaway sister's Chinatown apartment confessing to having killed her uncle. But enough about that. That's my quota for tonight."

"Chico!"

I turned my head and saw Uncle Dee entering from the kitchen with Olga at his side.

"Uncle Dee!" I shouted. I had not seen him since I had officially turned in my resignation at the HMD mail room.

Uncle Dee wore a sports jacket and black slacks, spotless and freshly pressed. He took a shot of rum from his silver flask, then he went and fiddled with the small radio on the counter until the sound came out smooth and clear, Duke Ellington's "Take the 'A' Train."

"What're you doing here, Uncle?" I asked him.

"He practically lives here," said Albert, "when he's not at home watching *Sábado Gigante* or in Atlantic City or working at the bank."

Uncle Dee added, "Used to play cards with Benjamin and Marcos and Albert and Samuel here for years before *that terrible thing happened*. But let us not talk about tragedy, let us talk of happier times." Uncle Dee crossed himself, gave me a thumbs up, turned, grabbed Olga, danced and twirled her and yelled, *"Ahora!"*

Olga rolled her eyes, looked at me, and said, "Help!"

"Vaya!" Uncle Dee sang and danced across the room with Olga.

Uncle Dee, still dancing, said, "Olga here does not believe in God or the Kennedys, Ronald Reagan or the Pope. This is America, a free country. But look at that face, she does not even believe in Duke Ellington!"

"I prefer Charlie Parker," Olga said.

Uncle Dee twirled Olga. "Charlie Parker *es* noise, *es* crap!"

"Everyone is entitled to their opinion," Olga said.

Uncle Dee dipped Olga. "What do you think, Chico?"

"Leave 'im alone," Albert said. "It's too late to start arguing."

Uncle Dee pulled Olga up, and dramatically grabbed Albert's hand. "Shall we dance?"

"No!"

The Chinese girls stopped their work and watched Uncle Dee pull Albert up. Uncle Dee and Albert began to dance.

"You guys are *loco* in the *coco*," one waitress said.

"Be of good cheer," Uncle Dee said, dancing. "What does it matter? Learn to laugh at yourself!"

Then Uncle Dee pressed Olga close to Albert and they slow-danced to someone singing a bluesy rendition of "Somewhere over the Rainbow." I watched as Olga hung on to Albert, her head on his shoulder, tears in her eyes. Tears? Why tears? Happy tears? Oh, she was hooked.

———

Next move. Central Park. Night. Albert was in Sheep Meadow shooting two naked trees and a moving shot of the open space that was supposed to be the surface of Planet X in another galaxy. I was standing behind Albert and the cameraman, leaning against a fence. The Serbian cameraman, Boris Popovic, who was almost seven feet tall, wore a loose suit and a pair of Adidas sneakers. They were dirty and and torn in places. Like their owner, they had seen better days.

Olga was standing twenty feet behind me, outside the fence, next to the lowered gates of the brick-faced Sheep Meadow Cafe. She stood beside a tall pretty brunette actress with pale green eyes. The actress was playing an alien. She was covered in green face and body makeup, shivering in a long silvery coat with a fur collar and nothing on under but a silvery bikini and silvery shoes with glass heels.

It was twenty below and after midnight when Kirk Atlas came swaggering up the stone path cut between the meadow and the café in silvery ski boots and a red, white, and blue leather motorcycle jacket. He was bare-chested, wearing only suspenders and baggy silvery pants with a glittery NASA logo just below the crotch.

Albert yelled, "Cut!"

Boris Popovic put down the digital video camera, lit up a Marlboro, and drank from a thermos as Albert stared at Kirk Atlas.

"You're late!" Albert yelled at Atlas.

Atlas stepped into the meadow, removing his large dark sunglasses. "All hail, spic Lee!"

"We said midnight," said Albert. "It's twelve-thirty."

I walked toward them, away from the fence and the girls, into the center of the field. Atlas checked his Rolex watch. "Sorry?"

Atlas looked at Albert Garcia, at his crooked teeth, hooked nose, barbed-wire hair, rumpled shirt, polyester pants, white sports socks, and black-leather waiter shoes. He stared at the wannabe director, short, sloppy, fake Orson Welles, who lived with his grandfather. It was his first feature film. Kirk Atlas was giving him an opportunity, and he was giving Kirk Atlas shit. That was the look.

Kirk Atlas looked at me and winked. "Good work flushing out Tiffany, my man. More where that came from. We'll talk."

"We have a very tight schedule, Marcos," said Albert through gritted teeth.

"Dude," Atlas said. "It's our final scene. Relax."

Albert looked back at the actress who was shivering patiently by the shuttered café and whispered, "I'm not doing the blow-job shot."

Atlas threw up his arms. "Why not?"

"Stick to the original idea," said Albert. "We need a romantic ending."

Atlas grabbed Albert's wrist.

"We have to do the blow job," whispered Atlas. "I know it sounds crazy, but there has never been a blow job in a science fiction movie. We'll make history."

Boris Popovic looked back at the pretty actress, grabbed the camera again, and whispered, "I think we need blow job."

I looked back at the green-eyed brunette in the silvery bikini, standing next to Olga. Taking all the conspiratorial whispering into consideration, I guessed that she knew nothing about Atlas's new and probably last-minute blockbuster idea.

"No!" yelled Albert.

"I'm the producer," Atlas whispered. It's my money. It's my film. If I say we do the blow job, we do the blow job."

"Good!" said Boris.

Albert pointed his finger at Boris. "No!"

Boris pointed at Atlas. "He is producer, not you!"

"I'm the director," said Albert. "Kubrick—"

"You no fucking Kubrick!" said Boris.

Albert turned his back on them and walked out of the meadow. "We're not doing it! Boris, pick up the camera, and follow me!"

Boris scowled but followed. "Is too much. I am no your slave, Albert. You can no just press a button when you want something."

Albert went toward Olga and the brunette. He stopped and stared at the lowered gates of the café and just stood there saying nothing. Then suddenly he ran and punched and kicked the metal gates with all his might. A loud BOOM-BOOM-BOOM-BOOM reverberated through Central Park as if someone was throwing sticks of dynamite.

"Is this filmmaking?" I asked Olga, as I went and stood next to her.

"Yeah," she said.

"Looks like fun."

Next move. Four days later. Pilar Menendez was dead and the funeral was next week, Irving Goldberg Jones was still in prison, Tiffany was reportedly with her aunt Josephine, and Kirk Atlas was throwing a party. Tiffany was not scheduled to attend the party because she was still torn up about Irving. That's what Albert said. Other than that, no comment. I tried getting into Josephine Rivera's building on Fifth Avenue. The Arcadia East. Albert was wrong about that joint. It was *tighter* than Fort Knox. The doormen looked at you funny for just walking *past* the marble hallway.

My cell phone rang. I answered, a few feet from the elevators.

"Hello?"

"Hey, chief. It's Salvatore."

"Oh," I said, fingering the End button. "Hi, Sal."

"How are you, Cochese?"

"I'm okay, *paisan*. You?"

"Listen, Oscar's outta the office, so I thought we could talk. Do you have time?"

"No."

"It'll just take a few minutes."

"Okay. How about no, is no good for you?"

"Look, Hannibal Rivera heard about you still hanging around his son Marcos—Kirk Atlas—even after he paid you and told you not to."

"Tell him I'm just spending time with an old friend. I'm a social animal. Nice talkin' with you, Sal."

"Is all this trouble really necessary, Chico?"

"No, I just like trouble. My mother was trouble. My father was trouble. It's a family tradition."

"Listen, spico!" It was Oscar on the phone now.

"How much is Hannibal Rivera offering you to chase me off?"

"Enough to put your black ass in a body bag," Oscar spit out.

My finger still hovered over the End button of my cell phone. "I don't like your tone, young man."

"Chico! Chico!" Salvatore came back on. "That's not right what Oscar said. I mean, look, let's have a beer, just you and me, someplace we can talk, man to man."

"I don't like appointments. If you want me, you might find me tipsy on Saturday night at Rudy's in Hell's Kitchen. Wear something nice. And bring your own quarters for the jukebox. Some blues. Some jazz. Some rap. Some country. No techno."

"Right." Salvatore laughed. "Listen, chief. Can we keep this phone call between you and me and Oscar? I mean, you know how the agency is about stuff. Protective and all."

"They wouldn't like you making side deals with Hannibal Rivera, huh?"

"No, chief, c'mon! Nobody's cheating the agency. They got

their fee. This is ours. You and me we go way back, we have a relationship. Do you report everything to St. James and Company? Of course not. Better off we keep this Rivera stuff between old friends, you know?"

"I don't need any more old friends, Sal. You missed the deadline. I got all I can stand."

I ended the call and walked into the huge living room in SoHo. A live DJ was spinning Tupac Shakur's hip-hop loud and without mercy.

The music pounded at my eardrums. It was so loud, I imagined shock waves pulsing down from the condo, past the marble lobby and its waterfall, through the laundry room and gym, past the pool and sauna, down through the private underground parking garage, past the building's foundations, down through the earth's surface, all the way to its core.

I swam through the twenty-something, young and rowdy, mostly white crowd, bouncing proud in their expensive designer outfits and shoes. Young and successful painters in jeans, fashion models in silk, working actors in leather jackets, and hip Wall Street suits crowded the bone-white halls of Marcos's cavernous penthouse. The wraparound terrace that looked out over West Side Drive, which sparkled like a sheet of black tar in the moonlight, was full of midnight smokers. Several bars were operating at full speed. Tuxedos were everywhere: taking coats, serving food on silver trays, passing buckets full of Cristal champagne.

The huge living room was now dominated by a giant *Doomsday* movie poster of Kirk Atlas posing triumphant in his red, white, and blue leather motorcycle jacket, the green actress in the silvery bikini on her knees before him, and a background of shooting stars and comets and other space junk with the planet earth in the distance. It was a bright and colorful poster, a cross between Van Gogh and *Star Trek*.

This was not just the home of Marcos Rivera, it was the

fortress of Kirk Atlas, and these were his people dancing and drinking, sniffing powders and dropping pills in dark corners. His cronies wanted a party, and Kirk Atlas was giving them one.

I saw Renata, thick, drunk, in a tight leather blouse and black leather pants, gyrating under the flashing lights, surrounded by drunk young white boys in untucked shirts and dark blazers. The boys were groping her breasts, her bottom, pulling her this way by the hair, pushing her that way by the back of the head, her arms pulled around their waists, her bottom pulled into their crotches, laughing, everyone drunk and laughing, Renata, too. Samantha's background check on Renata had turned up nothing but a couple of bounced checks.

Then I saw Olga Rivera. My old so-called buddy Albert Garcia was at her side, shaved, wearing a rumpled black suit. I looked at Olga, in her plain brown skirt, flats, dull gray blouse. She held a small brown knapsack in one hand and had a tight grip around Albert's arm with the other. Her face was red and wet with tears.

"She stabbed me," someone said. I turned and saw Atlas, drunk, wearing a dark suit, no shirt, and flip-flops.

"Olga stabbed me," Atlas said. He held up his left hand. There was a tiny wound on his thumb. "Passion. You don't stab somebody without passion."

"She stabbed you?"

"Family meeting in Connecticut," said Atlas. "After Tiffany came home. I said something nasty about Albert. Olga pointed a knife. I grabbed the knife. I practically stabbed myself. But still. It's the quiet ones."

Atlas stared at his cousin Olga, who was now standing alone and wiping at her teary eyes. Atlas was energized, sniffling. He said he had a cold and showed me a diamond-encrusted watch.

"Guess how much."

"How much?"

"Ten thousand."

"Weird what happened with Irving, huh?" I said.

"Yeah," said Atlas. "I was a little surprised."

"Any idea why he did it?"

He locked his eyes on my face and asked, "You ever see the movie *Blade Runner*?"

I nodded.

"When Rutger Hauer says to Harrison Ford, 'I wanna live, fucker,' you understand him. Evil or not, he wants to live. That's what we all want, Chico. And when Rutger dies at the end, bleeding to death, you wanna cry a river, because you know he won't live, they won't let 'im. That's what happened to Irving."

Atlas shook both hands at the ceiling and said: "I wanna live! I wanna live, fucker!"

I had no idea what the hell Atlas was talking about. I had no idea what Irving's situation had to do with Harrison Ford or *Blade Runner* but I had given up trying to make sense of what came out of the mouth of Kirk Atlas.

The creature looked at me, smiled, and said: "I'm a good actor, huh?"

"Unbelievable," I said. "There are no words."

"Anyway," said Atlas, "I thought Irving was a total fag."

"Why is that?"

Atlas raised an eyebrow. "Poetry? C'mon. Not that I got anything against queers. Hollywood is full of 'em. But that Irving he had passion. Who knew? That's the money shot. That's what I'm trying to do in my work on *Doomsday*—desire, hysteria, emotion, passion. You coming to my mother's funeral for Pilar?"

"Sure," I said. "What do you think about—"

"Dude!" Atlas said and put up a silencing hand. "Tomorrow we grieve and prosecute. Tonight we celebrate."

Kirk Atlas didn't give two shits about Pilar's death. One less lover to keep, I guess. And he didn't seem to give a crap about Irving's confession to killing his uncle Benjamin, either.

Kirk Atlas was a lovely young man.

"C'mon!" Atlas walked out to the terrace. I followed.

Olga was on the terrace, looking over the edge. The brown knapsack was now on her back.

"Hello, sweetie," Atlas said, putting his short muscled arm around Olga's shoulder and kissing her forehead. "Where's Albert?"

"He's inside," Olga said. "We had a fight."

Olga began to weep. "It's so awful. First Pilar. Now Irving."

"Don't cry," Atlas cooed into Olga's ear. "Don't think about that stuff tonight."

Olga wiped her eyes.

Then we all went into the quieter master bedroom where two pairs of boxing gloves and copies of *GQ* and *Playboy* sat on the king-size bed.

Albert Garcia, cradling a bottle of *Cristal*, was in the bedroom, stoop shouldered and staring at an object on the windowsill.

I went and stood by Albert and saw that he was admiring a small crystal sculpture, two figures on a pedestal. One figure was a woman with wings straining to hold up a crystal earth twice her size. The second figure was a fallen woman with wings, draped across the crystal silhouette of a city. The spire of a skyscraper ran through her chest.

"Struggle and loss," Albert said. "In the beginning and in the end. What can you do? Absolutely nothing."

"That cost me six hundred bucks," said Atlas, coming over with his arm draped around Olga. "I bought the painting in the hall from a man who died of AIDS. The nude in the poolroom I bought from the wife of an artist who died at the World Trade Center. And the one by the terrace was done by some South Bronx street kid who got shot and died in the eighties. This is the first piece I ever bought by an artist who was still alive. But you never know."

Olga elbowed Atlas in the ribs. Atlas dropped his arm from around her shoulder.

"Albert told me you box, Chico," said Atlas, sniffling.

"Not anymore," I said.

"We gotta box," Atlas announced, grabbing the gloves off his bed. "See if you still got any game, Chico. We got a crowd!"

Albert tapped Atlas on the shoulder and smiled wide and toothy, "Let's do it."

Atlas laughed at Albert.

Albert leaned forward, "You and me. Let's go."

"Same old Albert," Atlas said, sipping his *Cristal*, following Albert out of the bedroom. "I love that little guy. Always have."

I watched Marcos-Kirk-Atlas-Rivera who stood shadow boxing now in the empty center of his monstrous living room, just a few rows smaller than Madison Square Garden, as the partygoers lined up along the walls.

"Who wants some medicine?" Atlas called out.

"I do," Albert responded, standing, legs apart, directly across from him.

"Let's do this!" Atlas said, slipping out of his blazer and slipping on his red boxing gloves.

I looked at Kirk Atlas and then at Albert. The idea of fighting a man who was obviously outside your skill level. Disgraceful.

Olga Rivera entered the living room, eyes searching.

"You're just in time for the main event!" Atlas said, pounding his boxing gloves together. He flexed his muscular pecs. Albert put his gloves on, trembling hands and all.

"Don't be stupid, Albert," Olga said.

"Don't do this guys," I said. "This ain't a fair fight."

"I'll show you a fair fight," said Albert and punched his gloves together. "Let's rumble!"

"Please, Albert!" Olga came forward and kissed Albert's cheeks passionately over and over again and pulled on his arm. "Stop this. You're not a brute."

"Get a room!" yelled Kirk Atlas. Everyone laughed. He chugged back half a bottle of champagne, burped, *hoo-ahhed,* and the mob of partygoers cheered for blood.

Albert Garcia and Kirk Atlas squared off. The partygoers formed a ring around both fighters. Someone made the sound of a bell. Ding! Ding!

Albert took a hard jab at Kirk's face. Bam! It connected. Maybe Albert could pull a little David and Goliath outta his ass and miraculously whoop Kirk Atlas.

Maybe.

"Not bad," Kirk said and came forward and hit Albert in the stomach. Albert buckled a bit and Kirk gave him an uppercut that sent Albert stumbling backward into the crowd. They held him up and pushed him back at Kirk.

Maybe not.

Kirk punched Albert in the face and sent him reeling back at the crowd, who held Albert up again and pushed him staggering forward once more at Kirk. Kirk threw a punch at Albert's face. Olga jumped in front of Kirk's fist and took it on the chin, managing to say only: "Stop—"

The blow sent Olga slamming like a rag doll back against Albert, who stumbled with her into the crowd. But this time the crowd broke and Olga and Albert fell to the floor in a tiny pile.

"Coming through!" I yelled and pushed past the crowd. I pulled Olga up from the floor. I shook my head and threw a look of contempt at Kirk Atlas. A look he shot right back at me. I glanced down at Olga. Her eyes were closed. The blow had removed her glasses.

"Olga? Olga?" I said.

Olga opened her eyes slowly. She stirred and stared up at me. She placed her face near mine, gentle, soft, big black eyes, short black hair.

Then I saw that something had slipped out of Olga's knapsack besides homework. A .22, with a mother-of pearl handle.

Yeah, *primo*, it's true. It's the quiet ones.

TWENTY-TWO

Back home, cozy in my underground Pelham Bay nutshell, I was feeling grateful and lucky to be alive. I lay back on my bed, with Boo asleep on my chest. I thought about Olga Rivera and her mother-of-pearl-handled .22. The same kind of gun that Tiffany owned and the same kind of gun that Irving placed in his story. My cell phone rang and Boo went berserk barking like it was a tiny electronic intruder.

"Chico Santana?"

"Yeah," I said.

"Yes," said a frail and older woman's voice.

"Yes," I repeated.

"Hello, Mr. Santana, I've heard a lot about you. My name is Josephine Rivera."

"How can I help you, Mrs. Rivera?"

"I'd like you to come see me. Have a talk about my son

Marcos, and my nieces Tiffany and Olga. Get a pen. I'll give you my address."

"I have it," I said.

After saying so long to Boo, I took the N train into Manhattan and hopped off at the Fifth Avenue stop. I walked maybe half a block to a ritzy building overlooking Central Park. The white doorman in a dark blue uniform and hat with white gloves looked at me and said, without missing a beat, "Delivery?"

"Yeah," I said. "I got a foot to deliver, size twelve Rockport. Where should I put it?"

I have never had a doorman to greet my guests. Rats and cockroaches don't count.

"I'm a guest." I grinned at the blushing doorman. "Josephine Rivera. I'm expected."

A second doorman, with a Russian accent, escorted me up on the elevator to the penthouse. He told me that the Rivera's penthouse took up three whole floors and the elevator door opened up inside the apartment. He had seen nothing like it in Moscow.

"Mr. Santana?" the stunning young nurse said as she stood in the doorway, barefoot. She was wearing a white uniform over her shapely figure.

"Come in. Come in, darling," she sang with a West Indian accent. "Hurry, hurry. I have to run."

She asked me to remove my footwear. I slipped off my Rockports and followed the nurse through a white carpeted hall. It was a humongous apartment. We passed seven rooms, a home entertainment theater, a gym, a wine cellar, a music room with a Steinway piano under twelve-foot ceilings, on our way up the winding stairs to the second floor. We came to a stop in a waiting area the size of my whole apartment. Everything I had seen so far, the walls, the carpets, the furniture, everything but the West Indian nurse, was white. The Rivera apartment on Fifth Avenue looked like the original of what Pilar was trying to copy in her much smaller place in Astoria.

"Wait here, honey," said the West Indian nurse and disappeared beyond a pair of French doors.

I sat on the white leather sofa, but when the nurse was out of sight, I jumped up and scanned the waiting room.

There was a painting of a woman, young and beautiful, on the wall, just above the leather sofa. It was signed by Picasso. It was the real thing. Shit, they were all originals.

"Come now, sweetie," said the West Indian nurse, poking her head out of the French doors. "Hurry, hurry." I was escorted into a dark bedroom that smelled of menthol and talcum powder. Someone was lying in the darkness.

"Josie," the nurse said, turning the light on low. "That young man is here. He's very handsome. So you behave yourself until I come back."

The room was ringed by heavy white curtains that absorbed all sound and let in no light. Photos of Marcos-Kirk-Atlas-Rivera were everywhere, on the walls, over the bed, on the chest of drawers. Marcos, clearly recognizable at five, wearing a gold paper crown; Marcos on a pony; Marcos as a tree in a children's play.

Josephine Rivera lay quietly in a giant white bed, a white ribbon in her hair, a spot of red blood on her white nightgown. There was a bedpan by the bed; an intravenous drip ran into her arm, and on her bedside table was an asthma pump, fifteen pill bottles, and a book, *In Search of Lost Time*, by Marcel Proust.

She looked like Tiffany in many ways, same perfect oval face, same high cheekbones, same broad forehead, same green eyes. She was probably in her sixties but looked older, hair in a tight white bun.

"Pull me up, Kathy."

Kathy the nurse propped Josephine Rivera up on white pillows and leaving said, "I'll be back soon, Josephine."

"Take your time." Josephine Rivera's face was tense with pain. She looked at me and said, "Kathy has only been in America one week. Already, she isn't just my nurse. She's family."

I didn't have the heart to tell her that the definition of family didn't usually include a uniform and a paycheck. But I'm a private detective, not a dictionary.

Anyway, she put out her left hand and signaled for me to kiss it, like she was the Pope or something. I kissed it. It was warm and damp and smelled like rubbing alcohol. Like Hannibal Rivera the Third's hand, there was no wedding ring.

Josephine Rivera looked at me and said, "You look like shit."

"Thanks."

"*Hablas español?*"

"Not really. A bit, but it's rusty."

"Learn."

"Yes, m'am."

"Do you have a revolver?"

"No, m'am. Why?"

"You could finish me off," Mrs. Rivera said. "Pity."

"Sorry. I'll try and be more considerate next time."

The old woman broke wind without intent and said, embarrassed, "Lovely."

I shrugged.

"There are no peaceful deaths, Mr. Santana. Don't believe it. Dying is painful and stupid and ugly. Try not to do it."

"I'll do my best. Can't promise anything, though."

She picked up a large gold box marked Godiva. "Chocolate?"

"No thanks, m'am."

She patted the bed for me to sit and I sat.

"So," I said. "I finally meet the Wizard."

"I'm no wizard. I'm a witch."

"Are you a good witch or a bad witch?"

"That all depends on you, Mr. Santana. Do you know why you're here?"

"I shook my head. "Salsa lessons? Landscaping advice?"

She shook her head.

"I'm trying to protect my son."

"From what?"

"From himself."

"Explain, please, m'am."

"Marcos comes over here once a week. Every week. He is rough with me, sometimes cruel, but he is a good boy. A good son. I have not had an easy life, Mr. Santana. My husband Hannibal's family was nearly bankrupt when they came to Argentina from Cuba. My father, Francisco, kept them afloat long enough for Hannibal Rivera the First to get the family back on its feet. When I married Hannibal the Third, my father, my inheritance, and my money allowed his brother Samuel, a hard worker and a shrewd businessman, to eventually steer HMD from *just* agriculture to finance and real estate. Samuel works. Hannibal plays. We are all rich and unhappy."

"How rich?"

"Filthy. We have more money than the queen of England. Which isn't very hard these days."

"Congratulations. And I'm sorry."

"I love my son, Mr. Santana," she said, coughed, grabbed a handkerchief, and spit up blood. "I love him more than I love anything on this earth. I would do anything to protect him."

"Would you kill?"

"I would kill every last one of you."

"Including your husband, Hannibal?"

She smiled. "He would be the first. Oh, once upon a time I believed that Hannibal loved me despite the sickness. Now I am not so optimistic. I am speaking with you indiscreetly, Mr. Santana because I am beside myself. I have exhausted all means to get rid of you. I sent Hannibal. I sent Pena and Fiorelli. You're still here."

I looked around her shrine to Marcos.

"You've been paid to disappear, Mr. Santana. Why haven't you disappeared?"

"I'm a people person."

"And I'm unhappy, Mr. Santana. I'm unhappy that you're still here."

"Since we're being indiscreet," I said. "Did you know where Tiffany was?"

"No," she said. "Do you know why I was so upset by Pilar's news that Marcos was searching for Tiffany?"

She calmly took a photograph from the short dresser and held it out to me. It was an old and faded black-and-white photograph of what looked like Tiffany on a beach, wearing a one-piece bathing suit, sitting alone on a blanket in the white sand. The date was marked on the bottom: Cuba, 1950.

"Recognize her?"

I looked at the photograph again. Except for the Chinese influences in Tiffany's face, they were look-alikes.

"Hannibal married that girl in the picture," said Josephine. "His first cousin. Me. Why did I panic when Pilar came to report Marcos searching for Tiffany? Simple. I disapproved of his infatuation." ·

Infatuation? It took me a second but I got the picture. I was no longer puzzled as to why Atlas was so intent on finding his cousin. So that was it. Atlas was *romantically* interested in Tiffany.

Kirk Atlas had been Pilar's savior. Her alpha and her omega. Her higher power. The sun rose and set in the sky of his generosity. She wanted him all for herself and paying me not to find Tiffany or worse was just another strategy.

The poor girl was in love with a guy who didn't deserve her love. And Kirk Atlas was in love with his own cousin. I bet that wouldn't go over too well in Hollywood.

"How much money did we give you to disappear?" said Josephine Rivera. "I take it you have it hidden away in some account?"

"I don't keep a bank account. I keep my money in a sock. It's not big but it's clean."

"You're joking?"

"I wish. I don't joke about socks."

"You will stop harassing my family," she said, suddenly forceful. She shook a bony finger at me, like it was a wand, and pounded the bed with her frail fist. I actually felt sorry for her.

"I already have stopped," I said.

"I'm not a fool, Mr. Santana," she said. "My people tell me that you've been trying to get an audience with Irving Goldberg Jones in prison. That you were hanging about with Marcos in Central Park and at his home just the other night. Even after you were paid not to do so. Tiffany is back. The guilty have been punished. You will quit this silly investigation of yours!"

Then she lowered her head and sat so still that for a minute I thought she had dropped dead. Silence. After a long moment, Mrs. Josephine Rivera looked up at me again.

I didn't know what to think until she said, "Benjamin is dead. I am glad he's dead. We're all better off. You already know that Benjamin had molested children. What more do you want?"

So that was it. She wanted to convince me that even if Benjamin Rivera, as portrayed in Irving's short stories, had been murdered, he deserved it. But what about Pilar? Did she deserve it, too? Not by a long shot.

"Benjamin had dirty habits we didn't know about," Mrs.

Rivera said. "He inherited those dirty habits from his father. He had servants and a *thing* for young Asian girls. Very young."

"What about Samuel Rivera?"

"Samuel likes big girls, thank God. The point is: Benjamin is dead and no one cares, Chico. Nor should they."

She didn't seem to know anything about her own husband's "bad habits" or maybe she was just playing dumb.

"You think Marcos killed Benjamin?" I blurted out.

I hit a nerve. Her eyes popped and she went pale and I thought she was going to have a heart attack and quickly started running the lessons I learned in CPR through my head.

"I did not say that," she said. "No one has accused Marcos of anything."

"Why are you paying for Pilar's funeral after she blackmailed you?"

"It seems like an appropriate ending," she said. "I want to see it finished with my own two eyes. And now it's almost over and you're mucking about kicking up dust. And don't act as if all you ever cared about was that girl Pilar or that Irving boy or finding out the truth about Benjamin's overdose. I know all about you, Mr. Santana. I am sorry that your father was a drug addict. Perhaps you see something in Benjamin because he was also a drug addict."

"Hold on, lady."

"Your father was a doctor who helped the poor, Mr. Santana. That was his saving grace. Benjamin had no saving graces. Benjamin was not your father. You will help no one by digging into Benjamin Rivera's death."

Josephine Rivera gave me a sinister look. "Do you think I am sick *and* senile, Mr. Santana?"

Josephine Rivera knew about my father's drug addiction and death and God knows what else. I was investigating her family and she was investigating me. You wanna play hardball? Hardball it is.

"What about Irving? You feel comfortable sending an innocent kid to prison for a murder he didn't do?"

"Mr. Goldberg Jones is getting the best representation money can buy. I have already arranged it. I am not a cruel woman, Mr. Santana. There will be leniency once the truth about Benjamin is revealed in court."

"What about Olga and Tiffany's guns? The ones with the mother-of-pearl handles. They both got those guns from Marcos, right? I bet Marcos has one just like it somewhere."

"What do you want?"

"Where is the VHS cassette from the Chinatown Angel surveillance camera?"

She looked away. I'd hit another nerve.

I hit harder: "I think you know or suspect the same thing I'm starting to suspect or you wouldn't be giving me this story to suggest that Benjamin maybe deserved what he got because he molested your niece and I should feel sorry for the poor girl and take the money and shut up and just go away. Did Pilar find the VHS cassette, Mrs. Rivera? Was your son Marcos on that tape? Your son Marcos killing his uncle Benjamin in the Chinatown Angel?"

Her face went cold and frantic and white as a snowstorm and she said, "You're the detective, Mr. Santana. You're the one who's paid to deduce. Deduce. I'm just a sick old housewife."

"Good night, Mrs. Rivera."

"Will you stop your investigation?"

I took a gold-wrapped chocolate. "Good night, Mrs. Rivera."

As I left, Mrs. Josephine Rivera said in a childish voice, "How much?"

I kept walking.

Money could do many things. But it couldn't do everything. It *could* make murder go away, but maybe not. If I was smart, I would have taken more money and run. Why wasn't I smart?

That stuff about Benjamin being an addict and how that connected to my own father's murder, that was some mumbo-jumbo, right? Right? Damn skippy. I took the elevator back down.

But there was that lump in my throat again.

TWENTY-THREE

I ducked into the elevator and went up to the SoHo penthouse, ran down the carpeted hall and pushed open the door to Marcos's apartment, which was always unlocked—a dare to anyone who would try and violate the sanctuary of Kirk Atlas. Considering Josephine Rivera's worries, I decided to go in head first like a bull and see what broke.

Marcos stood in the doorway leading out to the terrace, shirtless and sweaty, wearing red jogging pants, diamond-encrusted cross around his neck, holding a drink in one hand and a phone in the other. His hair was starting to grow in. It was black and sharp, sorta like a porcupine.

"I don't care what he wants," Marcos yelled. "I'm negotiating with Sean Penn to appear in my next movie. Tell him I said he can go fuck himself!"

Marcos hung up the phone. "What's up, dude?"

"I'm gonna give you a five count," I said, looking down at him, accentuating my height and reach advantage. "And then I'm gonna give you a shot at that boxing match you wanted. And the only bells you're gonna be hearing are the ones ringing in your head."

"Listen." Marcos walked and reached into a drawer and pulled his .45 and laughed. "I could shoot you right now for trespassing."

"Where is the surveillance tape from the Chinatown Angel? The VHS cassette from the night your uncle Benjamin died?"

"What?" said Marcos. "What are you talking about? What cassette? What is your problem, dude? You're lucky I'm fond of you."

Either he didn't know, or he was the great actor he believed he was. Someone entered from the master bedroom.

Marcos turned. "Have you met Kathy?"

"Yeah," I said. "We met earlier today."

Kathy, Josephine Rivera's West Indian nurse, naked under a thin pink nightie, nodded, a bit ashamed, and turned to look out the wall-to-floor windows.

"Show him the rock," Marcos said.

Kathy held up her left hand and showed a giant ring, not on her ring finger, without turning to face me. Not a diamond. Jade.

"Did you think I got married, Chico? No way. It's just a friendship ring. Right, Kathy? I'm done with Tiffany and all that mess. And no more Brazilians. Kathy got all that crap outta my system. I figure she saved me a couple of hundred grand in therapy."

"Congratulations."

"Thanks, dude. I mean that," Marcos said, still holding the .45.

He lowered the gun and went over and slapped Kathy's behind. She flinched.

"Who knew? Right, Kate?"

Marcos took his new girl's hand in his.

"Who knew?" Kathy said and snatched her hand back.

"Time of the month," Marcos said and winked at me.

Kathy didn't react but kept her sad gaze on the river.

The phone rang. Marcos picked up. "I'll call you back, Mom. Yes. Kathy's here. Yes. I'm happy. Yeah, Renata's gone. Yes, I'll try and be good to Kathy. No. Chico's not here. Don't worry about it. Yes. Yeah. Okay, okay. I love you, too! Bye!"

Marcos hung up.

"Where is the surveillance tape?" I said. "Why did you murder your uncle Benjamin?"

Marcos looked at me with wide eyes.

"Murder?" He lifted his .45 again. "I don't know what your diagnosis is, dude, and I don't care. I've been more than patient and generous with you. I like you but I don't like you *that much*."

Marcos pointed the gun at my face. "Now leave, or I'll add some decorations to your tree."

I didn't move.

"Have it your way," Marcos said and started toward me, gun raised as if to hit me on the skull. I stood with my hands low, waiting for the assault. I had already been knocked out once on this case. One more time, and I'd have to turn in my private detective flashlight and matching key chain. Confusing action-hero fiction with fact, he lunged at me. Maybe that shit works in the movies, but I ducked and flipped him. I heard a loud thud when Atlas's head hit the floor as if someone had slammed a melon against a drum. Even Kathy said, "Ouch." He dropped the gun but got up. You almost had to admire his stupidity if not his lack of training.

"Don't hurt him!" Kathy yelled.

Atlas charged at me again. I punched him two times with a hard right and tried to lay him out for good with a nasty chop to the head. It was a lot easier than I thought it would be and a lot harder. Atlas fell back in a red rage and snatched the .45 off the floor and fired.

"Marcos!" yelled Kathy.

I felt nothing. I heard nothing. I saw nothing.

"Chico?"

Atlas and Kathy were staring at me like I was a ghost. I reached down and checked myself for holes. Nothing. I looked behind me.

There was a crater the size of an elephant's foot. Just above my head. Right between the *Doomsday* movie poster eyes of Kirk Atlas.

"Dude," Marcos said, in shock. "I'm sorry."

"Sorry?" I marched over to him, grabbed the .45, and hit him in the jaw. He slammed against a wall and slumped down to the floor. Kathy ran over and held him in her dark arms, rocking him like a baby, caressing his head, cooing, "It's all right, honey. Everything's gonna be all right. Kathy's here. Kathy's here."

"Benjamin Rivera," I said. "You killed him."

"What are you talking about?" said Marcos.

"Your uncle Benjamin was a molester."

Marcos held his bloody nose and yelled, "Why would I kill Benjamin for molesting Olga?"

TWENTY-FOUR

Olga Rivera returned to her apartment at the Arcadia West after spending most of the day at a place called the Bowery Poetry Club, reading and drinking coffee alone. She came back out of her building around 11 P.M. Freshened up and in different clothes. Strange fact, Olga Rivera left her apartment wearing a blond wig. I had not totally changed my mind about Kirk Atlas being guilty of murdering his uncle for love and profit but things didn't make sense again (if Benjamin had *not* molested Tiffany) and all roads kept leading back to Olga.

The small club was dimly lit. The kids were young. They danced or stood around talking in groups, sloppy drunk at two in the morning.

If you gave the disc jockey a few dollars or paid for his drink, he would play your favorite song.

I sat, sipped my White Russian, and watched the young dancers, feeling like the creepy old dude at the club who refused to accept that the days of the Hustle and the Macarena were over. I was watching her. I had been following her most of the day and then followed her to the nightclub. She was all skinny legs and hips stuffed into a tight, black, spaghetti-strap dress, no glasses, blond wig.

A boy in sneakers and jeans threw himself down at her feet and snaked across the dance floor on his belly.

As the music pumped away, I watched her shaking her groove thing, slapping her little hips, flailing her thin arms above the electric beer signs.

When the music stopped, I decided to confront her and deliberately caught her eye. She saw me and wobbled toward my table. She was wearing green contacts.

"Hello," she slurred.

"What're you doing?"

"Dressing up," Olga said. "Being silly."

"I hardly recognized you. Where's Albert?"

"I don't know," Olga said, adjusting her blond wig. "He broke up with me."

"Sorry to hear that," I said. "Why did he quit you?"

"I don't want to talk about it," Olga said, gesturing to the dance floor. "This is my night. My own thing. What are you drinking?"

"A White Russian."

Olga lifted my glass to her lips, drank, then said, "I'll get you more."

"No. No more."

She put a hushing finger on my lips and walked unsteadily through the crowd toward the bar.

She returned from the bar with two White Russians.

"Drink," she said.

I drank, and she told me that she was there that night to forget, to laugh, to dance.

"Let's dance, Chico."

Olga dragged me to the floor, and I moved with the music. She felt good in my arms. When the music stopped I looked into her eyes and said, "Where's the third story?"

"Are you going to tell my parents on me?"

"Depends."

"On what?"

"How much you're willing to help me," I said. "What can you tell me about Irving's Chinatown Angel stories?"

She sighed. "Is that what you want? The third Chinatown Angel story? What if I told you a better story? Would you leave me alone then?"

On 62nd Street, we went through the revolving doors of the Arcadia West, past the doorman, into halls that reverberated with echoes that seemed to start even before you entered. The halls were a hive of vanilla doors and chocolate walls, clean and glossy.

We got off the elevator and entered Olga's apartment, and it was like walking into a roll of fresh bread—warm and homey, and the air was sweet.

I'd already been there, but she didn't know that and it's not in my nature to search and tell.

Olga opened her purse and took something out, something I couldn't see. She turned to the right, and I saw it—her mother-of pearl-handled gun. She held it.

"Do you always have that gun?" I said.

"Not always. I was thinking of going to the shooting range on 23rd Street today."

"It is a dangerous city and you live alone now. Maybe you

should have a gun. I'm just not so sure you should be carrying it around as much as you do."

"Why were you following me?" Olga asked.

Note to self. Get better at following suspects.

"I didn't do it," she said.

"Do what?"

"Kill my uncle Benjamin."

Olga sat down on the sofa and placed her thin hands over her eyes.

"Irving's stories are true. Am I wrong? I've seen two so far. What is the third story about?"

Olga rubbed the top of her own head as if she were soothing a small child.

"I wanna help Irving. He was your friend once. How did you come to find your uncle's body?"

"I was looking for Albert at the restaurant."

"Tell me everything, Olga. Now's the time."

Olga took a crumpled letter off the coffee table. "I got accepted to Harvard Law School."

"Congratulations."

"Thanks," Olga said and gave a small cynical nod. "But I'm not going, I was only doing it for my parents. I'm going to be a poet. Tonight, I was nervous about Harvard, about my future. I couldn't sleep. I called Albert so that he could come over and comfort me and he told me it was over. So I went dancing."

"Why did you attack Tiffany that day in Chinatown?"

"Because she deserved it," she said.

Olga removed her green contacts, dropped them on the floor, and put on her glasses. Her eyes looked like two black marbles in a fish tank.

"Growing up Tiffany always had boys wrapped around her finger. She manipulates men. I hate her, she hates me."

"I don't think she hates you. She's your sister."

"Yes. She's my sister. I loved her once, too. I don't any-more. She never showed me any respect as an older sister. When she left, I was happy and I hoped she was happy wherever she went. But I was in no hurry to see her come back."

"Why?"

"She was the center of everything in my family. That wasn't good enough for her. She gets what she wants when she wants it. Always has."

"And you?"

"I have Albert," she said. "I *had* Albert."

"Did you have a boyfriend before Albert?"

"No."

"Nobody you liked?"

"I liked me. Albert was super-smart and down to earth and he liked me, too. So of course I liked him back. I wanted to expand my heart and mind in all directions and yet, for years, I cast my pearls before those spoiled rich swine at Dalton and Columbia. Then I met Albert at my uncle's restaurant."

"What did you do with your pearls then?"

"I cast them at someone who could appreciate them. I gave them to Albert."

"So he became your boyfriend?"

"The best. The first. My Albert. Mine."

There was a steady sadness in her eyes. She was much too thin, but the eyes. They were determined eyes. Eyes like a cam-era. Maybe that's what Albert loved.

"Talk to me," I said. "And maybe I can have a chat with Al-bert."

Olga dug out an asthma inhaler from her bag and took a pull on it. She looked at me.

"How did Irving get those stories for his trilogy?" I asked. "Marcos told me that you were the one molested by Benjamin, not Tiffany. He told me that the family knew but kept quiet about it. Made Benjamin apologize and you accepted and all was forgiven."

Olga's face was very still.

"So why did Irving think that Benjamin molested Tiffany? Didn't think you could drive Irving to kill Benjamin if he thought it was you?"

She looked around confused. "That's not what I wanted."

"It's easier if you don't lie," I said.

"I'm not lying."

"You and Pilar and Irving were good friends, right?"

"Yes," Olga said. "They were my best friends."

Tears welled up in Olga's big black marble eyes. I felt sad then, and Olga felt like no suspect, in that moment, and it wasn't phony, it was real. Her best friend was dead and another was in jail, and there was nothing she could do about it.

"Me and Irving," Olga said, "we had very different outlooks on the future. He was a socialist and, basically, I'm not. Neither was Pilar. But we all had a few things in common— we believed in poetry and art and music. We believed in friendship. I'm not a natural writer. Irving helped me write my first poem. He helped me realize that I don't want to go to law school. I never did. My parents want that for me. Because I'm the smart one. But if I ever become a poet, I'll always owe that to Irving."

I sat beside Olga. "He didn't do it, did he? Where is the tape?"

"Ask Irving," she said. "It's all up to him now."

"What do you mean?"

She folded her arms and rubbed her own shoulders.

"Who killed Pilar?"

"Nobody killed Pilar. She killed herself."

"Why?"

"Maybe she knew that no matter what she did—blackmail,

threats, love—there was no way she would ever have Marcos. Maybe she realized she was a fool and couldn't live with herself."

"Where is the surveillance tape?

"Irving," she said, shaking her head. "He has his own fate in his hands. He chose this, not me. There's nothing more I can do. I wish there was, there isn't."

"That's bullshit!" I said. "Why do you hate Tiffany so much? And don't tell me it's because she broke your Hello Kitty doll when you were kids."

"What does a girl who has everything want?"

"What?"

"The one thing she doesn't have."

"What does that mean?"

"My sister is not as wonderful as everybody makes her out to be. There is no mystery as to why she ran away. It had nothing to do with Benjamin's death. It had nothing to do with what he did or didn't do to her."

"Because of Marcos?"

"No," she said, and made a disgusted face.

"Why did she run away?"

Olga left the room and came back with a letter on pink paper. She handed it to me.

Dearest Albert,

As terrifying an experience as writing this letter is for me, I'm going to be honest. Okay, then: I was happy that day, after our midnight movie at the Angelika, and you explained to me how a certain scene was shot in *Touch of Evil*. I want to say that it was good for me to kiss you that night, after you told me about your rotten childhood, to open my eyes and find you there.

When I said that I had never been kissed like that before, I was being honest. Why did I run off when you asked me to speak in Chinese so you could watch my lips? No one has ever asked me to talk so that they could watch my lips move.

I don't believe this is happening.

I have developed this ridiculous love for my sister's boyfriend, an intelligent, passionate, filmmaker. An artist like me. My very own genius. I have tripped madly and willingly, irreversibly into the Albert.

So if you can make time, can I get a chance to know you and to let you know me? Could you cast me in your life? In time, Olga will understand. I think. I hope.

Tiffany

TWENTY-FIVE

On the day before I arrived at Rikers Island, Irving Goldberg Jones was declared a major suicide risk and placed in protective custody, where inmates are locked in their cells up to twenty-three hours a day. I called Samantha and she had arranged for me to see him at Rikers late that morning with a message I said I had from Tiffany.

Irving walked into the interview room, cuffed and shackled, wearing an orange prison uniform, and didn't say a word. The corrections officer nodded and left to stand outside the door. The room had a table and two chairs. Irving sat on a chair. I stood.

"Hello, gorgeous," I said.

"What's the message from Tiffany?"

"How are you?"

I noticed he had dark circles under his eyes. He stared at the ceiling of the room and said, "Buried alive."

"Thank you for talking to me."

"I've been stuck in a cell for twenty-three hours," he said, passing his hand across his newly shaved skull. "If they told me that Adolf Hitler wanted to see me, my only question would be what kind of wine I should bring."

"I'll take that as a compliment," I said. "Nice haircut."

Irving's Afro was gone.

"I'm worried about my parents," he said.

"Have you spoken to Tiffany or Olga?"

"I spoke to Tiffany on the telephone once," he said. "Since that time we've had no communication."

"Olga?"

"Nothing. What's Tiffany's message?"

"I'm gonna give you the short," I said, putting one foot up on the metal chair. "Make it quick and dirty. You're up shit's creek with a toothpick, son. And I'm the last sign of dry land you're gonna be seeing for a long time. I want you to get off your cross for a minute and tell me the whole truth."

"I don't need your help."

"You confessed to a murder. A murder I don't think you committed. Best case scenario, you get stuck in the system for a couple of years until they figure out what's what. Worst case, you're the next best thing they got to a suspect and you spend the next twenty years on a hard bunk, dreaming about revolutions."

"Nelson Mandela spent over twenty years in a South African prison."

"This ain't South Africa," I said. "And you ain't Nelson Mandela."

"I don't think I want to talk to you anymore," he said, and stood up. "Thanks for the message."

"I'm not saying you shouldn't use your anger, kid. I'm saying don't use it against yourself. Tiffany goes back to school

210

and a regular life. What do you get? A couple of visits and a sympathy hug? Not even that. Ask yourself. Is this worth it?"

"Yes."

"Benjamin Rivera molested Tiffany, right?" I said.

"Yes."

"You killed him as revenge. To show her how much you loved her?"

"Yes."

"But that's not what happened."

"How do you know?"

"Tiffany wasn't molested."

"Who told you she wasn't?"

"Olga."

"She's lying."

"Marcos says she wasn't molested, either," I said. "Says the family knew for years that it was Olga who was molested but since it only happened a couple of times everybody decided to forgive and forget. That's fucked up but I'm just the messenger."

Irving looked helpless, near tears. "Can't you just leave me alone?"

"That thing on your shoulders," I said, "is that a head or just a slab of meat with two eyes."

"It's a head."

"Then use it," I said. "A little booze. A little heartache. Damsel in distress. You run and get your shield and your horse and ride in for a rescue. I understand. But sober in a jail cell, floating in the East River between Queens and the Bronx in the world's largest penal colony, knowing that you are alone and abandoned, that Tiffany is out there free while you rot in here, must give you pause."

He grabbed his head. "Lemme alone! Do you have a message from Tiffany or don't you?"

"Yes," I said. "Tiffany is going to live happily ever after, Irving, and your life will be material for a Bruce Springsteen song. Is that what you want?"

"I like Bruce Springsteen," he said.

"You're losing the thread, my friend. You're a devoted martyr, I get it. But you got bad advice."

"I didn't get any advice."

"That's the worst kind," I said. "They were your friends—"

"I know they were my friends!" he yelled, his voice breaking.

"Do you really think Pilar just slipped off her roof?"

"Yes," Irving said.

"Let's say Pilar was killed. Who do you think was in a New York frame of mind to do it?"

"I don't know."

"Why was Pilar blackmailing Hannibal and Josephine Rivera?"

He sat back in his chair. "Pilar wasn't a blackmailer. She was a romantic."

"Did Pilar have any enemies that might want to see her dead? Besides Hannibal and Josephine?"

"No one killed Pilar," he said.

"Was it you?"

"No! Why would I kill Pilar? And if I did, why wouldn't I confess to that, too? I love Tiffany. She doesn't love me. Why? I'm not perfect. I'm not rich. I'm not successful. I'm a worthless poet. I know. But I'd do anything for her. She put up with me and my stupid scribbling. She's good. That's why I love her. I wrote the trilogy as a way to get everything off my chest."

He stood up.

"Did Tiffany tell you about Albert?"

"What about Albert?"

I placed Tiffany's love note to Albert down on the metal table.

He picked it up, read it, and looked devastated.

"With friends like that," I said. "Who needs enemas?"

He looked it over again.

"That's the message. What do you think?"

He shook his head. "I'm not stupid. You could've written that."

"Check the handwriting. You must know Tiffany's handwriting."

I watched him as he reread the note. He looked away.

"Where is the videotape? Where is the third story?"

He looked like a zombie, like I had ripped the life-force right out of him. "I didn't write the third story," he said, looking at the air, at nothing, as if in a trance.

"So who did write the third story?"

He paused and snapped out of it and looked at me. He turned and called for the guard and mumbled, "I never wrote a third story. I never finished the trilogy. That's what I meant."

But I knew.

That's not what he meant at all.

TWENTY-SIX

The first thing I heard was barking. The second thing I heard was my cell ringing. I woke up, fully dressed, after a long night of beer, Newports, and TV into the wee hours. I hoped it was Ramona calling about Irving's trilogy and the possibility that there was another writer at Columbia who wrote the third story. I rolled over on my mattress and grabbed my cell phone. A male voice said, "Chico?"

"Albert?

"Chico," Albert said. "What did Olga tell you?"

"What?"

I heard more barking. I said, "Where are you?"

More barking.

"Boo!" I yelled and sat up in bed. I saw Boo barking at Kirk Atlas, who appeared in my doorway. Kirk Atlas wearing a white sheepskin coat and a matching white baseball cap that said DOOMSDAY.

"Bad time," I said into my cell. "I gotta go. I'll call you back."

I hung up. I grabbed the dog and locked him in the bathroom.

I turned to Atlas and said, "What's up?"

"No hard feelings," said Atlas. "You're a detective. I get it."

"What do you need?"

"I'm almost thirty," he said. "I'm ready to get married, Chico. I want a wife. Someone I can trust. Children. House. Is that wrong?"

Atlas sat down on my one chair. "Tiffany's missing again."

"What about Kathy?"

"I have big creative balls," said Atlas, ignoring my question. "People don't appreciate big creative balls. They want small creative balls."

"Can we stop talking about balls?" I asked.

"I got a phone call from my cousin Olga saying that Albert is off somewhere with Tiffany. They're seeing each other. I think he knew where she was all along. I think they're having sex."

"Is that why you're here?"

"I want you to find them!" he said. "That short fat ugly little nothing two-face double-crosser will not end up with Tiffany."

"Why do you care?"

He looked around my room, angry, confused, as if he wanted to smash something or someone but didn't know where to start or why.

"I don't know," Atlas said and sat back in the chair. "I don't know why I care. I just do. He's a smart guy. Didn't have any advantages. He's a fighter. He always treated me like I was nothing. When all I wanted was his respect. I used to look up to him, you know? All that stuff he knew about film. I looked up to him and he treated me like shit."

So that was it, years and years of secret competition with Albert Garcia. Years of eating Albert's soup of contempt. Maybe Atlas secretly believed he deserved it, needed it to nourish his energy. And in the end, maybe Atlas saw only one last meal of victory, conquest over the burning derision that one boy fed him, a boy ten years older. A boy who loved movies, a boy with celluloid dreams, an older boy he may have loved and respected as a kid, like a big brother. And whose love and respect he needed and wanted. And couldn't get.

I saw in that instant that Albert Garcia had become, for Marcos, some kind of father figure. And now Marcos saw that he would maybe never get the chance to push Albert Garcia's face down into the glory of his accomplishments. He would never defeat his father, real or made up. He would never shed Marcos Rivera and become Kirk Atlas. He would remain at the table of childhood, eating the sour soup of self-hate with a short spoon.

Atlas dug into the pocket of his white sheepskin and counted out five thousand-dollar bills, placing them on my mattress. "That's for you. Find Albert."

I stared at the bills.

Pilar was dead. Irving in jail. Albert was gone. Tiffany was gone. Kirk Atlas was alone, handing me five thousand dollars in cash to keep him company on the deserted road he saw before him.

I moved toward the front door. I motioned for Atlas to go. "I can't do it. "I can't work for you anymore. I'm full."

"Why not?"

"Albert's a friend."

"You're not quitting on me, too!"

"I am," I said.

Then someone pushed open my front door and in stepped Oscar Pena and Salvatore Fiorelli.

"You know my new associates," Atlas said. "Turns out my

mother hired these two goons to watch out for me. I caught them snooping around my building. It's funny how two big guys like this on your mother's payroll will confess to almost anything when they're looking at the receiving end of a .45. I called my mother, she was sorry and said that she would make it up to me. Said I could keep them for a while. My own personal bodyguards. Say hello, fellas."

Oscar gave me a little wave, Sal just nodded.

"Let me shoot the bastard," said Oscar.

Oscar lifted his gun. Sal was standing behind him. Then I heard someone singing with a high falsetto voice, cracked and pitchy, "Oh, Chico!"

"Nicky?"

Nicky stood there, all dark and bearded, like a black lumberjack or a giant, stooped in the doorway, wearing a pea coat.

His girlfriend Willow Mankiller Johnson was with him, carrying a red, black, and green backpack. She was tall, almost as tall as Nicky, a black woman with dark Indian eyes and long lashes, long thick black hair, looking like a reddish brown Pocahontas—wearing cowboy boots and a white cowboy hat with a red corduroy dress.

If Atlas was a mini fridge, Nicky Brown was a meat locker.

"You see, honey?" Nicky said to Willow from the door. "The old me would be committing some serious violence right about now and asking questions later."

"Your nose is in business that doesn't concern you, dude," Atlas said.

Nicky stepped into my apartment. Willow was just behind his shoulder.

"What's going on, baby?" said Nicky.

I waved. "Same 'ol, same 'ol."

"Step outside, monkey man," Oscar said, pointing his gun at Nicky.

"Monkey man?" Nicky laughed. He turned to Willow John-son again and said, "And the old me wouldn't even have asked for clarification. I woulda opened up a can of whoop ass as soon as his mouth hit the K. I'm sure he meant *monkey* in the best sense of the word. Maybe he heard about our bonobo re-search?"

"Listen, gorilla," Oscar said, stepping closer to Nicky with his gun. "Take that big black bitch—"

Mistake. Nicky popped Oscar in the face so hard and so fast that sixty-six of his generations musta felt the pain. It sent him directly to the sandman, bouncing off my mattress and landing between my dresser and my chair. Knockout.

Nicky looked over at Sal, who put his hands up and said, "You got it, chief."

"That was amazing," Atlas said, staring at Nicky all wide-eyed.

"Sorry about the trouble, fellas," Salvatore said. He helped Oscar to his feet and then followed Atlas to the door.

When they all left, Nicky slammed the door behind them, stretched his arms out and said, "You really know how to throw a party, Chico."

We came together for a hug, back-slapped and traded rough kisses on both cheeks.

Willow, cutting Nicky off, kissed me on the lips and said, "Hello, Yankee."

Boo started barking from the bathroom and Willow walked to the door.

"What's the plan?" asked Nicky.

"I gotta find Albert," I said.

"Listen, brother, I promised Willow I'd change my old ways. I'm gonna be a married man soon. Time to grow up and be-come Settled Down Nicky Brown. I gotta look for a job, maybe the Bronx. But before that, we go make some visits."

"Yeah," I said. "Cool."

"Tell me more about that Hannibal Rivera the Third. Tell me more about that little Chinese girl at the Hunts Point Market. Ting Ting. Tell it slow. Make me angry."

"I'll tell it," I said. "But I need you to *hang back* until I say when."

"Of course, my brother," said Nicky and slapped my shoulder and smiled big. "I'm all about hanging back."

TWENTY-SEVEN

At the Universe Diner on West 57th Street, we sat in a booth, in suits and ties, under a wall mural—a cartoon version of the universe. Painted on the tabletop were cartoon men, in spacesuits, floating above the blue earth outside their ships as planets blazed pink and red in the distance.

"What happened?" I asked.

Albert grinned at me. "Sex happened."

"Just sex?"

"Yeah," he said. "Tiffany is a free spirit. You can't take her seriously. She's not Olga."

"Do you love Olga?"

He hesitated. "I do." Then, "She's nuts about me. Or just nuts."

He laughed uneasily. I said, "Was it worth it?"

"I don't know yet."

"If you had told me what was going on from the start, Albert. Maybe, I could have helped you. Not been so paranoid. Don't let my failed marriage fool you. Chico knows love."

Albert gave me a tiny smile.

My ideas about Albert were in a tangle—what to say and how to say it, what to share and what to keep.

I heard shouting and laughter coming from another table, voices of young girls and boys.

"Just wait," Albert said. "They'll see."

Albert crossed his short legs, revealing dark dress socks in black dress shoes. "We didn't mean to do it," he said. "Tiffany's excuse is that she's young and didn't know any better."

"What's your excuse?"

"Stupidity."

"And now you're back together with Olga?"

"Olga called me last week," said Albert. "She made a good case. We're *negotiating*."

"What did you think Olga was telling me?"

He paused. "I thought she was telling you about Tiffany," he said. "I wanted to tell you myself, Chico. But if Marcos or Olga found out about me and Tiffany, I was afraid my film would've been flushed down the toilet. I hated lying to you."

"What happened with Benjamin Rivera?"

"I don't know what happened," Albert said. "Irving says he killed Benjamin because of Tiffany. Says Benjamin molested Tiffany. I never heard that. Even Tiffany says it's not true. She says Benjamin never touched her. Says it never happened."

"Do you know about Olga being molested by Benjamin?"

"I didn't," he said. "I do now. She told me."

"What about Irving's stories and the surveillance tape?"

"I never saw any stories or tapes," he said. "The only thing I was hiding was Tiffany."

"Olga says that Irving's fate is in his hands," I said. "She didn't quite admit that he was innocent but almost."

"Let it go, Chico," said Albert.

Enormous gobs of awkward silence.

"So," I said. "Now that everybody knows about Tiffany, isn't your film still in danger?"

"No," said Albert. "We all made a deal. It's over with me and Tiffany. Atlas is appeased. Olga's satisfied. Tiffany knows it was just sex. Everything's not cool again exactly but it's bearable. Work in progress."

I tossed a gleam of doubt into my eyes and beamed it at Albert.

The waiter brought a cheeseburger with fries and a Coke for Albert and waffles with syrup and coffee for me.

"Diabetes, here I come," said Albert as I poured my syrup on the big stack.

"Man who lives in clogged heart," I said, pointing at his cheeseburger and fries. "Shouldn't throw gallstones."

Albert sank back on his chair exhausted.

"You can talk to me, Albert. I know I started this as a P.I. But I'm your friend. You say everything's okay but you don't look okay."

"I—"

Albert stopped short, as though his voice had failed him.

Then he picked up his soda, drank, and cleared his throat. His chin began to twitch and he slammed his fist down on the crotch of the cartoon astronaut.

Albert was about to spill his guts about something but stopped himself.

"I'm good again, Chico. I swear."

"Yeah." I grabbed a fry, chewed, and said, with my mouth full, "You look it."

That's when I saw Nicky march into the diner. He was wearing a black suit, white shirt, no tie. Willow Mankiller Johnson entered and stood at his side, wearing a blue winter coat. A black cowboy hat perched on her head.

"Nicky!" I waved. Nicky waved back and approached our table.

Albert turned his head. "Is that Nicky Brown?"

"Yeah."

"What's he doing here?"

"I don't know," I said. What the hell was Nicky up to? This isn't what I'd call *hanging back*. But Nicky Brown was a force of nature. You didn't tell the wind which way to blow. It just blew, as far and as wide as it wanted.

As Nicky came toward our table, Willow pulled open her coat. She had on a dark blue dress, close and tight to her reddish brown body.

"Albert Garcia," Nicky said, holding Willow's hand. "This is my lady. Willow Johnson. We're getting married."

"Congrats."

Willow put out her hand. "I'm sorry about your friend."

Albert stared at Nicky for a minute, jumped up and hugged Nicky with a "good to see ya, long long time, bro."

I looked out the window of the diner and saw a gold Cadillac.

Someone jumped out of the limousine and waved and it wasn't Olga.

"Marcos!" said Albert.

TWENTY-EIGHT

We rode to St. John's in the block-long Cadillac Olga had instructed Marcos to come pick us up in. I watched Atlas driving in his white Italian suit, gushing like a teenager in the Nicky Brown fan club. He wasn't angry with Nicky about the incident with Oscar and Sal in my apartment; he complimented Nicky on his fighting skills, asked if he did any personal training and even tried to give Nicky his ten-thousand-dollar diamond watch.

I looked back at Willow, who shook her head and rolled her eyes.

Albert watched the road, totally changed now, looking like he wanted to machine-gun everybody in the limo.

The church was filled with morning sunlight and tall stained glass windows. It smelled of incense and lilies. I saw mourners talking in little groups—wealthy friends of Olga's parents, all wearing black with their funeral faces.

The priest was near the coffin, his face long and thin, talking to some of the mourners. No one seemed to be listening to him; they either nodded politely or looked away. Josephine Rivera was wheeled in by Kathy. I watched Olga standing dutifully beside her mother, Mia Kwan, and her father Samuel Rivera.

Then I saw Nicky approaching Hannibal Rivera the Third. Not good. Hannibal saw me and scowled as if to say, "What the hell are you doing here?"

I went toward him and Nicky and shot out my hand. Hannibal shook it and smiled, all polite and phony. Nicky towered over Hannibal and put out his hand, too. "My name is Nicky Brown. I've heard a lot about you, Mr. Rivera."

"All good," Hannibal said, "I hope."

"Not really. Chico told me all about you and that little girl Ting Ting. You should be ashamed of yourself."

Hannibal's face dropped. Mine, too.

"Listen, son—" Hannibal Rivera said.

"I'm not your son."

The "son" bit always messed with Nicky's head. Considering that he had killed his own father, who could blame him?

Hannibal made a face and started walking off.

"Don't go away angry," said Nicky.

Hannibal turned with a sneer. "If my wife didn't insist I let you two stay and avoid any public embarrassment, I'd have security escort you into the nearest river."

"Thanks for the concern," I said. "But I took a shower."

Hannibal walked off and I looked at Nicky who was gritting his teeth like he was chewing on Hannibal Rivera's heart.

Later, we all sat and faced the front of the church. Marcos was going to give the eulogy. He had volunteered to do it. He had been instructed by his mother, Josephine, who wanted to see that Pilar was dead and buried quietly, not to mention "suicide," as the Catholic church where the services were being held was not extremely fond of this ancient practice.

I was seated in a wooden pew, at the back of the church, on the left side, next to Willow and Nicky. Up front, on the right side of the church were the Riveras. Olga and Albert sat between Samuel Rivera and Mia Kwan. Marcos made his way to the front of the church, waited for everyone to be seated, and began to speak.

"Who hasn't wished they were dead at one time or another?"

Olga began to cry.

"I myself am on a journey," said Marcos.

I winced. Albert looked up at the skylight and groaned.

"Let me tell you my story," Marcos continued. "I grew up pretty good, money, private school education, opportunity."

Marcos paused for effect.

"I wanted to be in the movies."

Albert shifted violently in his pew.

"But I took a detour."

Albert coughed, loud.

"I went to Yale," said Marcos. "I didn't graduate. I was a straight-C student, I'll admit it. I didn't apply myself like I coulda."

Albert had a coughing fit. Olga turned and hushed him.

Marcos put up one index finger.

"But at the age of twenty-seven I am finally realizing my dream, the dream of that little boy on Fifth Avenue."

Albert groaned, louder. Olga hushed him again. Nicky and Willow watched Marcos, horrified and fascinated, disgusted and awed.

"That little boy who is still inside me is truly living for the first time," Marcos said.

"I'm glad!" Albert yelled. Mia Kwan looked at him with fire in her eyes. Albert dropped his head.

Nicky and Willow looked at me.

Welcome to my world.

"We must be patient," said Marcos. "If Pilar were here, that's what I'd say. Don't go. Don't walk into the light. Maybe that's the only thing we can take away. Maybe that's Pilar's message for us, her lesson. Be patient."

Just when I thought it was over, Marcos looked up dramatically at the church skylight. Nicky's and Willow's eyes were riveted on Marcos's face. Albert was gritting his teeth, mumbling, fists clenched.

"Pilar, I know you are listening," Marcos said to the skylight.

Then Olga suddenly started bawling. I saw Albert, trying to comfort her. He whispered something.

"Pilar, please know that you are in our hearts," Marcos said. "And we will never forget you."

Then Marcos wiped at dry eyes, dropped to one knee, and made the sign of the cross.

I felt my cell phone vibrating in my pocket. I checked it. It was Ramona calling.

Then someone entered and I heard music and someone yelled from the back of the church: "Albert!"

I turned and saw Tiffany, walking down the aisle, in a long white winter coat, white scarf, and white boots, playing her violin. A white butterfly barrette perched in her long black hair. Every cranny of the church filled and reverberated with her playing. I felt as if I had been pierced. Tiffany's violin split me from the top of my head to the bottom of my shoes.

On reaching a pew Tiffany stopped playing and dropped and let her head sink down on the pew in front of her and closed her eyes.

"Tiffany," Albert said and jumped up and ran past Olga

and her parents toward her. And I saw Tiffany stand up, kiss Albert on the lips, and slump into his arms, weeping. It was a silent cry. The tears trickled down her cheeks, her mouth trembled, but not a sound escaped her lips, her face a melodious quiver of tears, impossibly green eyes glistening in the sunlit church.

I saw Olga watch as Tiffany's hand went behind Albert's neck, and she held his neck touched his eyelids, his nose, his lips. And she placed her mouth on Albert's face again and again and her youth and energy, stronger than death, seemed to pass from her into Albert, for a fleeting but noticeable moment.

And then I saw it flash, something close to ecstasy on Albert's face, as he stood holding Tiffany, all eighteen years of her, crying not far from the terrible glare of her older sister, Olga.

Jesus.

They were in love.

TWENTY-NINE

It was snowing. We walked briskly to Mimi's Cuchifrito to wait for Albert. I had agreed at Pilar's funeral to give Albert some time alone with Tiffany, to get his head and his story straight. I cared for Albert. He wasn't just some case. I wasn't afraid that he'd skip town. And if he did, we'd find him. No doubt. I made that perfectly clear. I couldn't say no.

A few men sat at the counter in front of the TV watching soccer as we entered. Mimi was behind the counter, standing over them. Mimi's eyes shot open when she saw him.

"Nicky!"

"*Holá*, Mimi," said Nicky. "Fattening the masses, as usual, I see."

Mimi came out from behind the counter and Nicky bent down. Mimi, on tip-toe, gave Nicky a big hug and sloppy motherly kisses on both cheeks. She ran a plump hand across his shaved head and said, "Chico should do this!"

"I'll just have a *Malta*," I said.

Mimi brought me one cold bottle of *Malta*. She poured a cup of coffee and sliced two hunks of *flan* and set them down before Nicky.

Mimi looked at me and said, "What is going on, Chico?"

"*Flan*," I said.

Mimi shook her head and looked at Nicky who just shrugged.

"Albert," I said. "We're supposed to meet him here."

"Be careful," said Mimi and took Nicky's large hand. "How are you, *hijo*?"

"I'm good, Mimi," said Nicky. "I'm getting married."

"I hear," said Mimi. "Where is she?"

My cell phone rang. I answered quickly. "Willow? Did you get it?"

I heard a female voice.

I looked at the cell phone screen. It wasn't Willow. It was Tiffany. Her voice sounded afraid, frantic even.

Tiffany said, "Albert wants to change the meeting place."

"What's going on?"

"I have no idea," said Tiffany. "Albert spoke to Olga after the funeral. He's got some videotape and he says only you can help him. Please help him, Chico."

I looked at Nicky, eating flan, and Mimi cheering at the televised soccer game. Willow walked in with a big brown envelope. She calmly placed the envelope on the counter to my left while Nicky introduced her to Mimi who gave her a paper menu and a kiss.

"Where are you, Tiffany?" I said. "I want to see you."

There was a long silence.

Then Tiffany came back on.

"The Willis Avenue Bridge," Tiffany said. "Albert wants you to meet us there."

"I'll be there," I said. "I could use a little frozen air."

"Come alone."

"Change of plan," I said to Nicky. "Albert wants to talk alone."

Nicky nodded and turned casually to watch soccer. Mimi was trying on Willow's cowboy hat. I looked at it and nodded. I stood up and grabbed the big brown envelope. It was marked HUNTER COLLEGE. Ramona had found it. She had found the third story. I walked outside and unfolded some pages: *Trilogy of Terror: Fire.*

It was the third story I had asked Ramona to try and track down. Only this story wasn't at Columbia or written by Irving Goldberg Jones.

THIRTY

Trilogy of Terror: Fire
By Olga Rivera

The boy ran out of the movie theater, past the gates of the local Baptist church, out to Longwood Avenue. He ran through the windy winter streets past garbage piled high, past howling cats and scurrying rats and busted tenements decorated with blinking Christmas lights, beer cans and liquor bottles on broken stoops. His heart was pumping confusion. There was pain in his legs, his backside, his belly, his throat.

He ran out into the street and a car screeched to a stop just before it hit him. People screamed, "Jesus Christ!"

"*Cono,* fucking kid!"

"Nigga, watch where you goin'!"

The boy kept running.

Run, run! Keep running! Don't stop! Don't ever stop! Never!

The boy ran all the way home and up the urine and graffiti stained stairway to the fifth floor of his building. He knocked frantically at his front door.

Ma's gonna kill me. Ma's gonna kill me. I'm gonna die.

The boy's young mother, blond, wearing a red bathrobe and slippers, opened the door, tears in her eyes. She gave his face a quick stinging slap and said, "Just like your father!"

The boy took the blow and looked down at the tiles of the hallway and said nothing. His mother pulled him into the apartment and slammed the door. A Rolling Stones record was playing: *"You can't always get what you want."*

The boy's stepfather came out of the kitchen holding a fried pork chop and a beer. He was handsome with black hair and sleepy green eyes. He wore a white T-shirt and jeans.

The boy's mother said, "How many times do I have to tell you to stop sneaking out at night?"

His stepfather bit into his pork chop. "That boy doesn't respect anybody."

The boy's mother looked down at the boy. "Where were you this time?"

"Movies."

"This late," his mother said. *"Mira la hora!"*

The boy looked over at the clock, in the shape of a black cat.

A cockroach scampered across the golden cloth in front of the Christmas tree with its red, white, and green lights. Four gift-wrapped boxes nested on gold tinsel.

The boy said, "I don't wanna live here no more."

"What?"

"I don't wanna be here anymore."

The boy's stepfather looked at the boy's mother and said, "You better teach that boy some respect, or one day you're going to be picking him up from jail or worse, the morgue."

The boy's mother looked at her husband and then down at her son. He looked up. He did not want to live there anymore. He would not.

His mother said, "So you don't want to live here?"

"No."

The boy's stepfather slapped a greasy hand against his upper thigh. "This boy is something else!"

The boy, thinking it was a compliment, smiled at his stepfather. He did not see his mother's hand coming as she slapped him, her forefinger stabbing his right eye, blinding him in a flash of white light.

The boy did not cry. He had had his fill of tears. He looked at his mother with his left eye, and he saw in her what he saw in his stepfather, what he saw in himself, what he was finally beginning to see.

He saw the light. And it was not good.

The boy's mother went into the kitchen and came back with a man's leather belt and a green tin full of uncooked rice. She grabbed the boy by the arm and dragged him to the small bedroom he shared with his half brother, the son of his stepfather. The boy's mother stood in the dark and scooped out some rice with one fist.

She spread the rice in a corner of the room. The boy's half brother woke in the dark and cried.

The boy's mother went over to the crib and cooed, "Sleep, sleep, sleep, *mi amor*."

The boy removed his clothes in the dark.

His mother whipped his bare bottom and legs with the leather belt. Then he knelt down on the uncooked rice she had scattered on the wood floor.

The boy's mother said, "You stay there until you learn."

She left the dark bedroom and shut the door. The boy knelt there, in the black, facing the white wall, kneeling on the rice. It cut into his bare knees.

The boy cursed as he knelt. He cursed his stepfather, his mother, the world, life.

When his mother entered the room again and sat on his bed and cried hysterically and said, "I only do this because I love you," the boy cursed her again, in his heart, and wished her dead.

His mother said, "It hurts me more than it hurts you."

"I know, Ma."

"Don't be like your father."

"I won't. Don't cry."

But still the boy's mother sat on the small bed and sobbed, so much that the baby began crying, too.

The boy got up and went to his mother and touched her blond hair, touched her wet cheeks, and kissed her face. He held her close to his small chest and they stayed there, a child holding his mother as she cried in the dark.

She picked the boy up and held him close. Then she put him down in his bed, stepped back and looked upon him as if she might have remembered something about herself and her own childhood.

She wiped her face. She kissed him and went over and kissed the baby and said, "Sleep, *niño*. Everything will look better in the morning."

When she was gone, the boy jumped out of bed, packed a small knapsack with comic books and old movie stubs.

He went over to the glass tank where he kept his hamster and fed him green pellets one last time. He had made up his mind. He would go to Hollywood. He would live with his real father.

Everybody would be happier.

He grabbed his coat, then went over, in the dark, to the old crib his half-brother slept in, kissed each of his cheeks, and closed the bedroom door.

The boy passed his stepfather asleep on the sofa. Matches, a spoon, and a freshly used needle lay on the rickety coffee table; he had a smoking cigarette in his left hand. He had fallen asleep in front of the TV watching *Sunset Boulevard*.

Saliva slipped from his stepfather's open mouth, down his white shirt. Cigarette ash dropped off the bright-red burning end of the cigarette, hitting the floor. The boy thought about stubbing the cigarette out.

But he'll wake up. He'll stop me. Maybe start touching me again like he does. Go!

The boy cracked the front door slowly, went out, and closed it slowly behind him. He flew down the staircase, to freedom.

Outside, he thought about taking the train at Hunts Point, but he had no money. So he walked in the opposite direction. When he reached a highway he would hitchhike, something he had seen someone do in a movie.

He walked not far from the wide steps and pillars of his public school, down the broad hill past rows and rows of tenements and lampposts dripping with

Christmas lights. He walked the deserted streets and came to a stop at the highway.

The boy stood on the corner, put out his hand, and tried to stop a car or truck that would drive him to Hollywood.

Ten minutes later a tall woman approached in a red wig and red heels, her large breasts sneaking out of a tight worn-out dress and red leather jacket. She looked at the skinny boy, surprised, and said, "Hey, you, what you doin' out here?"

The boy thought fast. "I got lost."

"Lost," said the woman, mistrust in her eyes. "Where were you goin'?"

"Find my father."

"Your father isn't at home?"

The boy shook his head.

"You don't know where your father is?"

"He's in Hollywood. He's a movie star. He lives in a house."

The woman's eyes turned to slits as she studied the boy's face.

"You're Puerto Rican, right?"

The boy said no, "El Salvador."

"That some kinda Spanish, right?"

"I think so. My mother and father is from El Salvador."

The woman screwed up her face and said, "C'mon."

The boy followed the woman to a small park where a tall, thin man wearing a dark coat and a knitted skullcap came away from a van parked at the corner. The man yelled, "What the fuck, Wanda?"

"Kid's lost."

The man in the dark coat looked at the boy suspiciously. "So what?"

"So he needs to get home."

"Send him home."

"He's lookin' for his father, Jason."

Jason looked at Wanda, eyes wide. "You either drunk, stupid, or crazy. I don't know which."

"Jason! He's a fuckin' kid. It's late. Let's get him home."

"What's goin' on?" said a short, fat man in a fur coat, walking out of the shadows of the small park.

"This is bullshit!" Jason said, no longer looking at Wanda but walking toward the dark van. He signaled for the man in fur to follow. Wanda grabbed the boy's hand and said, "C'mon."

The boy sat beside Wanda in the sticky front seat of the van, which smelled of cigarettes and car oil. They stopped and he happily took and ate a grilled cheese sandwich and drank a Coke that Wanda bought for him. When he was finished, Wanda pulled him close to her soft breasts. The boy smelled strong perfume and bath powder and sweat. Her warm thigh pressed against him. He liked it.

The boy looked up at Wanda and said, "Can I stay with you, Wanda?"

The three good Samaritans laughed and kept laughing. Jason laughed the hardest.

The boy looked at Jason and scowled. Jason stopped laughing. He lit his cigarette, and said to Wanda, "You see the way he lookin' at me?"

Wanda bent to the side to look at the boy's angry face and said, "What's wrong, little man?"

"He's laughin' at me," the boy said, pointing at Jason.

The fat man in fur, sitting in a back seat, took a hit from a small joint of marijuana. "He think you laughin'

at 'im, Jason. He gonna kick your ass. Float like a butterfly, sting like a bee!"

"Sugar Ray, Sugar Ray!" Wanda said, placing her
arms around the boy and squeezing him close.

The fat man in fur slapped Jason on the back and
laughed some more. Jason looked at the boy and raised
his cigarette hand as if about to slap him. Wanda
pulled the boy close to her breast and yelled, "Don't
you fuckin' dare!"

"I'm jokin', bitch."

When Wanda pulled the boy away from her breasts,
he had a big smile on his face. He tried to put his
face between them again. Wanda pushed the boy away
and said, "Niggas are all the same."

The fat man in fur took another hit of marijuana
and said, "A man after my own heart."

The fat man handed the boy the small joint.

Wanda looked back at the fat man in fur. "What the
fuck you doin'?"

The man in fur said, "He gotta learn sometime."

Jason took a drag of his cigarette and looked at
the boy. "Go ahead, little man."

Wanda looked at the boy disapprovingly, "Go ahead
if you want."

The boy took a quick hit from the joint. Then the
burning started, in his throat, in his eyes, in his
belly.

He doubled over and started coughing. Wanda
snatched the joint away from the boy and passed it
back to the fat man in fur.

Jason started the van and the boy said, "I don't
wanna go home," coughing as they screeched away from
the curb. "I don't wanna."

But he told them where he lived and they drove

until they saw the light of the tenement fire raging red and angry in the dark. Red lights from the fire trucks streamed across faces in the gathered crowd. Some were gawking. Some were crying. Some were standing out in the cold in bathrobes and slippers or half naked and barefoot.

Watching the blaze from the parked van, Wanda said, "Honey? You live in there?"

The boy pressed himself close to Wanda. He was speechless and helpless and sick as he watched his building burn, and he knew that his family was dead. He knew they had not gotten out. Not his mother, not his stepfather, not the baby, not his hamster. He knew they were dead before anyone could tell him, before the police knew, before the hospital knew. The boy watched his building and his family burn and he didn't say a word.

THIRTY-ONE

The Willis Avenue Bridge was covered by snow, a white slate of no-place-to-be-right-about-now. The dark streets of the South Bronx were a trail of brightly lit windows. Snow fell in great torn sheets, on wind that chilled me down to my Fruit of the Looms. I saw hints of buildings buried beneath white on distant Manhattan, and walked onto the bridge.

Albert and Tiffany were in the middle.

Albert wore no hat, scarf, or overcoat. He had not changed clothes since Pilar's funeral. He was holding something.

Tiffany stood still on the pedestrian walk when she saw me. Albert, at the railing, stared down at the river. He held up the thing he was holding. It was a black VHS cassette case. Tiffany, standing a few feet behind Albert, gave me a desperate look.

Man, Albert. I thought back to the kid he was at St. Mary's, wishing everything could've turned out different. But we were many miles away from Sister Irene and Father Gregory and those kids who called themselves the Dirty Dozen. No matter what you want, it's now, you're here, and time keeps on steppin'.

"Albert!" I yelled, standing a few feet away from him.

Albert stood still. Finally, he saw me, a look of agony, of despair, scratched into every crease of his face. "Clarence?"

"No," I said. "It's me, Chico."

"There is no moral order in the universe, Chico," said Albert. "I thought there was. There isn't. We're just a bunch of ungrateful and greedy bipeds."

"Speak for yourself, bro. Why you out here?"

"I just wanted to go somewhere and think. I can think out here."

"Let's go think somewhere else. We can all have some rice pudding at Mimi's. You remember Mimi."

"Mimi," said Albert and his face lit up. "Yeah."

"Let's go," I said.

"Yes," said Tiffany, "Let's go, Albert."

His face dropped again. "I can't."

He held up the VHS tape. "I could dump it," said Albert. "I could turn it over. Either way, I'm damned. I didn't know, Chico. I didn't know about Pilar's blackmail. I didn't know about Benjamin or Olga being molested or those stories. I didn't."

"I believe you," I said.

"Irving is innocent."

"Bro," I said. "It's me, Chico. Let's get off this bridge."

"What is going on?" Tiffany pleaded. "What is on that tape?"

I edged closer.

Albert leaned into the railing. I stepped back.

"If you're thinking what I think you're thinking," I said.

"I'm not going to kill myself," said Albert.

"That's right, you're not."

"You can't kill yourself when you're already dead," said Albert.

"Albert!" said Tiffany. "Don't talk stupid!"

"I'm dead, Tiffany!" Albert yelled. "I'm already dead!"

"You're not dead," Tiffany yelled. "Don't say that!"

"I died a long time ago. I died in a fire. I just didn't know it yet."

"Albert," Tiffany said in a soothing voice.

"I had nothing but my pride and my dignity," said Albert. "And I sold that out when I agreed to do *Doomsday* with Marcos. I sold myself. I cheated and I lied. So Olga killed me."

"What do you mean?" I asked.

"She killed me with the truth," Albert said, holding up the videotape.

Tiffany looked worried out of her head.

"Marcos is a snake," said Albert, "and Pilar and Irving were children. And I am nothing."

"I understand, Albert," I said. "You're all mixed up. You did what you thought was right to make your film. I'm your friend, Albert."

"Friend?" Albert laughed. And he went on laughing all the time he was leaning into the barrier, staring down at the dark and quiet waters.

"I never stood a chance," Albert repeated. "I just didn't know it."

"Stop it!" said Tiffany. "Stop it!"

Albert looked down at the water.

"Maybe I should just jump," Albert said. "Maybe Pilar had a point."

"Don't say that!" Tiffany said.

"Prison I'm not afraid of," said Albert. "I'll trade places with Irving."

"Albert," Tiffany cried. "Albert, please! What is happening?"

"Let's get off this bridge, Albert," I said. "I don't know what's going on, but we can figure this out."

Albert stared at the water. Maybe he was worried that he would be seen as he threw himself into the ocean, that people would stop their cars to stare and look round, as if they had nothing to do but to watch him drown.

"What do you want, Albert?" I said.

Looking around once more, with his hand still on the barrier, Albert closed his eyes. I could hear the traffic passing.

"Think, Albert," I said. "You're a smart guy."

"I am thinking, Chico," said Albert. "There is nothing left to film."

He hunched himself as though about to jump.

"Albert!" yelled Tiffany. "This isn't what we agreed to!"

"What can I do for you, Albert?" I shouted.

"We called Chico out here so that you could tell him," said Tiffany. "So you could both be on this bridge together one last time like when you were kids, remember? And you could tell him what Olga told you and show him what's on that tape!"

"I wish I'd never been born, Chico. Can you do that for me?"

"What's going on, man?" I asked.

"I want to tell," said Albert. His voice was filled with a great weight. "I want to tell everything and accept my punishment. I killed Benjamin. I'm tired."

He looked at Tiffany, face bunched up like a prune with teeth, lower lip trembling. "I'm tired."

"Why did you kill Pilar, Albert?" I asked.

"Nobody killed Pilar," said Albert, clutching at his head as if to stop it from flying away. "Pilar committed suicide."

"Why did you kill Benjamin?"

"Benjamin killed my family," said Albert. He banged at his chest and at his head as he spoke. "He killed my mother. I didn't remember, Chico. Olga told me. I remember, now. Benjamin Rivera was my stepfather! He killed my family! And I killed him!"

Albert lifted the VHS cassette and was about to fling it off the bridge into the ocean.

"Someone's coming!" yelled Tiffany.

I turned and saw someone walking briskly toward us in the snowstorm.

"Albert?" said Tiffany. There was worry in her voice.

"What the hell?" said Albert, squinting, trying to make out who it was. I saw the approaching figure's hand lift and then I heard and saw the flash of gunshots in the dark.

I saw someone else, a larger figure running behind the shooter. I felt a smashing blow to the side of my head. I heard more running and someone who sounded like Nicky yelling. I heard more gunshots and the screech of car wheels. And as I fell I saw a helicopter circling the skyscrapers and the million lights of Manhattan and then the waters that passed beneath the bridge.

I always knew I would end up like that, murdered like my father.

There I was and there was darkness and in the darkness there was a face. Ramona, sitting on our old sofa reading her manuscript, *The Detective*, a colorful rug at her naked feet. And on the rug, Boo, the Chihuahua you love to hate. And before there was nothing, there were pinks, reds, yellows, many shades of brown and black. Before the dark, before I felt my arms and legs go as light as though they had been cut off, there was Ramona, there was love. And then there was nothing.

THIRTY-TWO

Slowly waking, I heard a shower running and B.B. King singing "We're Gonna Make It." I opened my eyes. I looked around the room, confused. I was naked under a sheet, lying in a king-size bed. My head had a fat welt on it and felt like it had been a piñata at a birthday party for hyperactive children on steroids.

The room was dark. My neck and my back hurt. I felt as though I'd been lying there forever. I struggled to sit up, and eventually I stood and pulled open a curtain at the window. The sun came shining into the room, throwing streaks of light on the green walls and the polished wood floors.

Piles of books lined the walls. Outside the window was an endless row of buildings. Snow covered the rooftops.

I wobbled back to the bed, wrapped the sheet around myself and went toward what looked liked a bathroom door. The door was open. There she was, naked, between the claw-footed tub and the white sink, reaching slowly for a towel. She looked at me, dark, brown, glowing, and unashamed. Ramona Guzman Balaguer.

"I'm sorry," I said, covering my eyes.

"No. I'm sorry. I forgot to lock the door."

"Where am I exactly?" I edged out of the bathroom.

"You're on 135th street. You're in my new apartment."

"How'd I get here?"

Ramona threw on a thick robe. *"Cómo estás?"*

"I'm fine. Considering."

We walked back to the bedroom.

"What time is it?" I looked around, uneasy.

Ramona gave me a strange look and asked me to sit down on the bed. I went to the bed and sat, still wrapped in the sheet. I watched her robe ride up her thick brown legs as she sat down on the mattress.

Ramona put her right hand on my cheek and my forehead, feeling for a fever.

I said nothing, gave no resistance. I sank back on the pillow, trying to remember, something, anything.

"And will you have coffee, master?" Ramona said.

"Yes, Jeannie."

It was nice to hear her talk to me, playfully, like the old days when we were married *and* happy. I missed that. I reached out and kissed the palm of her hand.

Ramona left and returned with coffee in a blue mug the size of a giant soup bowl. I moved back on the mattress and began to sip. She smiled sadly. "You okay?"

I shook my head. It hurt like hell.

Ramona placed her hand on her chest. "Nicky and Willow brought you here. Nicky saying you had no one to turn to, that you needed me, that you needed me to make a man of you."

I frowned. She laughed.

"Don't worry. *Il est fou,*" Ramona said. "I know he's nuts."

"What else did Nicky say?"

"He said that you needed to begin from the beginning. He said that you needed to be in love again."

I sipped my coffee.

"Nicky said I was perfect for you." She gave me a big smile. "That he was wrong. That you were all mine. He said life is a book and that every relationship was a chapter, and that our chapter isn't finished."

"Sounds like Nicky, all right," I said, shaking my head. "I'm sorry about that."

"No biggie," Ramona said.

I looked down at the floor. "Do you have my clothes?"

Ramona went out, and came back with all my clothes, now clean and *almost* bloodstain free.

"You were shot," she said. "The bullet just grazed you but you fell over and banged your head."

During my life, I had been knocked out before, goes with the territory, but twice on one case? Jesus, Santana, you're getting old. What's up with those reflexes?

After I'd been hit, I remembered hearing someone yell. And then gunshots, and a girl screaming—Tiffany—and then wheels screeching and footsteps running away from me and another set running toward me. And then I remember Nicky helped me to my feet and we jumped into my Charger and Willow wanted to drive me to the hospital and call the police. And I had said no. And then we drove to Harlem.

We arrived at the back of Ramona's building, opened a gate, walked through a long hall.

Nicky rang and rang Ramona's bell. He yelled out, "Ramona!" Then everything went dark again.

Nicky was on the Willis Avenue Bridge. He had followed me from Mimi's. He had been watching me and Albert and Tiffany.

But who was shooting? Whoever it was had been walking

toward us all along, slow, hidden by the snow, waiting to make a move. When he saw his chance, he ran at me, shooting. If Nicky and Willow hadn't followed me, I'd be sleeping with the fishes.

"Where's Nicky?"

"He hasn't been back since he brought you here," Ramona said.

"Where did he go?"

"I don't know."

She handed me a piece of paper. "Nicky left this for you."

It was a note: *I got this. Stay with Mona. Nicky.*

"What did he do? Just before he left with Willow, did he call anyone?"

"Yes. He called a lot of people."

"Who?"

"I don't know."

"What else?"

"He put your car keys in your coat pocket."

"Anything else?"

"He took that 'Fire' story."

I grabbed my shoes.

"You can't go. You need rest."

"Lives are in danger," I said, buttoning my shirt.

"Where are you going?"

"Chinatown."

"You know why you gave up drawing?"

"Why?" I said, tucking.

"Because it was foolish. Like my love of reading and writing. But all the good things in life are foolish, Chico."

"Why are you bringing that up?"

"I'm afraid. I'm afraid something terrible will happen to you. You're not Nicky."

"I'm no Nicky Brown. But I ain't too shabby, once I get angry. Don't let what happened last night fool you."

"That was two nights ago."

"Don't nitpick," I said. The truth was, my legs hurt, my spine felt like jelly, and there was a Mexican jumping bean on speed bouncing around in my skull.

I turned and Ramona grabbed me and pressed up on me.

"Stop, Mr. Ramona. Don't go."

We stood in the middle of the room, and I gazed around me, at the piles of books that lined Ramona's walls. I looked at my face in a standing mirror; I saw my eye swollen, my lip busted, my nose scratched to hell. It looked like I'd been hit in the face with a steel bridge.

Ramona touched the hurt on my face. She leaned in and kissed my battered lips. It was a nice kiss, a healing kiss, a kiss that almost made me forget again as I put my hand on her plump bottom and she dropped her robe down boldly around her shoulders and pressed close against me.

"You're making this real hard, Madame Chico."

"I could make it even harder, Monsieur Ramona."

"If I stay somebody might die."

Ramona covered herself with her robe and kissed my face.

"We *can't* still be friends," she said as I reached the door.

"We *can't* be friends?"

"I want a husband and children, Chico. You can't give that to me. You never could. You're too busy trying to save the world one street at a time. Nicky said he didn't like you living in that basement."

"I don't either."

"There's room for you here if you stay."

"I thought you didn't want me?"

"I'm giving you a second chance, *idiota*," she said.

"I'll be back, sweet-talker."

"No," she said. "If you leave, don't come back."

"I can't stay, Ramona. Forgive me."

"I won't. I won't forgive you."

255

"I have to go."

"Don't come back, Chico," said Ramona. "Not if you leave again. Not ever. You can't come back again."

"Is that some kinda ultimatum, Mrs. Chico?"

"Something like that, Mr. Ramona," she whispered and smiled so sad and beautiful, her eyes full of all kinds of hope and promise. I fell in love with her all over again. I didn't know who was crazier, her, me, or Nicky, but I could've kissed her all morning in that green room and then some. A weaker man would have stayed. Or maybe a stronger man. Hell. Who am I to judge?

THIRTY-THREE

I found my Charger parked outside of Ramona's. I tried Nicky's cell. No answer. Albert. Nothing.

I called Samantha: "Can you get me any info on the mother, father, relatives, and siblings of Albert Garcia, marriage licenses, birth certificates, rental agreements, criminal background checks."

"Is that all?"

"With cheese, *por favor.*"

"Chico? It's my day off. Is this an emergency?"

"Somebody tried to kill me on the Willis Avenue Bridge last night. Is that enough of an emergency?"

"I'll call you back."

I put LL Cool J's "Mama Said Knock You Out" on the sound system and drove fast to Chinatown, to the apartment over the Wing Wok Restaurant. Albert and Tiffany were not there. No one had seen her.

I sped to the Arcadia East. Nothing. Arcadia West. Nothing.

Call me, Nicky.

Think, Chico.

Should I call Mimi.

No. Why? You're getting punchy, Santana.

I drove to the Bronx and thought about Albert.

Albert Garcia was thirty-seven years old and slowly discovering that he knew a lot less about everything than he suspected. He hated his job waiting tables. Without his own money to make his film, he was stuck with Marcos-Kirk-Atlas-Rivera. Maybe he was even beginning to think that he had no talent. He would have to face the writing on the wall.

He would never be a famous director. He would spend the rest of his life on the Grand Concourse, watching a film every night, getting fat, bald, and blind, waiting tables and bullshitting with beat cops at the Chinatown Angel and arguing with young Chinese waitresses.

Life would pass him by, and countless films would get made in a galaxy far far away. Just how desperate could a man like that get? How full of spite, envy, and a need for revenge?

Before my lungs collapsed from chain-smoking while driving, Samantha finally called back: "I discovered something strange about Marcos Rivera."

"What?"

"Albert's mother had a drug habit and a couple of arrests for solicitation. Her maiden name was Carmen Diego. Deceased. *Mira!* Carmen Diego had two children. Albert Garcia! And Marcos Rivera!"

"What?"

"*Nene!*" said Samantha. "Hannibal Rivera the Third and Josephine Rivera never had a child!"

"What are you talking about?" I said, driving.

"Marcos Rivera is not their biological son," said Samantha. "Hannibal Rivera wasn't Marcos's father. Benjamin Rivera was! And Albert Garcia is Marcos Rivera's half-brother. Same mother. Different fathers. They all lived together in the Bronx at one time. Benjamin Rivera's family owned the building on Hunts Point that Carmen Diego died in. There was a fire."

I hit the gas. "Criminal background check on all of Albert's family," I said. "The whole clan. Take it back to El Salvador."

He was sitting on the front steps with a cigar and his silver flask. He was alone. I was sitting in my Charger, waiting for Albert and Tiffany to show or Sam or Nicky to call.

I got out of the car. I yelled out: "Uncle Dee!"

Uncle Dee puffed on his cigar and looked down at me from the top stair of his short stoop like he had always been there. Waiting for me. His face was unshaved. His silver hair looked gray. His eyes were bloodshot. His clothes were wrinkled. "*Holá*, Chico. What happened to your face?"

"Bad blind date," I said. "She told me it wouldn't hurt a bit. She lied."

I walked up the short flight of steps. He put out his hand. We shook, all vigorous and manly.

"Where's Albert?"

"He hasn't come home. Would you like to come in for a cup of coffee?"

I nodded and followed Uncle Dee into the foyer and down the hall and up to his apartment. Uncle Dee turned on a dim light. There were old *El Diario* newspapers stacked up in piles along the walls, dirty dishes on the floor around the brown armchair, and the faint smell of dog shit but no sign of a dog. All bits of Albert, his movie posters, his milk crates full of films on VHS, even the television, all gone. Like he never existed.

"It's a mess in here," Uncle Dee said, standing in the middle of the room. "They're planning to destroy rent stabilization, cut the whole building into smaller overpriced apartments. Push the people out and call it SoBro. That's what the local communists are saying. Shame. It's a beautiful building. Do you know that they used to call Grand Concourse the Jewish Park Avenue? That was a long time ago."

"Yep," I said. "Long time."

"If you need a bathroom, it's down the hall."

"No thank you."

Uncle Dee removed his hat but kept his coat on. I sat down on the raggedy brown armchair on a broken spring. Uncle Dee went into the kitchen. I could see him clearly from where I was sitting. He put a pot on the fire and prepared a quick plate of sugar cookies. I was looking around at the now bare walls when Uncle Dee came back to me, carrying the plate.

I took a cookie, and Uncle Dee put the plate down on the coffee table. He sat on a chair, wiping his silver flask with a handkerchief, and examined my face. "I'm sorry, what did you say you wanted again?"

"I didn't say," I said, taking a bite of the homemade cookie.

My cell phone rang. I looked at Uncle Dee. "Excuse me."

I picked up. It was Nicky.

"Nicky! Where are you?"

"Here and there, baby. You know how I do. I lost my cell on the bridge or I woulda gotten back sooner. Heard from Ramona you were feelin' better. What're you up to?"

"Dodging bullets. You know. The usual. You and Willow?"

"Keepin' busy. Keepin' busy."

"What's up?"

"Albert and Tiffany," said Nicky. "Night on the bridge. They took off. Me and Willow tracked them down to the Chinatown

Angel in the Bronx. They were shaken up by what happened. They said you were right. Pilar Menendez *was* murdered. They didn't know. They do now. They were scared. Albert gave me the VHS cassette, the VHS cassette of the night Benjamin Rivera was killed in his restaurant. Olga kept it hidden inside of a white Steinway piano in her aunt Josephine's apartment in the Arcadia East. Olga gave the tape to Albert after Pilar's funeral as revenge. I have it now. Because of what happened on the bridge, Albert believes that Pilar was killed by the same person who murdered Benjamin Rivera. The person caught on the VHS cassette."

I signaled for Uncle Dee to hold on.

"Nothing criminal on Albert Garcia's biological father," said Nicky. "But I did find out about a murder in El Salvador involving Carmen Diego's mother. Albert Garcia's grandmother was found dead at the bottom of a flight of steps in her own house."

Uncle Dee stared at me from across the room.

"Uh-huh?" I said.

"Ready for the frosting?" Nicky asked. "Do you wanna know who's on the VHS cassette?"

I noticed that Uncle Dee had not removed his coat. I looked around the room. I saw a clean spot on the wall. I remembered what was on that spot and now missing. Not just movie posters. I saw the gun in his hand before I could say Boo!

"I am sorry," said Uncle Dee, his dark coat open and askew, pointing the Uzi.

He took and slapped my cell phone shut.

"Where is Albert? Where is my grandson?"

"I don't know."

Uncle Dee shook his head. "Are you wearing a wire, Chico?"

"I don't need a wire. I have the surveillance tape from the night you murdered Benjamin Rivera in the Chinatown Angel.

The police will be here soon. So no funny stuff like you pulled on the Willis Avenue Bridge. I'm not Benjamin or Pilar. Plus, I'm outta Tylenol."

"Benjamin Rivera got what he deserved," Uncle Dee said. "He was a child molester. I did not murder him. When you kill a good man, it's called murder. When you kill a bad man, it's called an execution."

"That night on the bridge," I said. "What were you planning to do? Murder? Execution? Tango?"

"Whatever I had to do," said Dee. "After Albert learned I had killed Benjamin from Olga at Pilar's funeral, I tried to convince Albert that you should not live. He would not agree. I followed you. I took matters into my own hands. I was doing what was best."

"You weren't planning on letting Tiffany leave that bridge either, huh?"

"I am a man who is not afraid of breaking eggs. What do you think?"

"I think I don't like the idea of being any man's omelet," I said. "No matter how well I go with hash browns. Albert wouldn't go for you killing Tiffany if he wouldn't go for you killing me. Don't you think?"

"I would make him understand."

"Why didn't you recover the VHS cassette? That was sloppy, Uncle."

"Very," said Dee.

"You killed your own wife?"

"I was a suspect. Nothing was ever proven."

"Smooth," I said. "You walk away from something like that. Murdering your own wife. Must make you feel invincible?"

"Not exactly."

"Killing your wife," I said. "I understand. Fifty years and one day you decide you don't wanna share the remote anymore. It happens."

"You do not know what it is like to live for others, Chico. You make fun. But I lived for my wife and daughter. And when my daughter left I lived only for my wife. And after my wife died—"

"After you killed her?"

"After she killed herself. Everyone knew she was cheating on me."

"There's a thing going around," I said. "It's really popular in the States. It's called divorce. Ever heard of it?"

"Dignity, sir. Reputation. Honor."

"So you killed your wife because it was the honorable thing to do?"

"I don't expect a boy like you to understand a man like me," he said. "Benjamin Rivera killed my daughter! He dropped the lit cigarette that burned the building that killed my daughter. He was passed out, filled with drugs, near the children's room when the fire started. He woke up and grabbed Marcos, his son, saved his life. But did not go back for Carmen or Albert. He did not even think of saving them. He thought Albert had died in that fire with Carmen."

"But Albert tried to run away that night," I said. "It saved his life."

"Yes. After my wife died, I came to America looking for my daughter. I found out that she too was dead. After a lot of searching, I finally found Benjamin Rivera with two little girls in Central Park. Olga and Tiffany. He also had a boy with him. Marcos. I looked at the boy's face. It was my daughter Carmen's face. The boy didn't know who I was or who his real mother was. They lied to him."

I took out my cigarettes. "What'd you do?"

"I told Benjamin that I wanted Marcos to know the truth about who he was, about his mother, Carmen, about me, about his brother, Albert, who I knew existed but had not found yet, before we finally made an arrangement. I would

263

get money to keep quiet about Marcos. Benjamin would help me find Albert, and Albert and I would be taken care of."

"What went wrong?"

Dee lowered the Uzi. "Benjamin promised that he would leave the Chinatown Angel to Albert in his will. Two months ago, doctors found a tumor inside Benjamin. So I went to Benjamin. I wanted to see his will, to make sure Albert had something when he and I went. Benjamin refused. Called me a greedy old man and said that Albert was not his flesh and blood, only Marcos was, that he owed Albert nothing. The tumor was not cancer. But Benjamin said he was going to cut Albert out of his will. So I cut him out first. But after Benjamin was dead, I found out he never did write Albert *into* his will in the first place. By then, it was too late."

"Did Albert know all this?"

"No," said Dee. "Not at first. Albert didn't remember the fire. He didn't remember Carmen or Marcos or Benjamin. He didn't know Marcos was his half-brother. Olga knew. I told Olga."

"So you killed Benjamin Rivera by forcing him to inject himself with a deadly dose of heroin."

"I adjusted his perspective, Chico."

"Olga found the body?"

"Olga found the body and the surveillance tape, which I did not have time to destroy because Olga showed up unexpectedly. Power over another human being is a terrible thing. Olga found the body and the tape when she came searching for Albert. She let herself into the restaurant with his keys. She found out from Pilar that Albert was cheating on her with Tiffany and that Benjamin knew about it. Jealousy. She found Benjamin dead and the surveillance camera videotape. Olga was silly enough to show Pilar the videotape and to tell Irving that Tiffany was the guilty party. Pilar was stupid enough to use her knowledge about the tape to blackmail the Rivera family. By lying and suggesting that Benjamin's killer was Marcos. Using the fact that Olga would not deny it to her advantage. Everyone had their own version about who the killer was and their own reasons for picking a horse. One day, Pilar and Olga came to tell me. They agreed that Benjamin was a monster. They wanted to reassure me that they were on my side, regardless of whether Olga and Albert were together, that they both hated Benjamin, that they would never turn me in."

"It was over," I said. "Why did you start it up again?"

"Pilar," said Uncle Dee and shook his head. "When Tiffany disappeared, Pilar came to me alone and asked me if I could make sure Tiffany didn't come back. She said that she had helped me. She had helped me by lying and would I help her. She asked me to kill Tiffany."

"Pilar asked you to kill Tiffany? What're you, dial-a-murder?"

"Pilar asked me to do her a favor. To make sure Tiffany never came back. She offered me ten thousand dollars."

"What did you say?"

"I said I would think about it. I began to watch her. Then Pilar called and told me Kirk was going to meet with you, a private detective, to find Tiffany and she might need my help sooner than she thought. I went to Astoria and when you showed up with Pilar, I knew what I had to do."

"You helped her off the roof?"

"In war, there are casualties, Chico."

"I understand, Diego." I couldn't call him Uncle Dee anymore. It felt dirty.

"Don't think I don't regret it," Daniel Diego said. "In El Salvador, when I was a police officer, I did many things. I don't apologize. I accept what I've done, what I've been, what I've had to do. Only God can judge me now, Chico."

"I don't know," I said. "I think I'd like a piece of that action. Professional curiosity. How'd you get Pilar up on the roof?"

"I held my gun on her and told her to go up. When she did, I pushed. I knew about her problems. I knew they would call it suicide. It was supposed to be simple."

"Look," I said. "They're taking attendance on Rikers Island. Put the gun down. That way, no regrets, and you won't be late for dinner. It's liver again. Sorry."

"Where is the VHS cassette?"

"It's too late," I said. "The police have it."

He was too far away for me to kick or punch.

Somebody started banging on the front door.

Diego turned away and as he raised the gun at the front door, I jumped, tucked, and rolled into the kitchen, threw over the heavy wooden kitchen table as if that would do any good against bullets, and heard shots hit the wall behind me. The front door was being pushed open. I peeked over the table and there were Nicky and Willow. Diego pointed the Uzi at Nicky, and I lunged and grabbed Diego's arm. The old guy was a lot stronger than he looked and his grip on the gun was like iron, like he was born holding it. The next thing I saw was Nicky going for a crescent kick as I twisted the gun in Diego's hand and something exploded.

And there was a flood of blood and bone and red spatter everywhere in the room as the bullets passed through Diego's skull, smashing holes into the ceiling, killing Daniel Diego instantly, sending his body slack and slumping to the floor.

And we just stood there. Me and Nicky and Willow. In silence. We stood there for what seemed like hours, all of us, half deaf, panting, ears ringing, covered in the old man's blood and bone, looking at the sad old corpse.

Uncle Dee.

Finally, I looked at Nicky Brown and shook my head.

Nicky went into his bloodied coat pocket and came out with the surveillance tape.

I looked down at the corpse of Daniel Diego as Officer

Samantha Rodriguez and a small army of Bronx police and homicide detectives arrived.

"I wasn't planning on killing him," I said, looking at Samantha and handing her the VHS cassette.

"He killed two people," said Samantha, taking the tape.

"How do you feel, Yankee?" asked Willow.

"Like I'm gonna vomit," I said.

"Good," said Nicky. "Try not to lose that."

THIRTY-FOUR

MOGUL FALLS TO HIS DEATH

Hannibal Rivera III, a wealthy property owner, died after falling down a staircase in his luxury apartment in the Arcadia East. Police sources said Rivera was found late last night by his wife, Josephine, who said that nobody was home when Rivera took the deadly plunge. Hannibal Rivera also co-headed HMD Financial.

University Place. My heart raced and my eyes darted around the lounge of the bowling alley. The joint was definitely not old school. Bright, colorful, with glow in the dark lanes and neon bowling balls. Not my style but Nicky knew one of the bouncers. A bowling alley with a bouncer?

Only in Manhattan.

269

It was Monday and the place was fairly empty, but they had a deal on cost per game and the Coca-Cola was served fresh.

I dropped the newspaper. It was over. Irving Goldberg Jones was free and out of prison and applying to the M.F.A. in poetry program at Columbia. Olga was off to Harvard Law School. Tiffany was also back at Julliard again. No sign of Albert. But his Kirk Atlas *Doomsday* movie did win Best Lighting award at the San Juan Capistrano Film Festival.

I quit smoking and drinking again and used my Atlas case money to start my own agency.

Earlier that day I had been outside on 149th Street, where the air was cold and the sky stretched bright blue over the Bronx rooftops. A chilly wind blew through the busy streets as I strolled to my new office. I picked up a package leaning against the wooden door with its new sign: SANTANA AND COMPANY.

Well, there weren't no "and Company."

Not yet.

Inside the tiny office was a desk, chair, phone, and two file cabinets. Samantha singing "Cielito Lindo" was stored on my new answering machine next to a photo of Boo the Chihuahua on my desk.

I didn't really have any business being in my new office. No paperwork yet. Hell, no paper. Nada. I just had to see that door with my name on it and sit in my office in my own chair even if just for a minute. It was small but it was mine. I opened the package on my desk, the first I'd received. Inside was a bulletproof vest and a card: *Good luck with Santana and Company! Mucho love!*

Hank and Joy.

I tried on the vest, opened the window wide, and saw the city of my birth; I took the Bronx air deep into my lungs and worried, only slightly, about developing asthma.

Below, the human highway passed by: good people, wannabe saints, monsters, fools, fanatics, maniacs, mystics, drunks, hucksters, rats, assholes, sleepwalkers, brutes, crackpots, impostors, illiterates, peddlers, the slightly insane, pickpockets, drug addicts, prostitutes, potential murder victims, potential killers, all scattering like shotgun blasts across the crowded streets of New York City, through mad traffic, burning, beating, hissing, rattling, railing, pushing, moving and merging, all breakable. Smoke rose in the distance, a helicopter circled overhead. Two teenagers kissed on a street corner.

Back at the bowling alley.

"So," asked Nicky, waking me up. "What do you think?"

I shrugged, looking around the bowling alley with its VIP rooms. "A little fancy for my taste."

"Nice shoes," said Willow, pointing down at my new black and silvers.

Willow was wearing a sleeveless shirt and I saw a tattoo on her reddish brown upper arm. I pointed.

"It's my web," she said. "It catches bad dreams that melt away in the morning sun."

"We're not getting married," Nicky blurted out as he sat down.

Willow said, "It's not the road for him."

I looked at Nicky. "What're you gonna do?"

"Maybe become a private investigator. Before my plane leaves tomorrow night for Atlanta, you can tell me everything you know."

"Can you spare the five minutes for my class?"

"A five-minute class?" Willow said. "You know that much, Yankee?"

"The first four minutes is a long joke and a short introduction," I said.

"How much would it cost me?" asked Nicky.

"I charge one million dollars," I said.

"That's a lot," said Willow. "How about some magic beans instead?"

"C'mon, it's everything I know." Pause. "Okay, five magic beans."

"Deal!" said Willow.

"How'd it go with Mona?" asked Nicky.

I handed him the crumpled napkin from my pocket: *I can't/ Ramona.*

Nicky shook his head. "I tried to hook it up for you but you wouldn't stay. What about Samantha?"

"I don't know," I said. "She has a good singing voice but I'm not sure that's enough to base a relationship on. Did you guys read the morning paper?"

"Sure," Nicky said, changing the subject. "How's your Spanish going?"

"*Es* muy good," I said. "I am going to *la biblioteca*."

"Ain't you ashamed?" asked Nicky.

"Humiliated, constipated, mortified," I said. "When I think about it, I hate myself. I try not to think about it."

"Hit the books. Practice, you lazy bastard!" said Nicky.

"It's not the lazy I resent," I said, looking at Willow. "It's the bastard."

"You both need therapy," Willow said.

"Did you guys read this morning's paper?" I repeated.

"Ah," Nicky said. "Hannibal Rivera the Third. Yeah."

"The creator works in mysterious ways," said Willow.

"Where were you while I was resting at Ramona's?" I asked Nicky.

"I kept myself busy. Caught up on the laundry, wrote a few e-mails, you know how I do."

"Oh, yeah," I said. "I know how you do. You said Willow called a friend at Child Protective. They took that little Chinese girl from Hunts Point, right?"

"Ting Ting. Yeah. It's done," said Nicky.

Willow nodded. "She's safe."

"You never did tell me what happened to Albert."

"I told you," said Nicky.

"Tell me again."

"I followed the old man to the Willis Avenue Bridge," Nicky said. "I watched and I waited until they got you down on the ground."

"Thanks."

"No problem," said Nicky. "I yelled out. The old man fired his gun. Everybody scattered. Willow came around with the Charger."

"I know that part. I was there. Tell me the part where I wasn't there."

"We caught up with Albert. Hiding out with Tiffany at the Chinatown Angel. I got in. They were just sitting there in the kitchen talking. Albert crying."

"How'd you get in?"

"Professional secret," Nicky said.

"Did you kill Hannibal Rivera?"

Willow looked surprised. "Say what?"

"Me," said Nicky, grinning. "I'm a lover, baby, not a killer. Maybe I had a meeting with Hannibal Rivera. But I just talked sense."

"You just talked?" I asked.

Nicky gave Willow a look. "Maybe I kicked Hannibal Rivera. Maybe once."

"You just kicked him?" I said.

Nicky gave Willow another look. "Maybe a little judo technique I've been working on."

"That's it?"

"Maybe some Hapkido."

"Hapkido?" I said. "What the hell is Hapkido?"

"I used a belt. But applied gently, really. Maybe I roughly questioned Hannibal about that little Ting Ting girl, but that's it."

"Where's Albert?" I asked. Nicky shrugged. "Maybe he's in Los Angeles directing his movies. Who knows? Life is a mystery."

Willow threw a piece of something into her mouth and said, "I'm staying in New York, Chico. On Parkchester. You can be my new best *amigo*."

"What're you eating?" I asked.

"Chocolate," said Willow. "Want?"

I held the small round piece of chocolate in my palm. It was gold. It was marked Godiva.

"Where'd you get this?"

"Nicky gave them to me," said Willow.

I looked at Nicky. Nicky winked at me. "A friend."

"It's good to have friends," I said.

"Yeah," he said as Willow popped another chocolate into her mouth.

Ray Charles's voice came on over the sound system: "Seven Spanish Angels."

"Here I go," I said. I got up, grabbed and rolled a neon bowling ball down the glow-in-the-dark lane. It was not a good shot. It was shaky and there was too much bounce to it.

As the ball rolled, I thought about Ramona. And I realized, at last, that it was over. The time for Ramona had rolled on.

"Gutter ball!" Nicky yelled. "Nice!"

"I can't believe I almost married you!" said Willow. I turned and saw them press against each other and kiss. It was a good-bye kiss.

Life.

You took your shot. You hit a pin or two or more. A spare. A strike. A gutter ball.

Life.

It was shaky and there was too much bounce to it.

Every night the game ended with the moon. Every morning the game began again with the sun. . . .

God willing. . . .

ACKNOWLEDGMENTS

Every book has an angel. This book has four angels: Caren Johnson, my agent, Carol Mangis, my first, Emily Adler, my partner, and Toni Plummer, my editor at Thomas Dunne Books. Thank you, angels. . . .